DECLARATION OF LOVE

"Do you know," she asked unexpectedly, "why I said I would go with you?"

Fox frowned and kept his attention on the car ahead of him.

"Did you hear what I asked?" Courtney said.

"Yes. You asked me if I knew why you said you would go to my home."

"I am going, Fox, because I fell in love with you." She waited a minute. He said nothing, not a muscle twitched. "I watched you, and I fell in love with you. So I had to go with you. . . ."

ELIZABETH SEIFERT won the $10,000 Dodd, Mead —Redbook Prize with her first novel. Since then she has written more than sixty novels of men and women of modern medicine, each one revealing the unique combination of emotional understanding and medical knowledge that have made her books so successful. In private life she is the mother of four children and the grandmother of eleven.

Other SIGNET Books You'll Want to Read

The DOCTOR'S REPUTATION

by
Elizabeth Seifert

A SIGNET BOOK
NEW AMERICAN LIBRARY
TIMES MIRROR

SIGNET TRADEMARK REG. U.S. PAT. OFF. AND FOREIGN COUNTRIES
REGISTERED TRADEMARK—MARCA REGISTRADA
HECHO EN CHICAGO, U.S.A.

SIGNET, SIGNET CLASSICS, MENTOR, PLUME AND MERIDIAN BOOKS
are published by The New American Library, Inc.,
1301 Avenue of the Americas, New York, New York 10019

FIRST PRINTING, MARCH, 1974

3 4 5 6 7 8 9 10 11

PRINTED IN THE UNITED STATES OF AMERICA

Chapter One

PEACH WAS making one hell of a row, banging his chairs against the doorframe, dropping one armful with a horrendous clatter. Dr. Creighton looked up in annoyed protest, and snatched his glasses from his nose.

"You done tole me to bring in chairs, Dr. Fox," said the custodian. "You fo'got they's to be a meetin'?"

No, Fox Creighton had not forgotten. He had called it himself. Full staff, or as full as possibly could be attained. And he had told Peach to bring chairs into his office. There was no staff room anymore. There wasn't room for a meeting in his office; there wasn't room, as such, for anything, anywhere in the hospital. Sun rooms, floor lounges, the staff room, all had been converted into wards for the patients which crowded them in these times. Medicare, hospital insurance, and just the fact of more people living and working here in this part of the Southwest. That, with the rising cost of equipment, building . . . Unless you charged the patients enough to drive them back to the medicine man, crowding was the only way to provide medical care. Or so it would seem.

The meeting had been called to consider this problem, among others. Chairs had to be brought into the office of the Chief of Medical Services, and the Chief could put up with the noise or go elsewhere.

He chose to brush his rough red hair back from his forehead; he even touched the lines which he knew would be deep between his eyes, and bent over the papers still piled thickly on his desk. He could concentrate, if he tried hard enough. And as the staff began to assemble, and saw him working at his desk against the far wall, they cut their chatter to a minimum. It got to be funny. They would come in,

5

two or three at a time, carrying with them the wisps and laughter of whatever they had been talking about in the hall; as they would see Fox at his desk, busy, not looking up, the talk would subside to murmurs, to whispers, to nothing beyond the inevitable rustle of selecting a chair and sitting down. The interns were the noisiest, and then the most quiet —they were scared to death of the Chief, which was a healthy way for interns to feel.

Fox kept one eye on his watch. A thread before the assigned hour, he stacked his papers with a sharp rap against his desktop; he removed his dark-rimmed glasses, and pushed his chair back for a quarter of an inch. Then he looked up and out across the crowded room. At the uplifted, watchful faces. He nodded.

"In the interest of nonsuffocation," he said, "will you please open the door into the corridor, Dr. Bechars? I shall . . ." He turned his chair and cranked open the window behind him. It was May, with sun and blue sky—a wind. They always had wind.

He turned back. "Good morning, ladies and gentlemen," he said then. "I believe we are all here. Except Miss Tunstall?"

"She went to her reunion, Fox," said Marion Clark quietly. She was sitting in the front row. Damn handsome woman, Marion.

"Thank you, Dr. Clark," said the Chief. His eyes traveled swiftly across the room, across the two dozen faces.

And in that one swift glance, he identified each of those present. Dr. Clark, staff pediatrician, Dr. Belze, chief of surgery, Dr. Forrest, their heart and chest man, the three interns, Ted Bechars, Arthur Smith, and Tommie—Dr. Pamela Thomas, training in anaesthesiology. The three sat together. Hank Blair, the fourth intern, evidently was the one chosen to remain on duty. Which worked out. He never had become chummy with these other three. The rest of the staff—o.b.-gyn, internal medicine, radiology, the dietician Carolyn Cotsworth . . .

And still during that swift glance, Fox thought, or brought up in his mind, the picture of this hospital, called simply "the Hospital" in this district, though it had a name. The Creighton Memorial Hospital, Fox's grandfather being the one memorialized. Way back in 1910 the thing had begun. A two-story stucco building then, with a wide and deep front porch, green shutters at the windows. Against blowing sand and hot sun. Thirty-five beds. A group of Carson businessmen had decided that the town was growing, and that it needed a hospital. They formed a corporation, they secured the money, and they built that hospital. Fox's present office had been its "parlor." His grandfather had been the doctor in charge; his father also had held that position. The hospital had grown gradually, ten, fifteen, twenty-five beds at a time. An X-ray setup went into the basement, new o.r.'s on the third floor, air conditioning, a sprinkler system. Now there were two hundred beds, and the place was crowded. The third Fox Creighton was the doctor in charge. Today . . .

"Yes!" said Dr. Creighton. "We should get this meeting done and over with, shouldn't we?"

He would have liked to stand; he said he would have liked to, but there wasn't any room.

"And there is the agenda of this meeting," he admitted. "The hospital does not have the room for much of anything we want to do. We have one lounge to serve all three floors, we don't have a staff dining room where we staff doctors could feel exclusive and important. In the past, when this hospital was faced with a similar need, we handled it by building on a few rooms to house a new department. But five years ago, to give us that program, we took the first floor lounge and made it into intern quarters." He glanced at the back row where these doctors-in-training sat. Dr. Bechars, who might be considered the chief intern, Arthur Smith, an older man, who had come back to do the intern training he had skipped on graduating from medical school, and still needed along with a couple of residencies, in order to take the specialist boards exams, and Pamela Thomas, far, far from the hen-medic type even this Dr. Creighton had known in his medical school days. A calm, pretty young woman, with short-cut blond hair; she got along fine with her fellow interns, and with the staff.

Dr. Blair, asked the Chief, was kept on stand-by duty?

"He's on ambulance call," said Tommie.

"He's always on ambulance duty," added Dr. Smith, laughing. "He claims."

"Yes!" said Dr. Creighton. "So that's the situation here at Memorial. Too much service, too many patients, not enough hospital. I don't hear any argument. Need I remind you that we more recently took over the third floor lounge for the newfangled intensive care unit?"

He didn't crack a smile, but everyone else laughed. They knew people in the town called it that. Dr. Forrest half-stood and made the suggestion of a bow. The cardiac-care unit was part of this newfangled business.

"All right," said Dr. Creighton. "So we come to the situation of the hospital in the town. We can't live without the town, and we like to think that the town couldn't function without us. But sometimes I, at least, wonder. The point is: one could state the problem of needed expansion, and expect the town to see our need and indorse whatever means we approve or decide upon."

"Won't it?" asked Dr. Belze.

Fox glanced at him. Their chief surgeon was an exceedingly handsome man, his thick dark hair was frosted with white above his ears. That silvering in no way made him look older.

Dr. Creighton continued to talk, about the town of Carson, and how it had grown within the last ten years. He mentioned the industries which had come in, extending the town's limits. This had meant more work for the hospital, and all, he said, were involved. Miss Cotsworth must determine how and where to feed the patients and the staff, the doctors must schedule their services very exactly, Mrs. Rice, the housekeeper—even Peach must know how often the halls must be mopped, how quickly a room could be scrubbed down.

"We have this problem," he said again. "It's like trying to fit a growing boy into the britches he wore last winter. Nobody is at fault. Both the boy and the pants are good; they just don't serve each other any more or very well. Now!" He lifted his head. "The town is well aware of our problems, the patients are; they carry the word out and about. We talk about it to them. And we all ask what we can possibly do.

"This morning—" He lifted his wrist and looked at his watch. "Outside, at this precise minute, is a man who believes he has a solution for this problem of ours. I shall have him come in and talk to us." Ignoring the sweeping stir of interest and speculation across the room, he picked up the telephone and spoke into it.

". . . Have him come in now. Show him the way if necessary."

Heads turned to the door, voices intensified, then stilled abruptly into shocked disbelief as the man appeared in the open doorway, and endeavored to make his way between the chairs to the desk where Fox Creighton stood, his face like a carved burl of wood.

Their visitor was a tall man, and a handsome one. His dark hair curled richly against his coat collar, the planes of his face were sharply sculptured. His eyes were deep set; there were marked hollows below his cheekbones, his nose was straight, his lips a straight line. That morning, this man wore a plaid jacket, a deep-toned shirt—and his manner was completely unperturbed.

Two or three of the staff rose to let him pass through and he thanked them courteously. He attained the desk and would have shaken hands with Dr. Creighton, but that doctor was entirely occupied with his pipe and a box of matches.

"I have introduced you, Dr. Hawthorne," he said between puffs. "The floor is yours. We can give you as much as ten minutes." And Fox sat down, carefully not meeting the eyes of anyone on his staff.

But Dr. Hawthorne did look at them. He carefully adjusted his shirt cuffs to the proper inch below his coat sleeve; he smiled a little, then the smile faded.

"I am glad that I have been introduced," he said. His voice was deep. He stood at ease.

"I thank you all for managing this meeting. I know how busy you are. Because I know how busy we are over at my hospital. Since I see a strange face or two here"—he was looking at the interns—"I shall identify myself. I am Perry Hawthorne, and I occupy the same position as Dr. Creighton does here. I am Chief of Services at Union Hospital. That is the somewhat large red brick building you pass as you drive north along the highway out of town. We are not quite so large a hospital as this one; but we do have the same problem of overcrowding and therefore limited services. As you have, I am sure, we have told ourselves that something must be done. I have given this matter great thought, and I have come upon one plan which I shall offer to you as a solution for your own problem of over-crowding and limited services. The two things go together. My solution is so simple that I wonder why it should have occurred to me instead of to all of us, all of you.

"Dr. Creighton gave me ten minutes, so I'll quickly get to the point. My suggestion is that Union Hospital, a non-profit organization, join forces with Creighton Memorial Hospital which is a proprietary institution, a corporation hospital."

He had expected instant comment, perhaps a gesture of some sort, though probably not wholesale enthusiasm, Fox Creighton told himself. But no one moved, or spoke. The white-coated, white-uniformed staff just sat where they were, silent, listening.

Dr. Hawthorne talked some more. He expanded on his "simple solution." The town did need more hospital service, he said. The best plan would be to build a new, and large hospital. Modern. Though either of the present institutions could be expanded if that was decided to be best. But the big thing was: if they would agree to close both existing hospitals, and build a new one, there would be Government money for a single hospital facility in Carson County.

That was the essence of what he said. His ten minutes used, he turned and thanked Dr. Creighton for his courtesy. He said he would await his pleasure. "The next move is up to you."

And he walked out. Four people this time stood and moved chairs so that he could pass. No one spoke. No face showed anything but the grave courtesy that had been shown him for ten minutes.

Dr. Hawthorne's footsteps retreated down the hall; his voice was briefly heard, then nothing.

Dr. Creighton tapped his pipe bowl against the big ash-tray on his desk. The creases which bracketed his mouth were very deep, and there was a brightness to his green eyes.

Dr. Clark fished in her pocket for a prescription pad and her pen; she began to write. Dr. Belze and Dr. Forrest resumed their chairs, and each lifted an eyebrow to the other. Carolyn Cotsworth fluttered; she touched her gray bangs, she smoothed the collar of her white uniform. The interns leaned their heads back against the wall and looked at the ceiling.

"Did you invite him here, Fox?" asked the radiologist.

With his question, the tension in the room sagged, and tore into tatters.

"No," said Dr. Creighton. "He called, he said what he had in mind, and asked to present his idea. I thought the quickest and the best way was to let him do it."

"I liked his coat," said Dr. Belze, who wore a plaid jacket of his own.

"You do the wrong kind of surgery," said his friend and crony Walter Forrest.

Relaxation complete, everyone talked at once. For several minutes, Dr. Creighton allowed this, then he rapped for attention. "We have work to do," he said, "lunch to eat, and a problem to be solved. If possible."

"Oh, it is possible," drawled the o.b. man.

"Joking is over," Dr. Creighton assured him. "I would like an opinion from you as to what the hospital can do."

"Expand," said a man's voice.

"We can't," said Fox. "The cost would be prohibitive."

"Could we join with Union?" asked Dr. Smith, the oldest of the interns.

"No," said Dr. Creighton dryly, "that cost would be prohibitive."

There was laughter, a few hands were clapped. Someone endeavored to explain to the interns about Union Hospital, and Dr. Hawthorne. Some of the charges were wild; most hit the mark.

"Yes," said Dr. Creighton after a short wait. "If we are in trouble now, and we are, we should be in deep trouble indeed if we would join Union as it now stands."

"There's no way," said Dr. Forrest. "The stink of that place and Hawthorne's reputation could not be buried deeply enough."

Dr. Creighton stood up. "Any action on our part," he said, "would need to wait on the Board. I called you together this morning to give Dr. Hawthorne a fair hearing. I shall report this meeting to the Board of Directors. I put his remarks on tape." He pointed to his desk drawer.

"And our response?" asked Marion Clark.

"And our response," said Fox. "I think now we should disband this meeting. I urge you each to consider our problem, talk about it to each other, and try to produce some constructive ideas. I plan to reconvene this session in a week."

"All of us?" asked someone.

"All of you," said Fox. "Perhaps a few more. I feel that the situation touches us all."

* * *

Peach, the custodian, orderly, janitor—his duties were multiple—was a giant of a man. He was black, and he wheezed a great deal when asked to do something he disliked doing. He was deft, for so large a man. This noontime, he steered one canvas linen cart down the hall with his left hand, drew a second cart behind him with his right. He pushed the first one through the door of the linen room, and began to lift the folded towels out of the cart, to set them neatly, precisely, upon the shelves. The linens were still warm from the mangle in the basement laundry. Peach worked steadily, swiftly, and talked to anyone who passed along the hall, or who came into the room. Bedspreads, hospital gowns, diapers for the nursery and pediatrics. It was told that Peach could neither read nor write, but that seemed incredible for so clever a man. He never missed the count in a stack of towels; he knew in a minute if a nurse had filched a gauze diaper to wrap around her hair before going into the delivery room.

"I hear they was a meeting, Peach," said the man with the floor waxing machine.

"There was," said Peach.

"I hear they was trouble."

"You hear too much."

"Ain't no trouble?"

"Not that you could fix by missing that corner."

Peach sent the empty carts back to the laundry, then went on to the kitchen and ate his mid-day meal. His choice was from a mixture offered to please the mixture of people who worked for the hospital, and the mixture of patients as well. They could count on a fair percentage of "Spanish," with an Anglo dietician who disapproved of too-spicy food. Still, beans and tacos played their daily part.

Peach could eat anything. Today the baked apple pleased him, and the sliced meat. He was asked about the meeting, about what had happened.

"They give me a front seat," he said solemnly, making a sandwich of his meat and two slices of bread.

"Aw, Peach . . ."

"They had a meeting," the big man agreed. "I lugged in two dozen chairs, I lugged 'em out. I heered some talk."

"Yeah, yeah, about us havin' to cook too much for too many people, but tell me, *was* Doc Hawthorne here? Right here in *our* hospital?"

"I seen him. He didn't stay long, and I didn't see no tracks when he left."

"I heard he wants in."

Peach laughed.

"He's a man to get what he wants."

"All right," said Peach. "So he gets in here. And what happens? Dr. Belze quits, Dr. Clark quits—we can't have no pretty lady doctors around *him*. You quit because you put chicory in the coffee."

"I—" began the cook, but immediately fell silent, and turned away from the counter where Peach was sitting.

Peach looked over his shoulder, and stepped down from the stool. "Yes, sir, Chief?" he said respectfully.

Dr. Creighton nodded. "I stick my nose everywhere, don't I?" he asked pleasantly.

Peach said nothing. Anyone in the hospital knew that the Fox could be expected anywhere.

"I overheard you getting rid of my key personnel," said Dr. Creighton, moving about the kitchen, looking into kettles and bowls, breaking off a corner of bread and eating it. "I hoped before I came in you had fired Peach. He'd be my first choice, because he talks so damn much."

He glanced at the big man in white, drew in one corner of his mouth, and walked out of the kitchen. Peach sighed and sat down again on the stool. "He ruins my appetite," he said, picking up his second thick sandwich.

"That will be the day," laughed the cook. Others in the room echoed him.

Peach still was shaking his head. "He scares me plumb to death," he admitted. "But I'd sure like to be him."

"So we'd all be afraid of you."

"Naw. So you'd all respect me the way we do Dr. Fox. He scares me, but still and all, we are proud of him. He puts a man down, but he never tromps you. Know what I mean?"

The others did know. "We all like the Chief," said the cook. "That's about the only way we work here."

This too met with agreement.

"But you know what I wish?" said Peach, glancing over his shoulder. He did not want Dr. Creighton bobbing up again. Not just now. "I wish the man would git himself married. He's at the age—well, if he don' git about doin' it, he may never marry. And he needs somethin' to occupy himself other than a big old hospital."

"He's also got that big old house," said the salad cook.

Peach nodded. "His grandpa built it, he says. And now who lives there? One man, two dogs, and a couple of old folks to take care of him. No wife, no kids—you bet he needs somethin' else but a hospital to fret about."

"He's got somethin'," said the dishwasher. 'Ef Doc Hawthorne is comin' around, wantin' in here, he *sure* got somethin'!"

* * *

Dr. Creighton would have agreed with the dishwasher. He did have plenty to occupy his mind. Not that his thoughts were immediately concerned with Perry Hawthorne. That man's visit had amused him, more than anything else. "Did he think we'd jump at his solution?" Dr. Creighton asked Dr. Creighton. He went up to o.r. where he expected to find, and did find, two of his interns. Tommie—Dr. Pamela Thomas, specializing in anaesthesia—and Dr. Smith, who was then working in surgery. Both were busy in one of the o.r.'s, checking and placing instruments in the autoclave, and on trays in the air-tight cabinets. When Dr. Creighton came in, Tommie was reading valves and writing on a pad of record forms.

"Why don't you wear a pant suit?" Dr. Creighton asked her.

Tommie looked around and up, smiled faintly, and stood erect, smoothing her skirt. "Pants are better for stooping and bending," she agreed.

He nodded, and crossed the room to watch Arthur Smith. "That's a nurse's job, you understand," he said.

"The surgical Head told me . . ."

"I know, I know. But since you are here, learning to do an M.D.'s work, I feel I must point out to you what that work properly would be."

"I'll remember, the next time I see you pushing a cart down the hall."

Arthur Smith was a large man, with heavy features. He wore steel-rimmed spectacles, and used unabashedly the speech and accent which he had known since birth. He had taken his M.D. five years ago, and had gone immediately into practice with an uncle in a southern small town. This past year, having acquired a family—a wife and two children—he had decided that whether his state required it or not, internship would be a help to him. He talked about doing a residency, and Dr. Creighton approved. He would recommend Smith without reservations.

"No surgery scheduled?" the Chief asked.

"Not till tomorrow mornin', sir."

Dr. Creighton nodded, and went out into the hall again. His eyes were busy; not one thing escaped him; but he was thinking busily, too.

He found Dr. Bechars on Medical, and busily at work. Dr. Blair came up from X-ray with a very sick old man who, necessarily, had been undergoing a g.i. examination. He might not survive, but the doctors needed to know what was behind the distress which had sent him to the hospital. Dr. Creighton stood to one side, and watched the interns manoeuver the cart and the i.v. bottle down along the hall and into the patient's room. Dr. Bechars was a very good man, settled, serious in his work. He had asked for service in a "small" hospital. Eye-glasses, pleasant, he had a wife and baby, both acquired in medical school, and everyone in the hospital called him Ted. Privately, Fox thought he would like to have Ted Bechars stay on at their hospital.

Hank Blair might be another matter. Miss Tunstall, Superintendent of Nursing Services, said he was their best man, and that well could be. He moved swiftly, got a job done with dispatch, and then could be found with his nose in a book of some sort. The other three interns were friends; they shared a free-time pizza and beer at the drive-in across the street; they relaxed together at meal times, or in the lounge. Blair was seldom seen with them except, as today, when at work.

"Who sleeps around here?" Fox asked when the young man came out of the patient's room.

"I do," said Hank Blair readily. "I did sleep until almost noon."

And then he had been assigned to on-call duty during the staff meeting.

Fox was ready to comment, when the floor nurse called from the desk. "Ambulance, Dr. Blair!"

Hank's head went up. He almost ran down the corridor, the men watching him.

"Does he really do all the ambulance work?" Fox asked Dr. Bechars.

"More than his share. He says he likes it."

Fox frowned.

"He thinks initial care saves a lot of lives." Ted was stowing the cart against a wall.

Dr. Creighton nodded. "I suspect he's right," he agreed. He should watch young Blair more closely. There could be something to the boy beyond soft, thick, overly long brown hair and a way of watching rather than talking.

"Send me word when that ambulance returns," he told the floor nurse as he passed the desk.

* * *

The ambulance driver was a young Mexican-American who got along fine with Hank Blair. He drove well, and might have been considered reckless. He used the siren, and a philosophy common to his countrymen. "It is dangerous to drive fast along the streets. Warn others that you are coming fast, that you have a heavy vehicle—then let them beware. I need to get where I am going. They do not."

Virgilio Almandarez had never put so much as a scratch on the ambulance belonging to Creighton Memorial Hospital. "But you need seasick pills to ride with him," Hank Blair told the emergency room staff when he brought their stretcher in.

"What do you have, Blair?" asked Dr. Creighton coming to meet the cart.

"I don't really know," said the intern. "Boy—six—fell off the house—"

"Off the *house!*" echoed three female and one male voice.

"Of course," said Hank gruffly. "Where did you climb when you were six?" He spoke again to the Chief. "He fell into a rosebush, sir," he said. "Sticks and prickles all over, but the bush saved his life."

Tenderly the two doctors lifted the big-eyed child to the table. Hank pointed to his jaw. "A big stick—a cane—went in there, sir."

Dr. Creighton touched it, gently. "Right into the jaw . . ." he confirmed.

"I think we need a surgeon," said Blair. "If we touch it at all there is bleeding."

Dr. Creighton turned to one of the nurses. "Get Dr. Belze down here, stat!" he said sharply. "And ask Dr. Clark if she can look in. If he's six, he belongs in pediatrics."

The child's mother was being detained in the hall. She didn't think Willie was hurt bad, she said. Just thorns. He didn't seem to have busted anything.

Marion Clark came in and confirmed this diagnosis. But when her hand went to the protruding rose stem, Dr. Blair restrained her. "Bleeds," he said tersely.

She looked up at Fox. "Yes, it does," he confirmed. "Where the devil is Belze?"

"He's not in the hospital, doctor. We are calling his home and his office."

Willie was being undressed, and Hank was pulling out rose thorns. "I'd get a surgeon pretty quick," he muttered.

Dr. Clark nodded to Dr. Creighton.

He stepped out into the hall. "I've sent for Crosby," he said, coming back. "Belze seems to have disappeared."

"Dr. Crosby won't work in e.r.," said Hank.

"He will, but there's no reason we can't take Willie upstairs."

There was no reason. The boy was conscious and able to tell his mother he was "fine." "He's got a stick in his jaw," Dr. Blair told her. "Here we go, Willie! *Wheee!*" The cart raced out of e.r., down the wide corridor to the big elevator.

Upstairs, on the skylighted, airy surgical floor, Dr. Crosby arrived within five minutes. He was an older man, small, neat, capable as a surgeon. He did not quite have Dr. Belze's skill nor his quickness. Certainly not his flair.

"Where is Belze?" he asked Dr. Creighton in scrub.

Fox shook his head. "Checked out at one. His answering service doesn't know."

They went into o.r. Dr. Creighton told Dr. Blair to stay close. "Get him some gloves. There's no time for him to scrub."

The child was anaesthetised. Dr. Crosby questioned the degree. He turned the head, found the end of the broken rose cane, fastened forceps to it, and pulled gently.

Immediately, out came a rush of blood.

"Shove it back!" cried Dr. Blair.

Dr. Crosby looked annoyed but he did push it back, and conferred with Dr. Creighton. Then he took his scalpel, and cut the child's neck open, down to the collarbone. "Through the jugular," he said in awe. He stepped aside to let Hank Blair see more closely.

"What do we do now?" asked the intern. "No wonder the thing bled."

Dr. Creighton was standing, with his head back, his eyes half closed. "I'm trying to remember . . ." he said.

"Get his blood typed," Dr. Crosby told the circulating nurse. "When you have the jugular to deal with . . ."

Hank Blair was watching Dr. Creighton in a half-amused, half-impatient way. A nurse tied a mask across his face and he hardly noticed her.

"I'm trying to remember . . ." said Dr. Creighton. "Way back—before I was born, but I read about it, or my dad told me. There was a ship—a big ship, loaded with passengers. On the St. Lawrence River, or maybe on one of the

Lakes—it was rammed by another boat. A freighter, or a tanker, maybe. And the captain of that boat got panicky at the hole he'd made in the Empress of something or other, and he backed out. That let the whole lake gush in, and the damned boat sank, with a terrific loss of life."

He looked down at the child on the table. A small bit of humanity to compare to an ocean liner.

Dr. Crosby was already back at work. He tied off the jugular vein, he drew the carotid artery out of the way, and he pulled out the stick. The thing had run from the boy's jaw, down through his neck and chest.

"To the fourth rib!" said Hank Blair in awe. He held the rose cane up for all to see. "This should go in a museum," he declared.

"I'm glad you didn't pull it out," said Dr. Creighton.

"I'm glad," Dr. Crosby added, "that you remembered that boat."

Above his mask, Fox's green eyes sparkled. "Hadn't thought of that in years," he confessed. "Can you men finish here?"

The surgeon nodded. "You be listening for fog horns," he said.

* * *

Dr. Creighton changed his clothes and went out into the hospital, then down to his office. He was puzzled about Dr. Belze. True, the man held office hours, and had other legitimate reasons to be away from the hospital, but he should be located always, reached without too much difficulty. Fox decided to do some telephoning on his own. He himself put the calls through, knowing that he felt that a little extra personal effort would get the job done. The Belze home did not answer.

Fox called the doctor's office. The secretary there said that he had not come in, and she was canceling appointments.

It was damn queer, said Dr. Creighton.

"Well, it's not like Dr. Belze," the secretary agreed.

The Chief put the phone down, and pushed the instrument away. He leaned back in his desk chair and gazed at the ceiling. Now where would he go if he were Belze? Where was his wife, by the way? Not at home, but that didn't guarantee a trip out of town. She might be shopping, be at the beauty parlor, at a bridge party. Jane Belze was reputed to be something of a swinger.

Fox dropped his chair forward, rested his elbows on his

desk, and put his head in his hands. At one time there had
been some story—talk, gossip—about Jane Belze and Dr.
Hawthorne. But Hawthorne could get any pretty young
woman talked about just by speaking to her on the street
corner.

Should Fox call Hawthorne? Oh, for the love of his Aunt
Maggie!

He'd better call Dr. Forrest. He and Belze were friends,
they shared an office . . . He pushed a button, and spoke to
the operator.

"This is Dr. Forrest's free afternoon, sir," said the switchboard girl.

"You mean, he doesn't hold office hours."

"Yes, sir, but there was another call for him earlier, and
his service said he was out of town. She thought."

Fox thanked the operator, then sat looking at his telephone. Had all his staff men decided to take the day off?

He decided that Belze and Forrest were together. Jane
with them, perhaps. Maybe even Dorothy Forrest, though
she was pretty pregnant and would not be playing golf or
driving to the city.

Now what did that leave? His mouth twisted wryly. Hawthorne. He knew the man. He had known about him for
fifteen years, really. Ever since Perry Hawthorne had moved
in at Union Hospital. Fox's father had called him a pants
merchant. But he too was called Chief of Medical Services.
He saw patients, held office hours, was subject to call, and
did some surgery. Though, a month ago, Fox had been told
that Union was doing almost no surgery. Which, in a way,
was good. Except that a hospital could not function without
surgery. "I was thinking of the populace," said Fox aloud.

He'd start over. Dr. Hawthorne was a successful man; he
made a lot of money. The town told of abortions, drug
accommodation, things like that, but so far, at least, there
had been no convictions. A town like Carson loved to fas-
ten such stories to a doctor's coattails. Hawthorne was a
handsome man, and was extremely popular with women. All
women.

At the meeting that morning, Carolyn Cotsworth, sixty,
had gone into quivers over the man, her cheeks pink, her
face smiling. Although even Carolyn must know that Hawthorne had entered hostile territory.

But other women—even so sensible a one as Marion Clark
—could find good things to say about Perry Hawthorne. He

adored his only child, a daughter of seventeen or so. He was successful in schooling horses and field-training dogs . . .

Fox reached for his buzzing telephone. He dealt with the call, and looked at his schedule for the rest of the day. Now he found himself thinking about Marion Clark.

She was supposed to be part Indian, and looked it. Her hair was jet black, and silky soft. Her skin was dark, her high cheekbones and aquiline nose could be Indian. Fox could ask her, and she would tell him. She had never denied the stories told that "George Clark had married a squaw."

Well, if so, she was a damn good squaw. With three children, she continued to be a doctor, and a good one. She now lived in a unit of the big apartment center built two years ago within walking distance of the hospital. Fox Creighton called their particular unit the Sorority House, because Miss Tunstall lived there too, and the two Cotsworth sisters, Carolyn and her widowed sister, Virginia Shelton, and Marion Clark with her three daughters, or such of them as were at home. George probably claimed residence, but Fox doubted if he came around very often.

George was Fox Creighton's cousin, another handsome and charming man. The old-fashioned term for such a man had been "ne'er-do-well." It fitted George. Marion had tried to make her marriage work, and when it didn't she had supported herself and her three girls. George was the son of a rich man who had, for his own reasons, refused to help him or his family. The girls were pretty well grown by now, though the youngest was still in high school.

George was a gambler, and by that profession he made such a living as he required. He dealt black jack, he ran illicit games. One day he would inherit his father's fortune, and he made out with that prospect always in his mind.

Well—

Fox clapped his hands flat on his desk, stood up and strode out of the room. "I'm going up to surgical," he told his secretary. He probably would find Marion there; she would now be watching Willie.

She was in intensive care with the little boy who was struggling out of anaesthesia. The mother sat white-faced beside the bed. At the Chief's entrance, Dr. Clark glanced up. "This is Dr. Creighton," she murmured.

The mother's lips moved, but no sound came.

"She's still badly frightened," Marion said softly.

"All that bandaging," the mother said pitiably. "And rubber tubes . . ."

"It's the way surgeons do things," Fox comforted her. He picked up the chart. "Willie's doing fine," he told the mother. "In a day or two, he'll be ready to climb up on the roof again."

"I'll whup him if he looks like it!" said the mother vigorously.

Dr. Clark laughed, and motioned to the nurse to attend to Willie. Marion followed Fox into the hall. They could see, and be seen, through the wide window of the intensive care room.

"Is something wrong?" Marion asked Fox.

"I hope not. It's just—remember we could not locate Belze early this afternoon?"

"Yes. Dr. Crosby did an excellent job."

"Her certainly did. But. Marion, I still can't find Belze."

She started to say something then stopped and looked at him alertly. "That's strange," she agreed. Her eyes were puzzled.

"It's damn strange!" said Fox Creighton.

"Maybe Alice Tunstall knows. I don't mean where to find him here, but she listens to gossip more than you or I do. He may have an interest . . ."

"Aggh!" Fox discounted the suggestion. "Anyway, you reminded me this morning that Tunnie is gone too. Remember? The reunion of her wartime buddies."

"Oh, of course. She left Sunday."

"Whole blamed hospital takes off at once," the Chief fumed. "Don't you go anywhere, Marion."

"Who me?" she laughed, and went back into intensive care.

* * *

Carolyn Cotsworth, the third of Fox Creighton's "sorority sisters," went through her final tasks of the day with an eye on the clock. She wanted to get home quite a bit early. Her hours were flexible. So long as she had her meals planned, and served, the special diets checked, orders in, kitchens inspected . . . Yes, she could get away by three, or maybe just a few minutes earlier.

She had so many things to do . . .

At three, on the dot, she closed her office door, and signed out of the hospital; Dr. Creighton was a stickler about checkouts, and today he was having kittens—his term would have been different—because Dr. Belze was gone and could not be located. Of course the dietician was not as apt to be needed . . .

Carolyn's car was a green compact, seven years old, as neat as a pin. She drove it as she did everything, quietly, competently. She parked it before the apartment unit, touched the horn twice as a signal to Virginia that she was home, and went inside.

She had to search for her keys again, because Virginia was not at home, probably gone to the library, or shopping —or even to the community house. She said she loved watching the "kids." Carolyn did not have time for that sort of thing, and the "kids" were not exactly to her taste. Their hair, the way they dressed and talked . . .

Well, Carolyn had a lot of things to do. Alice Tunstall would get home that evening, or the next morning, depending on plane connections. She went into the apartment, looked critically about, moved a picture frame an eighth of an inch—Virginia did well, but tiny things did not matter to her. Carolyn took off her head scarf, folded it, and put it into a drawer in her bedroom. She went through the dining room and out to the balcony. She cut a geranium from the long box inside the railing, and three green leaves. She knew just the small white vase into which she would put the flower. She would set it on Alice's coffee table, a gay hello to the traveler; its spicy perfume would greet her.

Carolyn picked up her keys and went out, up the apartment stairs to Alice's door, noticing that someone had left the utility room door ajar. Carolyn closed it. "Open drawers and doors drive me crazy," she said softly.

She unlocked Alice's door and went inside. The apartment was pleasantly warm, and quiet. A bar of sunlight slanted from the tall windows across the carpet of the living room. Carolyn sniffed suspiciously. Shut-up places could hold odors. But even she could find none beside the fragrance of the geranium in her hand.

She set the little vase down, and backed away to look at it. Yes, it was just right. Reflected in the mirror above the couch, the room looked very well.

There was no dust, but Carolyn dusted anyway; Alice kept everything quietly neat and pretty. No frills or fuss. But comfort, of course. Alice was a nice girl. Carolyn's sisters, Virginia and Clytie, thought there was a "thing" between Tunnie and Dr. Creighton. Carolyn knew that was nonsense. Fox was younger than Alice, for one item. Though both were beyond the age of silliness.

Finally she reached the kitchen. All was in good order there. She checked the refrigerator. Yes, there were eggs, bacon. Oranges and grapefruit both. Carolyn planned to bring down a salad, all ready in a sealed bowl, with a little jar of dressing to put atop the container. She had considered a meat loaf, but Alice would eat it cold, rather than bother to heat it. Alice ate her main meals at the hospital, which was fine, but coming in this way after a trip—yes, a bowl of chicken salad and some fresh bread. Miss Tunstall would eat that, and relish it. Carolyn would bring down a little plate of cookies, too, shielded with cellophane and set in the middle of the kitchen table. Along with silver, a plate, a coffee cup, a napkin . . .

The little woman moved happily about, doing these kind and thoughtful things. As she worked, she thought about the staff meeting which Fox had assembled at noontime. He certainly hadn't needed to tell his fellow workers that the Hospital was overcrowded, that it needed to find ways to add beds and services.

So he must have called the meeting solely to let Dr. Hawthorne present his offer for the joint action of the two hospitals in an appeal for Federal funds. Fox wouldn't take a stand; he just had let Dr. Hawthorne come in and tell the staff how expansion could be secured.

He had made a fine presentation, too. He was such a handsome, strong-looking man, his face was like one carved on a coin, or on a statue. And he dressed beautifully. Even Dr. Belze had commented on his handsome jacket; plaid it had been with a strong line of red marking off squares of black and white. Yes, Dr. Hawthorne was a warm and a beautiful man. He never failed to speak to Carolyn when he would meet her. He remembered her name, that she was a dietician—he would ask about her sisters—

The table set and ready, Carolyn hurried downstairs again to make her salad. She would make enough for her and Virginia, too, of course. She would add some seedless green grapes, and some slivered almonds, for prettiness and texture. Virginia would remark that she was doing something for someone again. Well, so Carolyn was.

She loved doing these things. She did them for all her friends. Tonight she might arrange a third plate of pretty cookies, and take it down to Marion Clark. As she did things for Alice and Marion, she wished she could find a way to do things for Fox Creighton.

For a second, Carolyn's busy hands slowed, and fell still, resting on the edge of her large salad bowl.

For goodness sake, that must be . . .

The radio had been softly playing ever since she had come into the kitchen, put on her apron and started to work, arranging the cookies, assembling the materials for her chicken salad. She had heard, without hearing, the songs played and sung, the announcer's voice advertising car service, fashion-coordinated clothes—then something—a change in tempo—had sharply attracted her attention.

"We are sorry to announce, on a bulletin just received, the death of Stephen Clark, industrialist and prominent figure in state affairs. Mr. Clark died at two o'clock this afternoon in the Medical Center of Los Hermanos after a lingering illness."

"That usually means cancer," said Carolyn, wiping her hands and turning up the volume of the little radio.

"Mr. Clark was seventy-six, and the father of George Clark, a well-known citizen of Carson . . ."

Carolyn sniffed. A *notorious* citizen!

"Also, he was the uncle of Dr. Fox Creighton, part owner and chief medical officer of Creighton Memorial Hospital. Mr. Clark is survived by three granddaughters, children of Mr. Clark and his wife. Funeral arrangements are pending."

Well! Maybe Carolyn should cook the meat loaf and take it down to Marion. If they'd be going to the funeral . . . As soon as she knew Marion was home, she would take the cookies down, and ask. But when she did go down, Marion said at once that she was not planning to go to Los Hermanos.

"But, Marion . . ."

Marion turned away to set the plate of cookies on the table.

"George will surely go, and you're the daughter-in-law," urged Carolyn.

Marion's lips twitched. "Look, dear. I know it will be no news to you that I, and my family, have never been, shall we say? *close* to George's father."

"I know, but at a time like this . . . Surely . . ."

"Surely George will go? Well, he may. And he may take the girls with him. I don't really know. Except that I shan't go. But thank you very much for the cookies. They are always delicious."

Carolyn stood, troubled. "I always think," she said, "that funerals are the best, and last, time to heal old wounds."

Marion smiled at her. "In this case," she said, "Mr. Clark's funeral would be the very worst time."

Because of the money, Carolyn told herself as she went upstairs again. She supposed Marion thought it would seem as if she and the girls were expecting to inherit. But— wouldn't they? George was the rich man's only son.

* * *

But Dr. Creighton . . . At the end of each day, his custom was to pick up an intern and make the full rounds of the hospital. Sometimes this went swiftly, sometimes the younger doctor survived, but only in a state of complete exhaustion. Fox was known to reach up seeking grease in a kitchen exhaust pipe, or to sit down and gossip for twenty minutes with the women in the large medical ward. The man was both feared and loved. A brusque man, a hard-boiled man, he took life much too seriously, thought young Dr. Pamela Thomas who was the "lucky" one on this day. Dr. Creighton followed no discernible pattern in selecting the intern. Pamela had not been called for a week; she might go again tomorrow, or the next day.

"You always learn something," Arthur Smith consoled her this evening.

"I'll choose books for my study," she assured the older man.

Also, her feet always hurt after one of these treks through the rooms and wards of the widely spread-out building.

But of course she picked up her clipboard and her ball point, praying that it would not die on her. As one had, several weeks ago. Dr. Creighton had waited on her *so* patiently while she found a replacement. Now she always took two, but . . .

Today they started up on surgical, in intensive care. Willie was there, and a very sick woman. She peered up at the two doctors; her trembling fingers picked at the edge of the bedspread. And she asked, "Am I going to die, Dr. Creighton?"

"Oh, no!" said the intern at the Chief's shoulder.

Fox Creighton straightened; he turned, and he looked sternly down at the young woman in the white jacket. "Well, doctor?" he asked gruffly.

Pamela felt awful. She wanted to run, she wanted to cry . . . Instead, her face white, she came to the bed, and she took the old woman's hand in her young, warm one. "Yes," she said softly, "you may die."

The next she was aware—they had covered the surgicals, and were starting on men's medical—Dr. Creighton was called to the telephone.

Tommie waited. It was impossible not to hear his side of the conversation. Someone had died. The doctor did not know where someone else could be located; he could give the caller the name and phone number of his wife. Yes, he would consider coming to Los Hermanos. If he could possibly get away.

He put the phone down, glanced at Tommie, and they continued their rounds. But now things went swiftly. The young woman had to run—or almost—to keep up with the Chief who was tall and had a long stride.

They finished at last, and Dr. Creighton gravely thanked the intern. Were there any questions?

"No, doctor. At least, not now."

"Yes, I am in a little rush. I may have to go away for a day or two."

"I'm sorry."

"Thank you." His reply was entirely courteous; he was always courteous, just as he was always withdrawn, uncommunicative.

"At some time," Tommie told Dr. Smith at dinner that evening, "people, or the world, have hurt that man. He has completely withdrawn from human contacts."

"Why don't you ask him what happened?" Dr. Bechars suggested.

"Oh, golly," said Tommie. "I got in deep enough this evening." And she told about the dying old woman.

"Yes," agreed her friends. They'd say that was deep enough.

* * *

Leaving the intern, Fox went to his office. His secretary had departed. He must, and could—did—put through his own call to where he thought he might find George Clark. The man was not there. Next, he called the one close friend he himself seemed to have. That this man was mayor of the town had no significance. Fox had labored to elect him to office, arguing that a good city government would start with a good mayor. But Pat Kern and he had been friends from

their youth. As boys they had hunted together, hiked . . .
One summer, when they were seventeen, the two boys had
explored the beaches of California and Oregon, on foot.
This was one person who knew Fox so well that there was
no need to explain anything to him. Pat knew why Fox
Creighton was a loner. It helped to have someone who
would know about the past years, and understand the doctor's self-isolation, who never attempted to bring him back
into close contact with the world about him. It was not a
matter of people. Fox dealt daily with the most intimate
problems and developments of *people*, and he did so with
sumpathy and understanding.

But never did he want anyone to attempt to deal with
him, attempt to solve his life-riddle.

So tonight when Fox called the mayor, the mayor listened. Fox's uncle, he said, his mother's brother, had died.
"George Clark is his son, but I can't locate him. Though
that is not my reason for thinking I should go to Los Hermanos."

Pat offered no advice. For all Fox's aloofness from human contacts, there were certain areas . . .

Pat remembered this uncle. With Fox, he had visited in
the man's home, and had gone on a certain memorable fishing trip with him. Pat remembered Stephen Clark's sister,
Fox's mother. One of the truly great ladies of the century.
Several years ago she and Fox's father had been killed in an
air disaster. This had brought Fox back to the hospital, to
the town—when he probably had not wanted to change the
course of his life, where he probably had not wanted to live.
Though Pat could be wrong . . .

Tonight Pat could said the usual things. He was sorry; he had
liked Uncle Stephen. When would Fox leave? "I don't
suppose you'll stay long?"

"I don't suppose I can go at all," said Fox gruffly. "Things
here . . ." Briefly he told of Hawthorne's visit that noontime,
and about what he described as the man's impudent suggestion.

Pat Kern laughed. "If he would seem to move in while
you are gone," he promised. "I'll get an injunction, or issue
something or other."

"You could just declare us a disaster area," said Fox, and
ended the call.

Failing in another attempt to locate George, he asked
Marion if she and the girls would want to drive to Los

Hermanos with him. "We couldn't go without George," she said. "Good luck, Fox. Don't drive too fast."

He did drive fast, however, across town to the outskirts where he lived in the large brick house built by his great-grandfather, enlarged—and then condensed by the closing off of one wing when Fox's parents had produced just the one child, and that child seemed disinclined to marry and put the whole house again into use. There was too much house, beautifully furnished, beautifully kept by the Storys, too much ground, the lawns kept green and mowed, the little lake sparkling, even the trees, tall cottonwoods, and such evergreens as liked their dry soil—and the single man driving homeward that evening, asking himself why he was going to his uncle's funeral. If the dead man's son would not make the effort . . . Fox had not seen, nor been in anything like close touch with, the man since his mother's death five years ago. So why . . . ?

The Storys asked him the same question. "I think it's nice that you will go," Mrs. Story said.

"I'm not being *nice*," He assured her. "I am doing it partly because my mother would have been pleased . . ." Just as he had returned to the hospital for his father's sake.

"That's being nice," the housekeeper assured him.

"If you say so. But there's another thing—this seems to be a good time for me to get away, to be concerned about other things than the hospital, Mrs. Story. I may be able to untie some knots, if I get clear away from the place."

"Yes, sir. Though what you need is a real vacation."

"And you don't think a funeral is any substitute. Well, you're probably right. The roast is perfection, by the way."

"Could I do your packing for you, Dr. Fox?" Fred Story asked when he presented hot rolls under their napkin.

Fox glanced up at him. "You could help me," he agreed. "I'll be gone only two days, I hope. I plan to start early tomorrow morning. But tonight I'll need to go back to the hospital for a time to get things tied down there."

"Yes, sir. You are very busy there, I understand."

Fox groaned softly, and buttered the roll. "Miss Cotsworth won't let us use butter at the hospital," he told the tall, blond houseman.

"I understand it is bad for the heart."

"Supposedly."

"You'll want your black suit, sir?"

"I think so. If I am going, I should do the thing properly."

"Yes, sir."

Fred Story had worked for Fox's parents. To him the doctor must still be the young man coming and going during his college and medical school years. Returning home much less often once he got busy with his profession. *Summa cum laude*, research in microbiology, had meant absolutely nothing to Story. But the tall, gruff-spoken man with the rebellious green eyes meant, literally, his world. If Dr. Fox had not returned to run the hospital . . .

Or try to run it, Fox told himself. "What does Mrs. Story have in the way of dessert?" he asked aloud.

"A chocolate soufflé, sir."

Fox smiled. "No whipped cream, Fred."

"No, sir."

Fox ate the soufflé, brought in, puffed and fragrant, served with a deftly wielded silver spoon. "Don't let the rest of that go to waste," he said, looking over his shoulder at Mrs. Story who had come to the pantry door.

"A half dozen kids would handle it," she ventured to tell him.

Fox laughed. "And give me a half dozen more worries to take with me in my bag tomorrow."

"There's no point in your getting away if . . ." she began.

"I'll not hope to escape the problems, Becca," he said kindly. "Just unpack them with my black suit and look at them in a different light."

"Yes, sir," said Mrs. Story. "How early . . .?"

"Too early for you to be up with coffee ready," he told her.

She waited. She would be up, and the coffee would be ready. She was a remarkable woman, and her idea of a half dozen kids was probably a good one. But Fox was right, too. He would indeed pack his problems along with his somber suit, the plain, dark ties, and his dull black shoes.

"I'd like to get off by six," he said.

"Yes, sir. I—I think you are doing the right thing," she added. "Your mother was fond of her brother. He was quite a bit older, and she respected him."

"I know. He was good to me when I was a kid. Pat Kern and I both remember the fishing trip he took us on, and other kindnesses. He did more for us, maybe, than he did for his own son."

"Oh, but George . . ."

"I know. Fishing was not George's bag. He was a rat then, and he's a rat now."

"What will he do with his father's money?"

Fox finished the last of his soufflé; Mrs. Story refilled his coffee cup.

"I wouldn't give it a thought," said Fox. "He could have already obligated some of it. You know? Got loans on the prospect of one day having money."

"Can you do that, sir?"

Fox laughed. "I couldn't. But George probably could."

The next morning, Dr. Creighton came downstairs to find coffee, orange juice, and two three-minute eggs waiting for him on a yellow linen mat at the end of the mahogany table in the dining room.

"She's just as apt to remind me to use the bathroom before I leave," Fox told himself, shaking out his napkin.

Story had his car out in front, the bag in the trunk. "Have a good trip, sir," he said quietly.

"Thank you, and thank Becca, will you? I couldn't get along without you two."

"Thank you, sir. Good-bye." The door closed, and Fox circled the drive, noting the way the early sun glinted gold on the windowpanes of the house. Since his parents' death, the Storys had occupied rooms in the wing—Fox had asked them to live there. "I don't want to be lonely," he had explained. But of course he was a lonely man, although he became angry when he was forced to admit it. To himself only. He would not say such a thing to any living person, nor admit that his decision to go to his uncle's funeral was, really, a reaching out . . .

When he got to the highway, he turned the car about and came back toward town, to the second-rate country club house where George Clark frequently conducted a poker game, and often stayed for days at a time. If he were there . . .

He was. Sleepy, disheveled, profanely angry to be rousted out at such an ungodly hour. "What the hell is wrong with you, Doc?" he demanded.

"Nothing is wrong with me. I am going to your father's funeral and I think you should go with me."

George's reply was obscene, and Fox winced. "You'll bring the lightning down on your head," he warned his cousin.

George leaned on the car door. His dark hair was tangled, the pajamas he wore were wrinkled, his color was bad. "I'll tell you what," he said insolently. "You go on to the funeral, you bring me a copy of the will. That is, if you stay to hear it read. It isn't going to mention you. Of that you can be sure."

Fox gazed at him. Then, not caring if George stepped back or not, he drove away, so fast that the car tilted at the turn into the main road. He had never been so angry. So furious.

Chapter Two

IT MADE A DIFFERENCE, the Man's being gone. The hospital was functioning. Temperatures were taken, meals served, the telephones rang. Nurses went swiftly along the halls. A new patient came in, another died.

All routine. But with a difference. For instance yesterday's problem now was blown up into a balloon of incredible size. Hawthorne was to blame. Before his advent, everyone in the hospital knew that some measure must be taken to expand the services, or to restrict them so they would fit into the space and personnel available. Everybody knew about that, and did a bit of talking, always with an ear and eye alertly on Dr. Creighton. Hawthorne had brought the problem into a sharp focus, and raised the level of the talk.

Sure, some said, the two hospitals should go together.

It was crazy, said others, even to *think* of operating with Union and doing the things that place did.

They talked, but always there was the thought, and frequently the statement: Dr. Creighton will figure things out.

But that had been when he was around, a big, warm body to stand between the hospital and all threats to it. With him gone, there was a difference.

Hank Blair wakened by a hand on his shoulder, felt an emptiness. He mentioned it when he went through the quiet hall, buttoning his sweater with one hand, carrying his bus bag with the other. "Something's missing," he told himself. The ambulance's engine was running, Almandarez behind the wheel. Hank opened the heavy back door and climbed in. He had not yet sat down when the big, clean car, red lights blinking, went swiftly out of the hospital "yard."

32

"Hang on to your hat, Doc," said the driver; he touched the circlet on the steering wheel which, in a car, would have sounded the horn. In the bus, this morning, the siren moaned. The driver looked in both directions, then swung the heavy car into traffic, picking up speed.

"You in a hurry?" Hank asked, though Virgilio was driving carefully, only a little faster than the street traffic—a few cars, a delivery truck, a small truck loaded with steers to make the early morning market. The ambulance driver made his time by swerving into the opposite lane, and using his siren to help him through the red lights. He used a searchlight against the fronts of the old flats down along the railroad tracks.

"This neighborhood . . ." he said to Hank. "You want me to come with you, Doc?" He brought the ambulance to a stop.

"You stay with the bus," said Hank, taking the pink bus slip, glancing at it, and going across the broken sidewalk to the small porch. He knocked on the door.

A man's voice called, "It ain't locked. Come on in."

The young doctor went in, listening for the heavy breathing, the gasping for air, which the slip promised him. The room he entered was small, and neat. A young man with a bad complexion, wearing an undershirt and pajama pants, was sitting in an overstuffed chair with a book on his lap.

Hank glanced again at the slip. "What seems to be the trouble?" he asked.

"I've got this cold."

A cold. "For how long?"

"Four days, five."

Hank motioned to the bed, and the young man pulled off his undershirt and lay down. The intern examined him. "Do you want to go to the hospital?" he asked.

"Oh, no!"

"Then why did you call for an ambulance? We were told . . ."

"Just give me some nose drops, Doc."

"You call me, and the ambulance and the driver, down here at four in the morning, to give you *nose drops?*"

"Well, you know how it is, Doc. Can't get one of you fellows to come see a sick man. And if I'd go to the clinic, I'd sit there three, four hours. I don't have that kind of time."

Hank felt the blood rising to his head. Dr. Creighton

said that "on ambulance duty, nine out of ten calls could be unnecessary, but the tenth one may save a life." He took his prescription pad out of his pocket, and wrote upon it. The young man complained that he didn't give him the nose drops, or maybe even a shot. Hank cut him short by leaving the house.

This was his second month of ambulance duty, which he should have rotated with the other men. He had not expected to do this duty for so long a period, but things had worked out that way, and he gradually found that he was liking the work. Dr. Creighton had noted his interest and suggested that he might go into the new field of emergency room service. A vital thing . . .

Hank Blair was soon going to have to decide what he would "go into." A graduate of medical school, and already a doctor, he, like hundreds of other good men, had elected to do intern service to gain practical experience. He had opted for a "small" hospital and had never regretted his choice. Now—did he want to stay small or go into a bigger institution, do a residency in, perhaps, emergency work, receiving, diagnosing, the whole bit? Soon he must decide. He was giving careful consideration to staying at Memorial Hospital, not knowing if the same suggestion had been made to the other interns. There was no conflict between him and the others; he just was not one to get chummy and talk about personal things.

As for Hank himself, he liked working at Memorial Hospital under Fox Creighton. The man made all the difference. So would Hawthorne's coming into the picture make a difference. Dr. Blair wanted no part of things he had heard and seen about that man.

The bus pulled into the hospital garage; Hank picked up his bag, and went back to bed. He could still get, maybe, two hours' sleep.

Arthur Smith, M.D., had problems which differed from Hank's. He was out of medical school for five years; he had a wife and family, and a practice back in Alabama. It had taken considerable thought and planning to decide that he needed intern training. By the time he applied, a small hospital was all that offered itself. Well, he would probably work in small hospitals. So, on this day, he philosophically accepted his assignment to the administrator's office, and patiently performed the paper work given him to do.

"You are pretty good," that woman told him at noon. "This could be your field. Besides . . ."

Dr. Smith looked up, and took off his glasses. "In this office," he said, "I don't run into patients who don't want a nigger working them up."

"Dr. Smith . . ."

"We do better back in Alabama, Mrs. Reuther."

"Our main problem in this part of the country . . ."

"I know. Chicanos and Indians. You don't have as many blacks."

"Not as doctors, no."

She could fight, this highly efficient, carefully disciplined woman.

"Did Dr. Creighton assign me here?" Smith asked. "To decide on pictures for the lobby, and to make out records from your figures?"

"He assigns all medical services, Dr. Smith. I understand you plan to join a group operating a hospital and clinic."

"That's right. And administration will be part of it."

He again bent over the desk. No matter why he was spending this day in an office, or this week, he would get credit according to the work he did.

Pamela Thomas—Tommie—was interning in anaesthesia especially, though in a hospital the size of Creighton Memorial, she had other duties as well, usually on the surgical floor. This day, however, she was helping in pediatrics. Dr. Clark had asked her to do this. Tommie liked that service, and wondered if she might do a residency specializing in children's anaesthetics. The baby over whom she was working offered arguments on both sides of her personal problems.

Dr. Clark asked Tommie: "Dr. Thomas, if you are not busy will you see what is wrong with Bettina's Freijka pillow? The night nurse had difficulties when she changed the baby."

Of course Tommie would see. Though she had not had too much experience with double dislocations, she told the nurse on duty.

"I'll help you."

"I suppose the way to check the pillow would be to take it off, and see that everything was functioning."

"I haven't had any trouble with it. But we'll do that. She's probably ready for changing anyway, and I'd have to remove it."

Two months old, ready to smile without coaxing, a fuzz of blond hair, firm pink skin, Bettina was a darling. Born with both hipbones dislocated, she would need to wear the big round pillow separating her legs until the bilateral dislocation was corrected, and stay in the frog position until the femur bones were firmly back into the sockets. Then she could and would resume a normal little girl's life of running and jumping.

"I couldn't be as cheerful about all this as she is," said Tommie."

"Bettina's never known anything else. She's been in this harness since she was only a week old."

"She's still a darling." And she still offered the arguments. If Tommie would marry, she might continue as a doctor, but there probably would not be any residency in infant anaesthesiology. If she decided on the residency, she could help and work with babies like Bettina . . .

She and the nurse checked the harness, the pillow. Bettina drifted off into sleep before they were finished. Bettina had no problems, and perhaps Tommie didn't either. She could always talk to Dr. Creighton. When he returned, of course. She definitely knew that she wanted anaesthesiology. To be what he called "the comforter." She liked that term. Big, brusque, unapproachable in a human sense, Dr. Creighton seemed to know a lot about people as well as medicine.

Ted Bechars was the fourth intern then working at Memorial. Usually the Hospital supported only two, or three. This year four were available, and Fox had put them to use.

Dr. Bechars, like his companions, was facing a crisis in his life. He too was married, with one child. He had borrowed money to complete his medical education; his wife was anxious, as he was, for him to begin to earn something like a living wage. He had planned on doing internal medicine; this internship would allow him to get a residency, with adequate pay, but nothing like luxury-class living. On taking this place, he had wondered if service here would hamper his chance for a residency in a big hospital. After several months he realized that training under Fox Creighton put him into a prime position.

Memorial was a good hospital; it had a staff of competent, even exceptional, men. Dr. Bechars was getting excellent training. He knew that he was doing much the same work he would have done in a big-city hospital four times this

size. Right now he was directly responsible for ten general
medicine patients, very sick people, which made for a load
to carry. He also accompanied the doctors who came to the
hospital to visit their private patients, studying the charts,
listening, asking questions, and answering them. To keep up,
Ted, like the staff men, had to do a lot of reading. The
intern often sat in on consultations with the hospital surgeons or the o.b.-gyn men. Ted's was a busy day, even his
breaks were used for study.

And the future was crowding in on him. He must decide
what next he should do. His understanding wife said that
he must himself decide. Of course, because of the way his
education had been financed, he was obligated to go into the
Air Force for two years. This would count as residency when
he was ready to qualify for certification as a specialist in
internal medicine, and up to the past month, Dr. Bechars
had thought his life was definitely cast into that mold.

But during that past month, he had met Perry Hawthorne,
perhaps not entirely by accident. There had been a party.
Marilyn had had her hair done; they had secured a baby-
sitter, and they went to the party, which was held at the
Carson Country Club; a couple in the same apartment house
had invited them. And there Ted Bechars had met . . .

.. That night, a whole new vista opened before him. Dr.
Hawthorne was quite a guy. Marilyn had fallen instantly
and completely under his spell. Ted found himself listening
to the man. He made quite a lot of sense. The Southwest
needed doctors, he said. Carson needed them. Why should
the town lose a fellow like Bechars? Oh, the Air Force
thing could be handled. Hawthorne had sources; besides, if
the district ever should have a Hill-Burton institution, Bechars, on the staff, would be indispensable.

For the past month, Ted Bechars had done a lot of
thinking and question answering. He and Marilyn had spent
his thirty-six-hour weekend at the Hawthorne country
place. Now, *there* was a layout! Horses, field dogs— a bit
of shooting, a little riding, a lot of sitting by a huge fire
with a drink in his hand, talking, listening, thinking. Hawthorne was neither the man, nor the doctor, probably, that
Creighton was. The town talked about him, the personnel at
Memorial talked—well, Bechars would not do, nor need to
do, the sort of medicine Hawthorne was said to do. Though
a lot of doctors did. With nice returns, too.

But what harm would there be in examining Hawthorne's

proposal, and using what voice and influence he had to push the plan for a merger? Marilyn was all for it, but Marilyn had been dazzled by Hawthorne's physical charms, and his home.

Ted must be more realistic. He should move cautiously, either way. He perhaps could talk to Tommie and to Smith. Their viewpoint would parallel his own. Blair probably would give the best counsel, but Blair was not a friendly soul.

Anyway . . .

Rather late that Tuesday afternoon, Dr. Crosby called a meeting of the interns. Blair came in last, eating a sandwich, bringing a glass of milk from the diet kitchen. He'd been on an ambulance call, he said. An old man with a stroke.

Dr. Crosby did a little quizzing on X-ray plates. He then spoke briefly on the subject of loyalty to the staff and the hospital where they were serving.

Ted Bechars sucked in his cheeks.

"You attended the staff meeting yesterday," said Dr. Crosby. "You heard Dr. Hawthorne's offer to Memorial. There was no action taken. Today there are rumors that the merger is going to be pushed. Perhaps advantage will be taken of Dr. Creighton's absence. Perhaps some of us at Memorial will be approached and asked to work from within. Perhaps some of you have already been approached. I suppose I need not say to you that, as interns, these decisions will not be up to you."

He excused the class. The four went out of the room and down the hall.

"Each one of us suspicious of the other," drawled Hank Blair.

The others stared at him. Bechars' cheeks got red, as they could from simply outraged anger.

"Makes for a jumpy atmosphere," said Blair blithely. "Boss gone, and all."

"Look, Blair," said Dr. Smith. Then he stopped.

"Ambulance call, Dr. Blair," the floor nurse was calling to them. Hank thrust the milk glass into Tommie's hand, and took off at a fast lope, his hair bouncing.

"I don't like that fella," said Arthur Smith.

"But I don't believe Hawthorne would either," said Tommie.

Ted glanced at her, then asked the floor nurse if she knew what this ambulance call had been.

"Not really," she said. "Just that a woman had been hurt in a car wreck; she must be pregnant because o.b. has been alerted."

"Oh, fine."

"Don't worry," said Arthur Smith. "Dr. Blair will take care of everything."

Tommie stared at him. "If I knew the words," she cried, "I'd tell you what I think of a remark like that."

Dr. Bechars touched her shoulder. "Simmer down, Tommie," he advised.

Then he glanced at Dr. Smith. "Things are tense enough around here," he said. "This crisis building for the hospital, Dr. Creighton gone . . ."

"He shouldn't have left," said the nurse.

"Oh, but a man has to get away!" protested Tommie.

"Have you seen the evening paper?" the nurse asked.

"Interns don't have time . . ." said Bechars, reaching for the paper she held up. He spread it out on the counter. On the front page, in heavy black type, was the headline: FEDERAL FUNDS ASKED FOR CITY HOSPITAL

Tommie read the account aloud, skipping words here and there. "Union Hospital announced today . . . asking Creighton Memorial Hospital to join their nonprofit organization . . . to secure Government assistance . . . building a large, modern hospital . . . a clinic to be part of . . . indigent care . . . extended care. Cardiac unit . . ."

"All run by Dr. Hawthorne," said the nurse dryly.

"It's what he suggested yesterday," Tommie pointed out.

"In the privacy of a staff meeting, he said that. Yes."

"I don't suppose," said Dr. Bechars," that Dr. Creighton anticipated this announcement."

"The town will be in a state," declared the nurse.

The town was in a state. The interns began to make evening rounds, and every patient was fired up. The newspaper, radio, visitors—word had come in. As many were shocked at the suggestion as were thrilled by it. Only the comatose, the very sick, had no opinion. Opinions of Dr. Hawthorne were freely given, and of his nonprofit hospital. What did Dr. Creighton have to say, they asked. Learning that he was out of town, several patients sank into despair.

What would happen to Memorial Hospital? Where would the new one be built? They guessed more room was needed, but—

Some would have no "truck" with a hospital which in-

cluded Union and the way they did things. But many more
thought the whole idea was wonderful.

Such a big, new, modern hospital would be a wonderful
thing.

* * *

The wreck had occurred miles away, and it was two hours
before the ambulance came back to the hospital. The o.b.
staff, standing ready, had time to eat supper, and then to
become restive about the delay.

E.r. was alerted. O.b. was alerted. Why the hell . . .?

Was Blair on the bus?

Oh, yes.

"Probably earning his pay," growled Dr. Kayser, the o.b.
man.

Everything continued to be ready, the e.r. was brightly
lighted, as was delivery. Three nurses, two orderlies stood
about, sat, drank Cokes from the corridor machine, visited
with other people on the first floor.

Dr. Kayser went off to the switchboard to talk again to
the Highway Police. The ambulance was on its way, under
escort, he came back to report.

"We're building this up," he said, "until we won't know
how to handle anything routine."

They did not need to know. Though, in any case, Memorial discouraged "routine consideration" of any medical
problem. When the first wail of the siren was heard—still a
mile away—the orderlies were beside the cart, a nurse—the
hall was clear, the emergency door was open, both leaves of
it.

Red lights flashing, the police car and the ambulance came
up swiftly, easily; Hank Blair had the bus door open, and
jumped down. "Kayser?" he asked the first orderly.

"He's here. Heard you had a pregnant."

Hank Blair helped slide the stretcher out, watchful. There
was a plasma rig which he held aloft as he followed the
cart inside. Dr. Kayser came to meet him.

"Pregnant," Dr. Blair told him. "Badly smashed up; she
wrapped the car right around a pole. The woman's in
shock; she lost a lot of blood."

"You took a time . . ."

"We couldn't get her out of the car. Watch the door,
sir . . ."

Dr. Kayser stood back while the orderlies and nurses
transferred the patient.

"If it's a ruptured spleen. . .?" Hank asked him.

"Do you think it is?"

"I think there is internal bleeding. A lot of it. And the shock I mentioned."

"Then we'll need Belze," said Dr. Kayser, going to the table. When he turned back, his face was pale green. "Call Dr. Belze," he said, "and find the man! Because he's needed here. But you'd better call Dr. Forrest, too."

* * *

There were a half-dozen motels in and near Carson. There was a flea-bag hotel down in the town's levee district. There was also a good hotel, twelve storys high, beautifully built in the fashion of the Southwest of stucco on brick, with arched windows framed in rough wood, a deep, cool portico sheltering the lower floor, Navajo rugs, silver artifacts, leather chairs and couches in the lobby. The bellboys wore uniforms reminiscent of the bull ring, the waitresses in the restaurants wore off-the-shoulder blouses and long, bright squaw skirts. There was a good, and popular, bar.

And there was also a drugstore, a large one, at the corner of the hotel building. Here was a long refreshment counter where anything, almost, could be bought and consumed. Coffee, tomato juice, Bromo Seltzer—ice cream sodas, corn beef sandwiches, soup—chili, tacos . . .

The place was large and bright, and popular. Several rows of dispaly cases offered bright and varied merchandise. Sooner or later, everyone met everyone else at the hotel drugstore.

Out-of-town hotel guests, of course, and the permanent residents, as well as anyone else who might be downtown and in need of aspirin, a cup of coffee, or companionship.

Pat Kern, the mayor of Carson, crony of Dr. Fox Creighton, came in that evening. A tall, well-dressed, friendly man, he greeted the first group he saw, answered a call from across the counter, and heard about the bad wreck out on the feeder highway . . .

Pat winced. "Who was it?" he asked.

"Woman. Alone. They are withholding the name."

"Sure, sure. It's always bad when the family learns of these things through the radio. I suppose she's been taken to the hospital."

"Yes. That is, their ambulance went out."

"Good," said the mayor, moving on.

"Good it's not Hawthorne's ambulance," said the man he

had left, loudly enough for the mayor to hear, but not need to make any comment.

But the pharmacist said the same thing when Pat went into his "office," to use the telephone. He could learn who the injured person was. When he hung up, his face was grave.

"Someone you know, Pat?" asked the druggist.

Pat waved his forefinger reprovingly.

The pharmacist nodded. "Well, at least she won't go to Union."

"Aren't you supposed to be neutral?" Pat asked him.

"I choose the folks I talk to. And, anyway, that Hawthorne, he's something else!"

"He made a very strong pitch in tonight's newspaper."

"Yes, he did. What does Fox have to say about such a merger?"

Pat laughed. "Fox is not the chatty type, as you well know, Tim."

"I am not a smart man, but I'd venture a guess on what he thinks of joining up with Hawthrone."

"I'll say this much," said the mayor. "Memorial's pinch for space is a big item with Fox."

"Building-on would cost an awful lot, wouldn't it?"

"Yes. And the cost would have to be paid by the customers."

"Would the Government really give us a new hospital?"

"If Memorial and Union both were to close down, or would say responsibly that they would do so, yes, a big grant would be made. The city would have to put up some money of its own."

"And who would run the thing?"

"Who runs any hospital? A board."

"That isn't what I meant."

"I know it isn't. And I couldn't imagine, any more than you can, Fox Creighton working with Dr. Hawthrone, or even having the man on his staff."

"He really is something else," said Tim again, shaking his head. "His hospital is in very bad trouble, I hear. They are crowded, too. Lately they've spent some money on new furniture in the downstairs waiting room, electric beds in a few rooms—and higher salaries for the staff. It's difficult for them to keep R.N.'s. They have never tried to qualify for intern service. I guess you know about the traffic in abortions."

"That's gossip, Tim."

"Do you know that it is?"

"No, I don't know. If I did I'd probably have to take steps."

"He got himself into something of a bind over the Medicare thing. Anyway, his hospital has only forty-five or fifty beds, and the building needs all sorts of repair and modernization. So he thinks the best solution . . ."

"But doesn't the man have brains enough to know that, if by some miracle of fate or happenstance, the two hospitals would merge, he could not possibly compete with Creighton? He'd be swallowed up! That guy, Fox . . . not only his abilities, but his character. He's the upright man, in all ways."

"He is," said Tim, accepting a prescription from a customer who had come to the pass-through counter.

"I heard," said this man, "that George Clark was Dr. Creighton's cousin. Is that true?"

"I believe it is true," said the Mayor.

"It's true, and maybe it's why Creighton is upright," said the pharmacist dryly.

"Clark doesn't work. Does Creighton do for his wife and kids?"

Pat Kern turned away, toward the door. "I'd better get home to my own wife and kids," he told Tim.

"O.K., Pat. See you!" Tim carefully poured small tablets into a small bottle. "I doubt very much," he said slowly, "if Dr. Creighton helps support George Clark's family. The wife, you know, is a doctor."

"And makes lots of money?" persisted the customer, who was well known to Tim.

"I wouldn't know," said the druggist. "Here you are, James. That will be seven dollars plus tax."

The customer got out his billfold. "You pillmakers do all right in medicine, too, don't you?"

"We're right in there trying," said the pharmacist good-naturedly.

* * *

Marion Clark, who sometimes suspected that she was talked about as George Clark's wife, but did not experience any burning of her ears that night, sat at the chart desk, impatient with herself for being late getting home. Her girls were able to take care of themselves, of course, and she would go home in another ten minutes. Sometimes it was difficult to explain delays even to herself. She had a full roster of patients in the hospital; her morning clinic hours had run late; lunch was eaten well after one o'clock. She had the usual office duties of mail, reports, paper work. She had made two house calls. Pediatricians still had to do that. She had not got back to the hospital until almost five. Rounds took time, Willie's mother had to be argued out of taking the boy home. And then, even as Marion had begun to write the night orders, freckle-faced Eddie had been brought to the hospital by a frightened and irate father.

The admissions clerk could not get a sense-making statement from the man, while Eddie refused to talk at all. Sulky, and frightened, too. His father alternately coaxed and threatened the boy. Finally she sent for Dr. Bechars who called Dr. Clark.

"On one symptom alone, I believe he's your patient, doctor," the intern said. "The kid's nine years old."

"All right. Send him over," said Dr. Clark, glancing at the clock. She called her home and told Nancy she would be late. "Fix whatever you want for dinner, dear. I'm sorry."

"That's all right, Doc. And I know how you would react to pizza."

Marion laughed. "Just air out the place. I hate the smell of the things."

Eddie's problem proved to be more time-consuming than serious. It was difficult for Dr. Clark to get a sensible account from father or son. But the boy did have stomach pains, and if it were true . . . Marion ordered X-rays, and went down with the child to help the technician take them. She would read them wet, she said. While waiting, she heard the ambulance come in upstairs, and someone out in the hall said they had a serious case in e.r. A pregnant woman in a car wreck. At that time, Marion was staring, not believing her eyes, at a polka-dotted picture of Eddie's abdomen. One didn't need barium to see what gave the boy his stomach ache.

She went upstairs again, and, this time shutting the father out of the room, she got the boy to talk.

Yes, he admitted, he had swallowed some marbles.

How many?

"Oh, four or five, I guess."

"Eddie?"

"Well . . ." The boy squirmed on his bed. "There was this kid—he bet I wouldn't swallow three marbles."

"And you did."

"Yeah. And then he made me a double-dare."

"For how many?"

"Eighteen, I guess." He began to cry. "You goin' to cut me open and take 'em out?"

"We'll see what we can do. But you have to promise me one thing."

"Yes, ma'am."

"Don't take any more dares, will you? And don't *ever* put a marble into your mouth again."

"Yes, ma'am. Will I get my marbles back?"

"I hope so," said Marion.

She spoke to the ward nurse, she spoke to Eddie's father, she wrote the order at the floor desk for a special diet, and mineral oil.

"And Eddie can sit and wait," said Dr. Bechars.

Marion smiled at him reprovingly. "I am going home," she said. "What do you hear about the accident case?"

"Not much. It was a woman, badly hurt. They've taken her to o.r., but Dr. Belze hasn't come in yet."

"I hope he isn't missing again this evening."

"He won't be, will he?"

Dr. Clark walked down the hall, thinking. Fox would be amused at her emergency. *Marbles,* she said softly, below her breath. She looked in at Eddie. He was all right. And she came out into the hall again. This time was a lull between supper trays and evening visiting hours. The corridor stretched before her, shining, green-white, quiet.

And Marion Clark, dark, slender, walked silently along the pale green brightness, between it, below it—thinking.

Not of green hospital halls, but of Fox Creighton who had left his hospital—because it definitely was his!—to go to his uncle's funeral. Marion must think about him there. She could imagine every detail. She had grown up in Los Hermanos. All through her childhood, she had seen the big Clark home. Built by Easterners who had come to the Southwest to live, and designed through their nostalgic memories of what a proper home should be. The city had grown up and around the house, but it still stood, dark red brick, white stone window trim, gabled roof.

The Clark home was rightly called a mansion. Fox too had known it as a child. His mother would have brought him

there on visits to her parents, and perhaps later to see her
brother. Fox's mother had inherited an equity in that home.
Through a lifetime trust, she and Stephen Clark had deeded
it to the state historical society, for by then George's father
knew that his son would never honorably live in it. And he
would not tolerate anything but an honorable use of the
handsome home.

Marion could remember going into that house the day
after her marriage to George. She was a young girl then, and
pretty. Her great-grandmother had been an Indian, which
was a handicap in some circles, but her family was an old
one in Los Hermanos. They were not rich. Not rich at all.
Marion had her degree from the state university, and she
wanted to study medicine.

Instead she had fallen in love with handsome young
George Clark. He had demanded that they quickly be
married, a step which went against everyone's will or wish.
George Clark was a wastrel, a gambler. The police once
had asked him to leave Los Hermanos.

Marion's mother had opposed the marriage in every way
she could. She talked to her daughter, she threatened her
and begged her. Finally she went to Stephen Clark and
found that he was as opposed to the marriage as she was.
Not against Marion as a desirable wife, but sternly against
George as husband to any nice girl who knew him so slight-
ly.

She now remembered every detail of the dinner at the
Clark home after the wedding. The cut-glass salt dishes, the
tall-backed dining room chairs, roast beef carved at a side
table, and asparagus handed round on a silver dish. It had
turned into a gathering of disapproval.

Why had she done that awful thing? Why had she not
listened to those older and wiser people? Twenty-five years
later, she could not think of a single reason. And already
she wished she had gone to her father-in-law's funeral.

* * *

The hospital in Carson was facing the crisis of its life; as
a hospital did have a life, a vitality given to it directly in ac-
cordance with its concern for the lives of the people cared
for beneath its roof, by the doctors and workers who labored there. That concern should be and usually was an in-
tense awareness of life such as could be found in few other
places.

For a hospital itself to be in crisis was a fearsome thing.

"If we don't expand," Alice Tunstall told herself, "we can go on. But it will be marking time. And five years from now, we'll have gone downhill, slowed."

She should not have left the hospital. As superintendent of nurses, one of the vital services of Creighton Memorial, she should have stayed at home, in the hospital, to look after things. She could have helped Fox. She could have encouraged him, and he would have known that she supported him. Perhaps together they could discover a way. Fiercely defensive, she did not want to give up the hospital as she knew it. Fox must not get discouraged. The Board and the town must not be allowed to go to the Government for help and reorganization.

Such a place could be a good hospital; it would do good work; but Fox Creighton would not stay with such an institution. He had come back to Carson, at great personal sacrifice, to carry on the tradition which his father and grandfather had built and maintained. The cost to him had been great. Tremendous.

But when his father and mother were suddenly killed in that terrible plane crash, he had come home. He took over the work to be done. Big, brusque, and kind, he had chosen to isolate himself, and so work with the hospital, for it.

Of course he had been young—but he acted ten years older than his age. He still did. He had taken on a tremendous job, one strange to him. But the task was there, he accepted it, and he did it, though the cost had been high.

But it was the way life's die had been cast for him, and he lived with it, not happily often. But he managed.

However, if anything should happen to the hospital, the whole project would blow up and away. Fox Creighton would return to his laboratory, his microscopes, his test cases and controls.

And the hospital—that would be another "airplane crash" in his life.

Though that could not happen! Alice Tunstall must do all she could to see that it did not happen. Right this minute, she should be dressed in white linen, a starched cap on her head, busy at her desk, or out on the floor, perhaps conferring with Fox, instead of hundreds of miles away, getting out of this bus, waiting to see that the skycap had her bag —she showed him her airline ticket, received the check. Her back straight, she walked into the big, airy building, sought the proper desk where she would determine her gate, and the time of her plane's departure.

She was anxious to board, to get home. She had left her car at the Carson airport. Her apartment would welcome her with warmth and comfort. Carolyn Cotsworth would surely do something wonderful to welcome her. She hoped not with an invitation to join her and Virginia for supper. Tunnie wanted to unpack, and go over to the hospital for a quick check.

But Carolyn would have a plate of cookies, a casserole in the oven—something. Nasturtiums in a little green vase, perhaps. Carolyn was really remarkable. And Tunnie did want to see her, if only to ask about Clytie. Clytie had been asked about at the reunion, and Tunnie had had to report that she was very ill. Without anyone's saying so, she knew that Clytie would not get well. Did Carolyn know this? She had never talked about it.

* * *

Clytie. Clytie Cotsworth Whiteside. The youngest of the three Cotsworth sisters. And the sickest, she would have said wryly that sunny Tuesday morning.

Really sick, she half-whispered to herself. She should, really, give up and go to an apartment, or even to a nursing home near her sisters. They were all the family she had. Donald, her husband, had been dead for six or seven years. Oh, dear Donald! If only he could have lived. But there it was, dead of a heart attack with Clytie summoned to his law office by telephone.

As a former nurse, she had known these sudden things to happen. But to have her beloved Donald— The experience still could shake her.

With Donald gone, Carolyn had been anxious for Clytie to move to Carson. She would not need to live with her sisters, though Virginia seemed happy enough living with Carolyn. Clytie could perhaps have a little house and a flower garden.

Clytie should have done that. Then, now, she would not be alone, and frightened. During the intervening years, before this horrible cancer had gnawed its way through her body, she could have helped the "girls." Donald had left Clytie plenty of money; she had learned to manage it well.

But, the truth was, three hundred miles away from her sisters, she could live alone. And until just lately, she had liked living alone, in her own apartment, with her pretty things. She looked fondly at her green silk damask couch, with its little pink tuck pillows. She liked her friends, playing bridge with them, going to lectures, and taking trips—to Switzerland three years ago, and Majorca the next year. She liked having pretty clothes and lots of them. Carolyn called her extravagant. Clytie liked hunting for antiques, and buying them. Things like her handsome mahogany desk with its original brass. She did write a letter to Virginia. And again she was struck with a faint pang of remorse. She should have done more for her sisters. Had she been too selfish? Maybe she had ...

She drew an envelope out of the pigeonhole and addressed it. Then she sat thoughtful for a minute before she began to write the letter. Virginia might have to show it to Carolyn, and Carolyn would be hurt. But there were things Clytie wanted to say, and she must say them soon.

She bore down on the pen point and wrote darkly at the top of the note page, "For Virginia only."

Of course Carolyn could find the letter and read it anyway, but if she did, any hurt would be her own fault. So—

"Dear Virginia," Clytie wrote.

"I am not doing very well, and I want to tell you something. I want you to know that I am making a new will. My old one leaves everything to Carolyn. She has been kind to me, and for a while I thought she should have what money and property I own. But lately Carolyn has gone religious. She is obsessed with going to church and doing things for the church. Then there is some man; she writes some pretty silly letters about him, how handsome and charming he is. He is a doctor and it may be the one she works for. But I don't think that Donald's money should go to Carolyn's church or to this doctor. I don't want it to, at any rate."

Clytie sighed, and leaned back in the chair, to rest. She looked across at the couch. Should she do the remaining part of the letter in her lap? She was tired. No—she would rest a little, then finish here. Make it short ...

She put her head down on her arms folded on the desk leaf. My God, she thought, how thin I am! Just ugly bones. Old at fifty-one. As short a time as two years ago, I was watching my weight. She could laugh at that, if she could laugh about anything. She sighed and picked up the pen.

"So I am going to leave my estate in trust, Virginia. First to Carolyn, then to you, and finally to Judy and your grandchildren. I think that is more fair, and, really, they are my family. All I have.

* * *

Across the city of Los Hermanos on that hot Wednesday morning, a desert of heat stretched between the earth and the white-hot sky. The final events of Stephen Clark's funeral were proceeding in due order.

Fox Creighton dreaded the rest of the day, the heat was only a part of it. His black suit, white shirt and somber tie were proper for the occasion, but scarcely for the temperature.

Here in his grandfather's house, the darkened, high-ceilinged rooms still held the coolness of the night. But he wished he were back in the hospital, able to check on things there, able to be informed about Perry Hawthrone and whatever devious schemes the man might be devising. It was ridiculous to think that such a doctor could threaten Fox Creighton, or that his small hospital should not only compete with, but swamp, Memorial. But there were ways to accomplish such things, and in a time of trouble . . .

He turned up his shirt collar and measured the length of his tie. He should not have left. The problems at home were too great to be left untended for forty-eight hours. One thing was certain; he would go back as quickly as he could. Leave by midafternoon, surely.

He picked up his suit coat, and went out into the hall, down the wide stairs. His hand cupped the newel post.

From now on, the undertaker and then the lawyers would determine what he did. Where he stood, or sat . . . He had agreed to stay for the reading of the will.

There were a dozen people in the wide lower hall. His uncle's business associates, their wives—the mayor of the city—the honorary pallbearers. Fox was introduced to several people. One, gray-haired, neatly mustached gentleman was a physician. Fox was to ride in the car with him, he was told.

It was a long, black, shining car; the cortege was forming. This other doctor—his name was Ball—said he had been a friend of Steve Clark's.

"And you're the antigen fella, aren't you?" he asked Fox, as soon as the two men were seated in the car.

"Well . . ." said Fox. He was feeling ill at ease. Burials were uncomfortable relics of the tribal rites.

"I-heard you lecture at an AMA meeting in San Francisco," said Dr. Ball.

Fox nodded. "But that was several years ago, sir."

"Yes. Yes, it was. Five or six. I was greatly impressed."

"Thank you."

"What are you working on now?"

The cars were beginning to move, slowly.

"Well, nothing," said Fox. "Not in antigens, that is."

"Oh, but that's too bad, isn't it?"

"I don't know, sir. I—things happened. I am now Chief of Medical Services at the Creighton Memorial Hospital in Carson. And that job doesn't leave much time for research."

"Too bad, too bad. You had a fresh, and bold, approach. I know your hospital, of course. Is it good work you're doing?"

"I certainly hope so," said Fox.

"I didn't know that you and Stephen Clark— But I understand he was your uncle."

"Yes. My mother was his sister."

"He was a fine man. We are going to miss him. I wonder —there has been talk—and I suppose you'd know—what is going to happen to the girl?"

They were approaching the cathedral. "What girl?" Fox asked.

"Why, the girl—her name is Courtney something or other —she was your uncle's ward, his protégée. She lived in his home. Surely you've met her."

"I may have," Fox agreed. "Everyone here has been a stranger to me."

"Yes, of course. Well, Steve took her into his home several years ago. I don't know if she was related, or if she might have been the daughter of a friend—just that he has been kind to her."

"As he would be," said Fox. "And surely he has made some provision . . ."

"Oh, yes. He certainly would have done that. But this Courtney would be of an age when a girl needs a family. She's eighteen or nineteen."

"Neither retarded nor handicapped?"

"Oh, no. She's entered the University, I understand. But if there is no one in the relationship . . . Perhaps Steve's son . . . I understand he has daughters of his own."

The car drew up to the steps, and Fox prepared to get out of it. "Before I'd let George Clark take care of my uncle's protégée," he said firmly, "I'd take her into my own home." He turned to let the older man join him on the steps.

"Now that would please your uncle," said Dr. Ball, standing beside the tall man. "If the son is out, I don't believe there is anyone else in close relationship."

Standing there, with a wind beginning to whip up dust around them, watching the mourners join the lines of escort, or go into the church, Fox critically studied the women, trying to pick out one who might be his uncle's ward. There were only a few young women—Courtney might already have gone inside—Fox should be able to recognize another lonely soul in this crowd.

* * *

Courtney had indeed gone inside. She had come alone to the cathedral, and early. She wanted to face her loss and her grief alone in the dim, silent church before the people began to fill the pews. She sat in the space allotted to her; she knelt for a minute in prayer; she listened to the soft organ music, and gazed up at the colors of the rose window high above the altar.

She saw the pallbearers come in and take their places. She looked closely at the tall, red-headed doctor whom she knew to be her benefactor's nephew. She had seen him at the house, from the stair landing, from behind the screen in the dining room. Hurt and shyness had prevented her from going forward and declaring herself. The young doctor must feel no obligation . . .

But she wished she could know him.

And she watched him, all during the service, and then at the cemetery where things were being hurried because of the sandstorm which was whipping up.

This man was tall, with wide shoulders and narrow, flat hips. His coat collar fitted beautifully, showing just the right edge of white above it. His neck was thick and strong. His hair was red, and would feel coarse to the touch, the girl felt sure. It was uncompromisingly straight, thick, and not long. The features of his face were rocklike, there were deep creases between his eyes, and wide, double brackets about his mouth. His hands were big, and strong-looking. At the minute, they were clenched tightly at his sides, and his face showed no emotion.

"I love him," Courtney said to herself. "I love that man . . ."

She turned on her heel and walked away from the gathered people, from the grave. The man with the red hair watched her go. Beyond her the sky was angry. Clouds were rolling across it, hiding the mountains. The sun was one red gash in their heaviness. Then tree, mountains, nearby buildings, and the people who mourned, dissolved into the darkening air. He saw Courtney running toward a car; someone tugged at his sleeve.

"We'd better get out of here, doctor!"

Chapter Three

CLYTIE COTSWORTH WHITESIDE frowned at her need to snap on the lamps as she escorted the young attorney to the door. The whistling wind, the darkening sky, spelled sand-storm, and despite all precautions, there would be little ridges of dust on the windowsills, against the doors.

She held out her hand to the young man from Donald's office. The other clutched the blue-bound fold of papers against her breast. "Thank you so much for coming here," she said, summoning all her graciousness, even managing a smile. "I am afraid a storm is coming up. Perhaps you should stay . . ."

He shook his head. "I think I can make it downtown. Take care of the will, Mrs. Whiteside. It should be kept in a safe place."

"I know. I'll take it to the bank tomorrow. They will take care of it for me. Perhaps I'll go later today."

"And see that the former one is destroyed." The young attorney smiled engagingly at his client. She was a very sick woman; her eyes were sunken, her smile ghastly.

"I'll destroy the old one," Clytie promised.

"All right. Now, I'd better run."

Clytie closed the door, set the chain in place, and turned back to the living room. She would lie down for a time. Later, if she were able, she would dress, call a taxi, and try to get to the bank. Perhaps a friend would take her, or the apartment manager. He and his wife had witnessed the sign-ing of the will. It would be safe enough here, but things happened. If she became very ill, and had to return to the hospital . . .

Yes, but surely by tomorrow she would go to the bank.

She would not attempt to drive, of course, but she surely could go by cab, have the driver wait . . .

She lay down on her bed, and unfolded the will, read it through again. Yes, that was the way she wanted things to be. Carolyn could use the income from her money—that was all she would use anyway—then Virginia and the children . . .

Lying there, Clytie frowned. She had written to Virginia —this morning? No. Yesterday, wasn't it? Well, in the letter she had explained that she was making a new will. But until Clytie could give it to the bank, unless she could, something might happen to it.

Should she phone her sisters? So they would expect to find the will if she became ill. She could call Carolyn at the hospital. Only, she was so very tired. She would rest for a time.

It was still dark from the storm when she found strength and will to get off the bed, go out to the kitchen and warm a can of soup. It was too late to go to the bank, but she could phone. . .

After she had eaten, she felt a little better, and remembered to take her medicine. She could think more clearly. She even put in a call to Carolyn's number. And got the busy signal.

She could call that nice woman doctor who lived in the same apartment house . . . What was her name? Clark. That was it. Marion Clark. Dark, slender, good-looking. She knew how to dress.

Above the sisters, there lived a nurse. Her apartment was quiet, uncluttered, and rich-looking. Clytie knew Miss Tunstall, and she would not call her for a thing like her will and not wanting it lost.

Carolyn's and Virginia's apartment was filled with bric-a-brac, shadow boxes, knickknacks.

Dr. Clark's had all the clutter to be expected when there were young girls in the home, books about, records, somebody's crewel embroidery, a tennis racquet—a nice, homey place, with a nice, understanding mother. The girls . . .

They were cute girls, modern girls. Clytie could figure their ages though it didn't really matter. She did know their names. The oldest was Laura Ann, pert, pretty, and smart. She'd got into trouble when she was fifteen. The mother, the woman doctor, thought she should have her baby and put it out for adoption, but not be saddled with the boy who had

got her into that terrible spot. Carolyn had been shocked at
such a suggestion. And the father, too, evidently, because
there had been a wedding to satisfy Laura Ann's father.
Clytie could not remember what had happened to the child,
but Laura Ann was now divorced.

* * *

The cars quickly left the cemetery because of the sandstorm. Many of the people would return to the Clark house,
for lunch, it was announced, and the reading of the will.
Dr. Ball rode back with Fox but said he would not come in;
he had many things to do, as the other doctor would
understand.

Fox groaned a little when he agreed with him. "I don't
dare to think of all the things I should be doing," he said.

"If this wind drops you should be able to get away this
afternoon, but don't start out in a sandstorm."

Fox nodded, shook hands, and dashed up into the
porch and house. A dozen people were staying for lunch,
two lawyers, men who seemed to know about a foundation
to be set up for the vocational training of local boys . . .

So George Clark would not fall into "all that money."
Good!

Fox served as host. He sat at the head of the luncheon
table. The inside shutters had been closed against the sand,
and lamps were lighted. The lunch was good. Sliced meat
and eggs in aspic, fresh peas and tiny mushrooms—good
coffee, and wine for those who wanted it.

The girl, Courtney, did not come to the table. But Dr.
Ball had been busy. He had spread the word that Dr.
Creighton stood ready to assume responsiblity for Stephen
Clark's ward.

"Yes," he heard himself say to one of the attorneys for
the estate, a pudgy man of fifty or so, with a slow, deliber-
ate way of talking. During the meal, he sat at Fox's right
hand. "I said she could come to my hideout. Oh, really, it
isn't that. It's quite a large house, actually. Comfortable. It
was my grandparents' home, and I grew up there."

"In Carson."

"At the edge of town, yes. But this girl—Courtney?—
perhaps she is old enough to care for herself. Though she
would be welcome to come to my place for this college vacation, and others. I owe that much to my uncle for the
vacations he made pleasant for me. When she's older, or
even now, she possibly could find employment in our hospi-

tal. If she would like that sort of thing. The main idea of course would be to give her roots, a sense of belonging to someone."

"That is very generous of you."

Fox made a slashing gesture with his hand. "Generosity has no part in my suggestion," he protested. "Besides, the young woman may want to be on her own."

"There is provision for a small trust fund," said the attorney. "She'll never go hungry."

"I should think there would be provision, but if she would care to consider my home as hers, a place where she belongs . . ." He reached for his water goblet. Why in the devil was he arguing for this thing? He didn't really want a girl—any girl—living in his home. That could bring about all sorts of complications. The thing was, quite simply, he would have done the same thing for his uncle's beloved dog.

His uncle, Fox's family, had assumed this obligation. George would not, and should not, take it over . . . So . . .

"Where *is* Courtney?" asked the woman who sat at Fox's other side.

"She'll be in," said the lawyer. "I believe she is helping in the kitchen."

"Is the girl shy?" Fox asked.

"No. Not at all. Just now, she is sad. And of course with your uncle's death, she feels that she no longer has a place here."

"But that is exactly what I have in mind," said Fox strongly. "To give her a chance to feel that she does have a place."

"You are very kind," said the woman.

"I am a doctor," Fox answered. "It is a part of us to prevent or to heal hurt."

"I still don't see how you can do it," said the lawyer. "You are young . . ."

"I'm thirty-eight," Fox said. "But I am a busy man, weighted with responsibilities, if not years."

"And I understand you are not married . . ." The woman still smiled at him.

"No," Fox agreed. "But it would be nonsense to make an issue of that fact."

"Others will make an issue of it."

"Then it would *be* nonsense."

"Perhaps you could marry her."

Fox growled, soundlessly, and turned to accept food being offered at his shoulder.

This arrangement he had offered—it made no difference to him if it were accepted, or not. Or if it did make a difference, the balance would have to be on the negative side. He had, so far, managed to keep himself free of other human entanglements. He would handle this one, however things turned out.

* * *

Late on Tuesday night, Marion Clark's silent green halls of the hospital were again quiet. The floors gleamed, the curtained half-doors were closed, and the nurse at the floor desk sat, busy, in her pool of lamplight. Over the stairs, and at the elevator, a red light bloomed.

Up on surgical, the intern and the orderly drew the cart slowly along the hall. The men wore the baggy, wrinkled trousers, the smocklike jackets, the tied caps, for o.r. The patient lay covered, doubly strapped. Outside o.r., the floor nurse looked up, accepted the sheet of paper which Dr. Blair handed to her, and nodded. The cart turned, gently still, and entered the room.

Here too was a sort of quiet, though people moved about briskly, noiselessly. There were soft beeping and hissing sounds. The brush of canvas-covered feet against the tile floor.

The cart was brought exactly against the operating table, cranked up to height, and three people put out their hands, their bare arms. The straps were loosened and fell free. Still under the sheet, her silver-blond hair falling free, the woman was lifted, only a matter of inches; the bare arms extended, and laid her very gently upon the table.

The sheet was folded back, and someone lifted her arm . . .

"Dr. Blair, will you scrub?" It was Dr. Crosby, ready to shoulder the intern away from the table. Since Creighton Memorial did not have a supervising resident, Fox directly took over the instruction of the interns. Other doctors substituted when he was away.

"Kayser?" asked Hank, going toward the scrub room.

Crosby's head jerked. "With Belze in scrub," he said gruffly.

So Belze was there! He was standing on the far side of the circular basin where the bright cone of water rushed downward. Dr. Kayser, the o.b. man, was briefing the surgeon. "Sure to be her spleen . . . Blair here suspected that."

Belze looked terrible. He was a big man, with graying black hair, a heavy-featured, handsome face. And he was a prime surgeon. But—tonight—

Hank wanted to ask where-the-hell he had been. Instead, he scrubbed his left arm, rinsed, and scrubbed his right. A thousand and sixty, he counted, a thousand and . . .

White gown, gauze mask, gloves—he'd do what he was told to do. Belze might just save the woman.

He tried. The baby was dead, but so long as there was a flicker of life in the mother . . .

It was not enough. He stripped his gloves, and sighed heavily. "Will you close, Kayser?" he asked. "Where is Dr. Forrest?"

"He's in the hall, doctor."

Belze nodded, shrugging his chin up out of his gauze mask; he looked again at the woman on the table. He wished she had not driven so fast, and under such emotional strain. He wished he had been where he could have been reached, not —not—

He dropped his gloves, and, mask dangling, he shouldered through the door to the hall. Dr. Forrest waited there, leaning against the wall. He looked terrible too. He straightened when he saw Belze, with Dr. Crosby right behind him. "Where the hell have you been, Vil?" he cried roughly, loudly.

Dr. Belze pressed his lips together, and swallowed. When he thought where Forrest had been . . . He shuddered, and looked vaguely about. He was badly shaken, not just over the loss of a patient. This time he must fight remorse—that he couldn't save Dorothy, that he had not stopped her . . .

Ignoring all this, Dr. Forrest lunged toward him; his hand fell roughly and heavily upon Dr. Belze's shoulder. "She was *pregnant*, man!" he shouted. "And you had to disappear. For hours!"

Dr. Belze seemed not to notice what the other doctor said or did.

"Take it easy, Forrest," Dr. Crosby managed to intervene.

"Take it easy!" screamed Walter Forrest. "She was brought in here, and everybody stood around for two or three hours waiting for the chief surgeon to show up. In that time, he could have saved her child, and *her!* But, no—she just lay there . . ."

"I was here," said Dr. Crosby, "and Dr. Kayser. Even the ambulance intern did all that could be done, Forrest."

"But, *Vil!*" cried the anguished man; he seemed frightened by what had happened. "Where was *he?*" He thrust his face into Dr. Belze's. "Where *were* you, fella? *Where were you?*"

Dr. Belze straightened. He wiped his hand down along his face. "For that matter," he said wearily, "were *you* here?"

"I got here before you did!"

"Did you save her? You could have, couldn't you?"

"You know damn well I couldn't operate on her. But you —I've seen you do exactly that surgery."

"But not on Dorothy," Belze attempted. "She—"

"Damn right. Not on my wife! And that's the main thing, isn't it? That she was my wife. Well, I'll tell you one thing, Vil. I am going to sue you in court for this. I'll file suit tomorrow morning."

He talked wildly and loudly. Dr. Belze listened, woodenly, for a time; then he turned and went back into the operating room, and from there to scrub, where he would change. He looked at no one, he spoke to no one. A young nurse said that there were tears in his eyes.

Out in the hall, Dr. Crosby sought to quiet Dr. Forrest. He had the whole third floor, maybe the whole hospital, in an uproar, he said. He was to go to the lounge, have a cup of coffee and settle down.

"You think I'm not going to sue that character?" Forrest demanded.

"I think you can't do such a thing," Crosby told him. "You two are friends, man. You men and your wives have been friends for years!"

Everyone said the same thing. Forrest was in shock. Understandably so. But he would not sue . . .

"I wish Fox were here," said Dr. Crosby, preparing to go home. "Belze is in shock just about as deeply. Forrest is noisy. But Belze looks like a man ten weeks dead."

A dozen people said they wished Dr. Creighton was there. The third floor of the hospital, the whole hospital, and, by morning, the town, certainly were in an uproar.

What had happened at the hospital? What *could* have happened?

*   *   *

The hospital itself well knew what had happened. Tuesday night had been a wild one. "I think even the window frames are out of line," said Tommie at breakfast the next morning. She was wearing the hideous o.r. gown, her head was wrapped in gray-blue gauze, and she was without make-up.

"If your best beau could see you now," Ted Bechars teased her.

Tommie's head went up sharply.

"Hey," laughed Dr. Smith. "I think she has a best beau!"

"Well, of course she does," said Ted soothingly. "Hank's her deepest love."

"Where is he?" Pam asked, not thinking his rib worth noticing.

"Sacked in, I suppose. I heard he had a rough night."

"You can hear anything around this place," said Smith. "Even that Blair was a hero."

"They say . . ."

"But the patient still died."

Nobody said anything to that. The patient had died, but she also had been the wife of a staff man. The less talk about that the better where the interns were concerned.

"You don't suppose that Belze is operating this morning, do you?" Tommie asked finally, unable to bear the silence longer.

"He's scheduled."

"I heard he was terribly shook."

"Mhmmmn. But hospital stories—can you really imagine him with tears running down his face? I even heard that!"

"I heard it too," said Tommie soberly. "He's a wonderful surgeon, you know."

"If available," murmured Ted Bechars.

"Now, Ted . . ."

"I didn't say a thing. Except among friends."

"You hope."

And again they fell silent, each one worrying—about themselves primarily.

Dr. Bechars thought about the big medical school which he had attended, and the big hospital where he might now be interning. He thought about his wife and baby here in Carson, and the good chance that he would be going into the Air Force in the summer. Unless Hawthorne did have ways and means. If the prospect of a really big hospital here in

Carson lit up the sky, Ted would just as soon hitch on to that sort of thing. A man could do well for himself if things started right.

Pamela Thomas fetched another cup of coffee, and considered her place in the life she seemed destined to live. She thought about marrying the "boy friend" the men had just teased her about. Marriage, a home, and babies. She looked down at her hands, slender, sinewy, not always as strong as she needed them to be when asked to administer a sedative to a struggling patient, but she hoped she was approaching the ideal of having them as sensitive as the hands of a violinist. If she did opt for child anaesthesiology, she must be able to restrain a fighting child, and to handle a baby as gently as a glass blower handles a goblet. She must be quick of hand and eye, able to dart her glance to every dial and meter in o.r., all the time knowing by feel exactly how the patient was doing. Calm, sureness, to communicate to the anxious patient—sometimes Tommie wondered why she had wanted to be a doctor, why of all things, she wanted anaesthesiology. But the minute she was in o.r. and saw what went on there, the reliance of the patient, the doctor and his helpers, on the doctor behind the shield at the head of the table . . .

Arthur Smith was not given to retrospection. He was doing what he felt he was required to do, and that once decided, he took things as they came. He only hoped Creighton Memorial held on until he could be certified as having done his internship. He'd felt the same way the first time he was needed to deliver a white woman. Let the baby come safely, let him be able to care for the post-partum hemorrhage— subsequent things could be handled.

Hank Blair was much in the same spot as Smith, and both men would have objected to such a pairing. At breakfast time that morning, Hank was dead asleep, and if he dreamed it was not of the way he had clawed his way through premed and med school, but of the struggle he had had with and for that woman the night before. Caught in the twisted wreckage of her car, gasping for air—warning everyone about the baby—bleeding—her forehead gashed, her chest crushed, her abdomen . . . Hank found himself praying that she would lapse into unconsciousness. As she did, helped by the morphia he gave her. Next time—Next time he would do the same things he had done last night. Get the patient out of the wreck with as little further trauma as could be managed. Stop the bleeding, ease the pain, administer plasma—oxygen—and wait to get her to the surgeons as fast as Virgilio could drive. Which was *fast!* Hank could tell all these things to the Fox, when asked, and know that even the great-and-wonderful could not have done more.

The young doctors went on about the morning's duties, Tommie up to o.r. scrub, Dr. Smith to duty in o.b., Bechars to the lab for test reports, and Hank continuing to sleep, one ear alert for the next ambulance call.

Wherever they went the interns' troubled thoughts were echoed by everyone in the hospital. "There's trouble all over," Peach summed up the state of things.

At nine o'clock, the ambulance went out. "Blair will take care of everything," said Dr. Smith, watching it go. And found himself in trouble with Dr. Clark, who generally was a pleasant, soft-spoken woman.

This was a child, she rebuked the intern, probably poisoned, or with an overdose of some medication. The mother had reported collapse after two days of nausea.

"Would you be ready to diagnose it, doctor?" she asked crisply.

"I'm sorry, Dr. Clark."

"I know you rag Blair. But so long as he is doing his job, he probably does not deserve your sarcasm."

It did not surprise Dr. Smith, nor Bechars and Tommie, to be summoned when the child came in, to stand by while Dr. Clark made her examination and diagnosis. The case was one of salicylate intoxication. If the baby was younger —she was four—death would have been certain. As it was . . .

"Aspirin," said Dr. Clark, "should never be given to children under one year, and only very cautiously to those under six."

"I heard some talk upstairs," said Tommie thoughtfully. "You know, I was in o.r. when this case came in; that's why I reached here late . . ."

Her companions nodded. "In o.r.," she continued, "someone was telling that Dr. Hawthorne—he's the one from the other hospital, you know, who wants to—"

"We know who he is," said Ted Bechars testily. "There's gossip enough about him, probably one hundred and ten per cent true."

"You never saw smoke without fire?" asked Dr. Blair.

"Well, I mean—these stories do grow," Bechars said sulkily.

"They do," agreed Tommie. "But three deaths from aspirin since last November! That's a lot, Ted. Three babies!"

"So the o.r. crew says."

"I hope they were wrong. I'll admit that a prescription of five adult aspirins to a baby four and a half months old sounds exaggerated. But they said in o.r. there were two other deaths . . ."

"You'd think the coroner would move in," said Blair. "Though I suppose the infants died technically under medical care."

"If he was responsible," said Tommie hotly, "he should be in jail."

Hank Blair started down the hall. "Some people think he is wonderful," he said over his shoulder.

The others gazed after him. "Some do," Tommie agreed. "Miss Cotsworth, the dietician, does. But then, she is probably head over heels in love with the Fox, too. These desiccated spinsters . . ."

"Do you know him?" asked Ted. "Hawthorne, I mean."

"Me?" asked Tommie in surprise.

"Well, you might. My wife met him, and like Carolyn, she thought he was great."

"Do you suppose we could be wrong about him?" asked Tommie, her face troubled.

"That depends on who 'we' are. Some think he's all black, some, all white. I'd suggest that, like the rest of us, he might be only a shade of gray."

"Mhmmmn," Tommie agreed. "And because three babies died in his hospital of aspirin poisoning doesn't mean that Dr. Hawthorne poisoned them."

"That's what I mean."

Ted Bechars continued to think about Hawthorne and the stories he heard about the man, on both sides. He mentioned the matter to his wife when Marilyn came past the hospital at noon to bring him a letter from his mother. "I think she sent a check," she told Ted.

He laughed. "And that's better than a special delivery stamp, any day."

"Certainly is." She shifted the heavy baby in her arms. Ted took him and said he'd walk downstairs with them.

"Aren't you busy?"

"Oh, yes. Marilyn, you never give the tad aspirin, do you?"

She said the tad never needed any kind of medicine, besides, with a doctor in the family . . . So he told her briefly about the aspirin case, and mentioned the gossip which seemed to follow Hawthornes name in almost any conversation.

"I've noticed that," she agreed. "At the beauty parlor, one day, I heard some women talking about a time when he was supposed to be parked with a woman, not his wife, and for some reason he got into a fight with a bunch of kids who went past and heckled him."

"Hmm," said Ted, thoughtful.

"Didn't you tell me that he wanted to consolidate his hospital with this one? Of course, by the time he'd do that, we'd be through here, and off and away."

"Yes. I was just wondering . . ."

"Wondering what?"

"Well, I rather like the man, from what little I've seen of him. I was wondering if I could work with him."

"Is there any chance you would?"

"I don't know, Marilyn. He's said he could get me out of serving in the Air Force."

"But you agreed to do that."

"I know. It's a debt. Don't worry about it. I'll probably be handsome in a blue suit. That's worth a try, maybe. I've never been handsome before."

She got into the car and took the baby. "The tad and I like you," she said.

But the whole thing worried Ted Bechars, as it worried other people in and out of the hospital. If Dr. Creighton were on the job, perhaps things would not have grown so tense. He was expected home later that day.

* * *

The mayor of the city, when questioned, said that certainly Memorial Hospital could handle any crisis which might arise over Hawthorne's move for a consolidated hospital.

How would the hospital handle it, he was asked.

Pat didn't know, but he should think Fox would avoid their being a crisis at all. The hospital was evidently ticking along, and he personally felt certain that it would not tie up with Hawthrone and Union in any project whatever.

A lot of people thought . . .

The mayor knew what a lot of people thought and said.

They said those things to him, on the street, in the drug-store, over his office telephone. He hoped a popular vote on the matter could be avoided, and finally he let himself speak of that hope.

"Ordinarily a referendum is the best," he agreed. "But this thing might get rushed through, and the people as a whole won't have time to become entirely informed on what the proposition means.

"Well, for one instance, take the term 'nonprofit hospital.' Union is a nonprofit hospital. That confuses their good sense. They forget the style in which Hawthorne lives, his big, expensive cars, his home. When Union plows back its profits, he gets a good deal of that dust on his shoes.

"No, I don't call him a crook. He's a smart operator, and there should be a way to put such a man under control."

"Do you think Fox Creighton can handle him? On this joint-hospital arrangement, I mean."

"That's probably the only way or time that Fox would dirty his hands. But he's out of town just now. Only for a few days, and the hospital Board won't make any move until he's back."

"Delay could be dangerous, give Union, which is Hawthorne, of course, a chance to undermine—drop bombs—or whatever warlike term applies."

Pat Kern laughed. He was having lunch with the president of the town Council. "I hope this table isn't bugged," he said, looking around.

"You're going to have to take a stand on this, aren't you?" asked his friend.

"Not in words, I hope. Though my friendship with Creighton is pretty generally known here in town."

"I know that. Look, Pat, would it be possible for someone to talk to Hawthorne?"

"And advance the subject of ethics?" asked the mayor dryly.

"No, but perhaps try to convince him that he'd not gain a thing by any alliance with Creighton."

"Hospital or man?" asked Pat. "Talk on that level would not penetrate Hawthorne's ego, I'm pretty sure. Nothing would convince him that he is not on a par with Fox."

"It would take doing. All right. Could he be threatened?"

"Do you have any gangster friends?"

"I meant rather along the lines of legal investigation of

some of the shady things the town says he and his hospital does, and have done."

"Striking when the iron is cold is shoemaking the hard way, my friend. Besides, I think you should know, as I do, that a lot of people—and I mean a *lot*—like the sort of doctoring Hawthorne does. He is generous with his drug prescriptions, he will declare an abortion justified, he accepts troublesome seniles for hospitalization and quiets them down for indefinite periods. All this for a price, of course."

"Price," mused the councilman. Then his face brightened. "Money. Would it be possible to buy the man off?"

"Creighton Memorial would use any such available money for expansion on site," said the mayor.

"I didn't mean the hospital. I meant civic-minded businessmen, the banks, the industries . . ."

The mayor shook his head. "That is a possibility, and would certainly involve some intricate financial operations— fascinating to watch. Not that I would know what was going on. But—Fox should be home tonight. I hope he is at any rate. Since he's been gone, there's been the announcement, and a tragic death in his staff family."

"Dorothy Forrest. Yes, I know. That really was bad. I even heard that her husband was going to sue the surgeon who operated on her."

"There isn't going to be any lawsuit," said Pat firmly.

"How do you know?"

"I don't know. But with Fox home—he wouldn't like fighting among his staff members. And such a lawsuit would give the hospital a black eye."

"Could the hospital weather such a scandal?"

"Union manages. But—no! Strike that. This is a regrettable matter of one staff doctor suing another. The surgeon —Vilray Belze—you know him? It seems he turned up missing for an hour or two when he was needed. Forrest claims that the delay caused his wife's death. Now, with Fox home, someone could do what should have been done, talk to Vil Belze, find out where he was, what happened to cause the delay."

* * *

Dr. Belze was at work on Wednesday morning. He was a strong man, physically, and his fifteen years of practice as a surgeon had taught him self-discipline. A bad highway wreck could keep him at work around the clock; he could work with a headache, a cracked rib, or when worried sick about some personal development. The things that had happened to him and around him in the last two days were undeniably bad. They set stern lines of self-control into his handsome face, darkened and hardened his eyes. And it took real effort to bring his attention, his thoughts, to focus on the case in hand that morning. It took massive control to steady his hand and to strengthen it.

But Vil Belze was a good surgeon. Now, he did the surgical tasks which he had scheduled for this day.

The tendon transplant for the fifteen-year-old boy injured in schoolyard football. The removal of a woman's breast which had shown a lump that almost certainly was cancerous. In both cases, surgery had needed to be sold, the patient prepared mentally as well as physically. Especially for the woman, this surgery had great psychological impact. She had not wanted to have it done, now if there were delay she might never again be able to summon courage enough to go through with it.

Dr. Belze thought about such things, he thought about them that morning. And he tried not to think of himself at all. His hands in the red-brown gloves were instruments which his mind guided. They accepted a knife, a clamp, a suture needle at fixed times in a fixed program of surgery. The man did not matter.

Only—he did matter. The patient on the table at that hour of the morning was a boy. Fifteen years from now, it could have been Walter Forrest's boy . . . killed when a six-month fetus.

The next patient was a woman, lying on the table where Dorothy Forrest had lain—and all the discipline, all the practiced skill in the world could not have saved her. All of Dr. Belze's discipline and skill could not save her, or her son.

And the doctor—he straightened his shoulders, and drew a deep breath, the nurse swabbed at his forehead.

Last night—this morning—Vil Belze should have told the truth about yesterday and last night. He should finish here, find Forrest and tell him . . . But he could not. He would not.

The hospital was in trouble enough. Should he speak out, the place would go to pieces completely. And that could not happen. Belze might not be able to save Creighton Memorial, but he certainly would not, and could not, be the means of destroying it. Often morale was more important to a hospital than any amount of new wards and new equipment.

Chapter Four

MRS. RICE, the housekeeper, was making a round of the hospital, poking her inquisitive eyes and nose into corners, opening doors and drawers, tipping her head back to look at ceilings.

"The patients in bed see more of the ceiling than they do of other views," she would explain, and did explain that morning.

"It ain't the day to inspect," Peach reminded her.

"That's why I am inspecting, Peach."

"Yes, ma'am."

"If you've got any bottles of gin tucked away, now's the time to run save them."

Peach laughed aloud. "You find any bottle, you give 'em to me?" he asked boldly.

"I certainly will."

She counted towels, she frowned at a patch on a patient's bedspread, and shook her head. They had to patch bedspreads—though not sheets. Fox Creighton would not let a patient lie on a patched sheet, the seam would make trouble.

Mrs. Reuther, the administrator, also asked her why she was inspecting on Wednesday.

"Wednesday's a good day," said Mrs. Rice comfortably. She was a "comfortable" woman, tall, large of waist and bosom. Her face was pretty. And she knew a clean hospital when she saw it.

She had been told by various people and in various connotations that the hospital was falling to pieces. Not, she determined, through any fault of hers. She knew about the crowding and she understood about the need to economize, and to cut corners where possible. But she saw to it

69

that the patched bedspreads were spotless, the floors free of dust, the windows sparkling.

Things beyond her control should not concern her, but they did. The hospital was her home, and when things went wrong in a woman's home, she worried about those things. This story about one of the doctor's suing another one—right inside the family! That was a terrible thing to happen.

Mrs. Rice knew both men. And she liked them both. Dr. Forrest was a tall, hawkish-handsome man, who liked to tease, who told naughty jokes, and laughed loudly when she blushed. Dr. Belze was more quiet, but such a *good* doctor! He did marvelous things in the operating room, and people adored him out of their gratitude. He worked too hard, of course, and that could be why his wife . . . Well, the least said, even to herself, about Jane Belze the better. She was certainly a pretty young woman, and when a girl is pretty, and young, she wants a good time.

As for Dr. Forrest's wife, poor dear. Dead with her baby. The old days, when pregnant women stayed at home and behaved themselves certainly were not so dangerous. A tragic thing to be killed that way . . .

But the lawsuit made everything else seem just too bad to endure. Of course medicine and the town, perhaps, could take another lawsuit. People, grief-stricken, or feeling guilty themselves, were often inclined to blame the doctor for a death, and often they went to law.

This Dr. Hawthorne everybody was talking about—he'd had several lawsuits brought against him. One was a paternity suit, Mrs. Rice remembered that quite well, and she believed one was for an illegal abortion.

Perhaps he was guilty, perhaps not.

But Dr. Belze—just by being absent from the hospital—could he be thought guilty of Mrs. Forrest's death? He'd *done* nothing, she was sure of that.

* * *

It would have helped Vil Belze to be that sure. He had been stunned by the promise of a lawsuit. In Forrest's place —good Lord! The man was crazy! Though, perhaps, in his place, Dr. Belze might have been crazy too. When he thought about it, as he did think about it, over and over, the whole thing, he told himself as he changed after surgery that morning, the whole situation, up to and concluding with the promised lawsuit, was unreal, and—crazy. It was driving him out of his skull.

Skull was a fair word for the way he looked, he agreed, as he combed his thick hair. He looked like the very devil. His eyes—what was the phrase? Burnt holes in a blanket. That fitted.

Lunch trays were being served, and the fragrance of food filled the hospital halls, even permeating the elevator shaft. Lunch would be available in the staff dining room, and usually Vil ate there before going over to his office.

But not today. He had a desire for neither food nor company. He checked on his post-operative patients, then went downstairs, and signed off the roster; he cut across the hospital grounds and the street to the clinic. He spoke briefly to his secretary and went into his office, closing the door. Gratefully he sank into his chair, and sighed heavily. At last he was alone; he could not, he felt sure, have managed so much as one more civil word to one more person. He had to be alone. He had to think.

He leaned forward and picked up his telephone. "Miss Austin," he said, "please don't pass any calls in to me, or send anyone in, for the next half hour. Thank you."

There. That was done. Barring some extreme emergency, he had secured a time to think. To be alone, go back . . .

It had begun on Monday. So, let him think. He had worked in surgery that morning. At noon he had attended that staff meeting—it seemed a thousand years ago!—when Hawthorne had offered a way for Creighton Memorial and Union Hospital to join . . . Oh, the details of that no longer were important to Vil.

He had gone through the routine of that day, office patients, a couple of telephone calls. One of them was from Dorothy Forrest. He'd been surprised to have her call. She was pregnant, Kayser's patient . . .

But she said she had to see him. No, she'd rather he wouldn't stop at the house. But could he meet her—she mentioned a certain road, it led to the Boy Scout camp. There was a restaurant . . .

He'd made a joke about meeting her at such a hideout, but Dorothy had been dead-serious.

He shuddered, and wiped his hand down across his face. He got up and took off his jacket, tossed it on the patient's chair. The air conditioning was on; his perspiration was pure nerves. He poured himself a glass of water, and sat sipping it.

Let's see . . . Monday. He finally had agreed to humor

Dorothy, and to meet her at the restaurant. Pregnant women needed to be humored. He remembered, six years ago, before the twins were born, Jane . . . He choked on the water, and coughed heavily.

The restaurant was a typical roadside place, neat and clean. There was a long counter, three or four booths. Dorothy was waiting for him, and Vil ordered Cokes.

As he expected, Dorothy was teed off about something. It took a little time for her to speak so he could understand her, or even begin to grasp what it was she wanted to tell him. But finally he sifted through her excited words, her confused phrases, her side comments—"We've been friends!" "I never dreamed, did you, Vil?" Things like that. Twice he urged her to calm down, people were noticing them. Perhaps they should go out to her car?

But finally he came to understand that she was warning him about his wife, who, Dorothy insisted, was two-timing him.

"And with Walter! With *my husband*, Vil! With your friend. She sees him, they go places together. Two months ago when he was supposed to go to that meeting of chest surgeons—Jane went to see her mother that weekend, too. Remember? Wherever they did go, they were together. And since . . ."

Vil had refused to believe her. He reminded Dorothy that her pregnancy could make her distort things. Women at such times often experienced depression, and got strange ideas . . .

Finally he persuaded her to go home; he followed in his car until he saw her safely into the house. Then he tried to decide if he should talk to Forrest about her ideas.

He decided at once against mentioning it to Jane. But he also found that he could not go home for dinner and the evening. He had driven about, stopping once to eat and for a couple of drinks. He forgot to call his answering service. He didn't believe Dorothy, but the possibility fogged his mind.

Then, yesterday—Tuesday? Yes, last night—about six or so—he was still at work—Dorothy called him. That time she spoke with cold calm. Walter and Jane, she said, had gone to a motel just outside of Ravinia. Near the dam and the lake, he knew? Yes, she was sure. She had overheard Walter making a reservation. Would Vil go there with her, and confront them?

No, he said, he would not.

"They are there."

"I don't believe it."

"Do you know where Jane is?"

"I hardly ever know where she is, Dorothy, not at any precise time. We have the children's nurse. Jane plays golf, and bridge . . ."

"She goes to meet my husband."

He argued, and tried to persuade Dorothy. Even if what she had dreamed up was true, he was not about to stick his neck out . . .

"Well, I'll stick mine out. I am going to Ravinia, if you won't. And do you know what else I'll do, Vil? I am going to take Walter's gun with me. I am going to kill them both!"

He should have called the police. He had not. Still only half-believing that Dorothy would do any such thing, he drove to their house. Her car, and Walter's, were both gone. Then, a half hour late, he started for Ravinia, taking a road that cut cross country; he could perhaps get to the motel before Dorothy did, and could stop her, prevent her . . .

In any case, he would bring his own wife home.

He did bring her home. She was, indeed, at the motel—and with Walter. He wouldn't want to go through that scene again. It was only after they reached home that he found out about Dorothy's wreck, and that he was needed at the hospital. Walter had got the word earlier—not the two hours he claimed, but earlier.

The man was wild, with all sorts of emotions. Vil had his own assortment. But there could not possibly be any lawsuit.

*   *   *

When Pat Kern returned to his office midafternoon, he found a memo on his desk. He was to call the president of the city Council. He told the secretary to put the call through, and she did. What could have come up in the two hours since he'd eaten lunch with that same man? He soon found out.

"Look, Pat, could you come over to the city hall about four-thirty for a Council meeting?"

Pat frowned. He looked at his desk calendar, and still frowned. "We have a regular meeting Monday night, Ralph."

"I know, but the other members think this is urgent. Time seems to be important."

"Do you know what the hell you are talking about, Ralph?"

"Yes, sir, I'm afraid I do."

"And enough members want the meeting to get one called. You'd need some special agenda, you know."

"I do know, Pat. They have their special agenda. They are going to decide on an early election date for a bond issue to pay the city's share on a new hospital for Carson County."

Pat groaned. "I suppose Dr. Hawthorne has looked into the matter."

"Now, Pat—we all know you're a Creighton man."

"Mhmmmn. So I'll have to agree to the special meeting, won't I?"

"Maybe the Council won't vote to have an election."

"Yeah, and maybe the citizens won't vote for the bond issue." Pat sighed. "But, yes, I'll have to agree to that meeting. What time did you say?"

"Four-thirty."

* * *

At five the local radio station issued a special news bulletin saying there would be a special election Tuesday, May 16, to vote on a revenue bond issue for the erection of a district hospital. The announcer said the district comprised Carson County, and that this would be a community project. Union Hospital in Carson already had signified its willingness to close. Creighton Memorial was expected to do likewise.

So the crisis had not been avoided.

"When do we quit?" asked the people who worked at Creighton.

"Will we be moved right out?" asked the nervous patients.

"Will Dr. Creighton run the new hospital?"

"Will Dr. Hawthorne run the new hospital?"

The town had many questions to ask. If it took two years to build a new hospital—a lot could happen in two years. Why would they need to build an all-new one? Creighton was overcrowded, but it could be expanded.

Some people wept; some people joked. It was a fair guess that there was no one in the district, hospital personnel or town citizen, but what talked about the upcoming vote and what it would mean. If the bond issue passed, or if it failed.

"We've got us a nice kettle of fish waiting for Fox," Pat Kern thought.

* * *

In Los Hermanos, in the cool dining room of Stephen Clark's big home, the ceremonial luncheon was drawing to a close. They would, the attorney said, move to the library for the reading of the will. Dr. Creighton, and others, had pressing need to get back to their offices.

The guests crossed the hall; Fox's shoe tip traced the parquetry of the floor, his eyes went up the stairs. This, probably, would be his last visit to this home. He would have left immediately; the storm was over. But there was the girl . . .

The lawyers sat at the table with their papers and brief cases. When the luncheon guests were all seated—the entire Board of the historical society was there—the servants came in and stood against the paneled wall. And, finally, the girl, Courtney, came in from the hall. She was, Fox Creighton told himself in surprise, the most beautiful young girl he had ever seen. One minute in the full sunlight through the window, the next in the light shade from the pine tree beyond it, so that sun and shadow played in a rippling pattern across her head and the white dress she wore.

"Jeune fille en fleur," thought the doctor on the window seat.

She sat down on a low hassock, and the lawyer began to read the will. The usual opening, mention of the deed of trust concerning the home, and its transfer now to the Historical Society. There was the provision for grave upkeep, modest bequests to the servants. There was a trust fund for Courtney Armstrong, "my beloved ward." It was not a large trust fund . . . There were a few other bequests.

The residue of the estate was to go to establish a foundation for the education of worthy students in engineering. Fox Creighton was named to be on the board of this foundation.

Through the reading of the will, the girl Courtney had sat with her hands clasped around her knees, her light brown hair falling forward across her face.

"He could have done more for Courtney!" said one of the women present. "What's to become of her?"

Courtney's head went up. "I can go to work," she said. "Don't worry."

Fox moved enough to attract her attention; she glanced at him, and a faint smile lifted her lips. "Don't worry," she said again.

The attorney cleared his throat. "I told you, Courtney . . ."

"I know you did," she said softly.

But the attorney went on to say to those assembled, "Dr. Creighton—Dr. Clark's nephew, as you all know—has generously offered to take Courtney into his home."

"She couldn't accept that offer!" said one of the women.

Courtney turned to look at her, then, still with that faint smile on her lips, she stood up and walked across to Fox. He was standing, and he looked down at her.

"I offered you roots," he said quietly. "It is not charity, or anything of that nature. Young people need a place of their own. That is what I said I would offer you."

He held out his hand, she looked up at him. And everyone in that quiet room saw what passed between them, the tall, stern-faced man, and the young woman waiting for the sternness to melt. When it did not, she spoke, her voice low and clear. "I'll go with you," she said. "Thank you. I'll be glad to go with you."

There was a stir throughout the room. The lawyer said yes, in answer to some question, he was finished. There were details of course, appraisal of property, various things. He would communicate with individuals as necessary.

"When do you leave, doctor?" someone asked Fox.

"As soon as I possibly can," he answered brusquely. "I must get home tonight."

"Carson?"

"Yes. I am medical officer of a hospital there, you see. And the place has probably fallen into ruin."

"You're joking, of course."

"Well, not really," said Fox. "Hospitals these days have problems, you know. Rising costs, increase in patients, decrease in available help. Though the doctor shortage hasn't touched us as yet." He laughed shortly. "In fact, in Carson we seem to have one doctor too many. There is a man there who thinks he should join our staff and work for a Government financed hospital . . ."

The people around him asked polite questions. Courtney stayed in the background, but she listened and watched him intently.

And when the guests began to leave, she walked beside him to the front door, to thank them, to say good-bye.

The servants were clearing the dining room, a maid was straightening the library. Fox turned toward the stairs, Courtney put her hand on his sleeve.

"Something?" he asked.

"Oh, a lot of somethings! First, tell me. Does your hospital always fall into ruins when you leave?"

He laughed. "I don't know. I don't leave it often enough to tell."

"But you left at this crucial time? Why?" Her eyes were dark, and straight of gaze.

"Well," said Fox, "I let myself get sentimental. I don't do that very often, either."

"I know."

He bent his head to look into her face. "How do you know?"

"I've watched you. Just now—and ever since you came here—this morning."

"Mhmmmn. Well, you see, Mr. Clark was my mother's brother, and he was the last contact I'd had with her. This house—oh, all sorts of things. He was good to me when I was a kid. He taught me to fish, and how to ride—"

"Yes, I know," said Courtney. "He was good to me, too."

He looked at his watch. "I'll have to leave in an hour," he said. "If you want to come with me—or you could come over later."

"I'll be ready," she said softly. "When someone told me that you had said you would take me to your home, I got my personal things together. I'll be ready when you are."

She was, too.

Her bags, and Fox's, were stowed in the trunk of the car, she sat in the front seat beside him, ready if he wanted to talk, able to maintain a companionable silence when he did not.

She should be no bother to me, Fox told himself, settling down for the long drive. The Storys would take care of her physical comfort and well-being. He would be back in his hospital, deep in its claims upon him.

He probably would not need to give the girl a thought. She could spend the summer, safe and comfortable, and go back to her college work in the fall. There, some chap would fall in love with her—she was a real beauty. Or she might decide upon a career. Women did these days . . .

"Do you know," she asked unexpectedly—they had driven for fifty miles—"why I said I would go with you?"

Fox frowned, and kept his attention on the truck ahead of him.

"Did you hear what I asked?" Courtney said.

"Yes. You asked me if I knew why you said you would go to my home."

"Do you know?"

"I suppose you felt it was an honest offer. Perhaps you see in me something of my uncle."

"Well, there is something of course. I am glad there is. But I am going, Fox, because I fell in love with you." She waited a minute. He said nothing, not a muscle twitched. "I watched you, and I fell in love with you. So I had to go with you."

Fox still said nothing. In the mirror he could see the girl smile a little.

* * *

After the sandstorm had cleared itself away, leaving its usual sifting all over everything, Clytie saw the dust, and she talked about it to herself. Later perhaps she could get a cloth and work on it. Her "woman" would be in tomorrow, or maybe not until Friday. Clytie might feel better tomorrow, too. Well enough to get to the bank . . .

Only, she didn't think so. The storm, the pressure, or maybe the soup she had eaten—something was making her feel very shaky and depressed. If she did not get better by morning, she would talk to her doctor; he probably would want her to go to the hospital, and just at the minute she thought of those smooth white sheets, someone to take care of her, was tempting.

But first she must . . .

A half hour later she was walking down the street, a frail-looking woman in a red linen suit, much too large for her thinness, a net scarf tied about her hair. Clytie Whiteside had been a beauty all her life, so even on this day when she felt so bad, her only strength that of her determination to do this thing, she had carefully made up her face; her lipstick was precise, her skin glowed with the various lotions and powders she had used.

She wore short white gloves on her hands, and a long white envelope was held tightly in one of them. She came to the end of the block; the mailbox was across the street, and she hesitated. Their streets were so wide . . . If she made it down the curb, she could, she thought, cross the expanse of concrete. She looked to the left, and to the right —if no car turned the corner . . .

She grasped the mailbox gratefully, and clung to it for a

long minute. She had not guessed how weak she was. She never would have made it to the bank.

She lifted the envelope, covered almost, she told herself, with stamps. But she didn't really know how much special delivery service cost—she had written those words large above the address. She lifted the box lip, and stopped.

Oh, dear. She had meant to address the envelope to Virginia. But there she had written Carolyn's name! She supposed Carolyn was on her mind. Well, it really didn't matter. Carolyn would take care of Clytie's will; she was very precise about doing the proper thing.

Clytie dropped the envelope into the box, and, relieved, she again faced the perilous journey across the street. She felt so trembly; webs of fatigue blurred her eyes. If someone would just come along, she could follow that person . . .

"Why, Mrs. Whiteside!"

She started violently, and looked around. It was a neighbor, a woman who lived in the next entry of the large apartment house.

"I haven't seen you for a long time!"

"Yes," said Clytie. "I—I have been ill. Are you going home? The strong medicine I have to take confuses me. If I could walk along with you . . ."

"But of course." The woman's strong hand took her thin upper arm; they crossed the street, and started along the sidewalk.

"I'll see you inside," said the neighbor. Clytie could not remember her name . . .

* * *

Alice Tunstall was tired; she told herself that she was, marveling. For a woman who worked, often, seven days a week, anything from eight to twelve hours of each of those days, to be tired by a three-day trip, a comfortable plane ride . . .

But—why else would she look forward to the job which she had thought was overly tiring? She had needed a rest, a change, she had told people—Fox Creighton, Carolyn Cotsworth, probably a good many more in the hospital.

So she had had her change, if not a rest, and now she could take up the hospital tasks again. Fox, and others, would ask if she had enjoyed her trip, and she had better say yes. It would save a lot of explaining. And, really, she had enjoyed it. Seeing and visiting with all the old girls, seeing how they had changed.

Most of them had come to the reunion, even pert little Jennie Crawford who had hated nursing, and still could make them all laugh with the reasons she gave for hating it. Maggie Clark always reminded Tunnie of Jennie. She had the same straight, flyaway blond hair, the same pert little kitten's face, and a mind of her own. Maggie had been a very popular girl. Heavens yes! From the time she was twelve, boys had swarmed about her. They had about Jennie, too. Marion, Maggie's mother, had fretted and worried about the girl; she so often had to be left alone.

Marion need not have worried about her second daughter. Maggie did very well in school, and having married, when she graduated from high school, a boy also in his teens, she had stayed with her marriage. Tunnie saw her often; she was working to help her husband get through law school. He was home only on weekends. But Marion said he was sticking to business. "Maggie sees to that!" Marion added, laughing.

Maggie Clark had a hard core to her, which was a good thing, Tunnie thought.

Chapter Five

THE ROAD stretched wide and straight across the tawny desert. Tumbleweeds had piled into the shallow ditches. There were stretches of green, the oases of towns to be seen, and the mountains in the distance, but it all made for monotony. The girl Courtney, still wearing the white dress, with a bright green scarf tied about her hair, holding its length back from her face and throat, had made a comfortable corner for herself in the right-hand seat of the car.

The man, Fox Creighton, drove steadily, easily, his eyes hidden behind his dark glasses. His red hair now was somewhat rough, and the open collar of his tan shirt showed the strength of his throat. His shirt cuffs were folded back, and his hands and arms too spoke of strength.

Courtney watched him, rather than the scenery, and he was well aware that she did this.

"You know," he said abruptly, after another twenty-five miles had been covered in silence, "I live a rather isolated life."

"You run a hospital."

"I am Chief of Medical Services in a hospital."

"How big?"

"Two hundred beds. We have a board of directors and an administrator. The heads of all services. All those people *run* the hospital. What I started to say was . . ."

"You did say it. You live an isolated life."

"Yes. And I do. I am with people, I contact people all day and every day. Few of them contact me."

"Don't you have friends?"

"I have friends. No intimates. You might say that I am concerned but detached from the people around me."

"That will include me."

"Yes. I am afraid so."

"And *that* is what you started to say."

The muscle in his right cheek twitched; it was not a smile. "You are welcome," he said, "to stay, to live, in my house. It is an old house, with a lot of ground about it. Orchards, gardens . . . There are large rooms, and many of them."

"Mahogany," said Courtney, "silver, and mural wallpaper."

Fox glanced at her. "Yes," he agreed. "It was my grandfather's home, it was my mother and father's. Now it is mine. I have a couple, Mr. and Mrs. Story, who take care of the house, and, they think, of me."

"Do they know I am coming?"

"Yes. I phoned them before we left. They will make you comfortable. You can stay around the house and grounds, amuse yourself, or you could perhaps find something to do in town. For pay, or as a volunteer. There's a day-care center, a Head Start school, things like that. You'll make friends."

"Could I work for you at the hospital?"

He started to ask if she would like that, then bit back the words. "Of course," he said steadily. "I understand you left spring term to be with Uncle Stephen, but you will want to resume at the University in the fall."

She shrugged. "That takes care of me, doesn't it?" she asked.

"Isn't it all right?"

"Yes. It's all right. It is what I could expect. But you are forgetting one thing. That I am in love with you."

He laughed. And for the next seventy-five miles he said nothing more. Courtney laid her head back and closed her eyes. Perhaps she slept. She had gone through a difficult few days. Fox thought forward to the hospital, particularly to the interns in his charge. Their term was about completed, and for all his vaunted isolation, he was deeply concerned about their future.

He considered each one in turn, conjuring up their faces, their mannerisms, their skills, their faults. He knew their backgrounds, he himself had largely cared for their present, now he must consider their future plans. Of course only in an advisory capacity, but he did have responsibilities.

"It's five o'clock," he said to Courtney, speaking abruptly. "We'll stop for a sandwich . . ."

Within minutes he turned into an exit ramp, and they

stopped before a large service station and restaurant. Fox pointed out the restroom to Courtney. "I'll meet you in the coffee shop," he said, and turned his attention to having his car serviced.

When she came to the table, he rose and seated her, then handed her the menu, but his first attention was on the notebook open before him.

"You look as if you were cramming for exams," she told him.

He laughed a little, and turned the pages of the book. Before he really knew what was happening, he was telling her about the four interns. "I feel like a biddy hen who hears her eggs about to crack," he said.

"You're responsible for these men?"

"In that I should have done some preparing them for their next steps. One of the 'men,' incidentally, is a girl."

"Pretty?"

"I don't—really know. Yes, I suppose she's rather pretty. She has blond hair, which she wears cut off short and raggedly. She wants to specialize in anaesthesiology."

"Is that a good field for a woman doctor?"

"Very good, if she is conscientious. Tommie . . ."

"Tommie?"

"Her name is Pamela Thomas. The men call her Tommie."

"And you do."

"No, I call her Dr. Thomas. Hospital protocol is very strict, you know."

"I'm learning. Will your Tommie go into anaesthesiology? What a word!"

"She's filed for residencies. Though I believe there is a man in the picture."

"And you'll advise . . ."

"Oh, I shan't advise. I'll summarize her record, I'll let her talk to me—and she will make the decisions."

"Poor Tommie. All right. Who are the other ones?"

Their sandwiches and milk came, and she had to ask the question a second time. But Fox, somewhat to her surprise, did tell her about the others. Dr. Smith, and his family, his racial problems.

"He makes some of them for himself," Fox said. "He expects resistance . . . But he was treating white patients, and delivering white women, before he left Alabama."

"Why did he decide to go back and do an internship?"

"To be eligible for the staff of a new hospital-clinic at home."

"I see. Then he doesn't have any problems you need handle."

"No, nor does he, except that someone—Bechars, probably, because Smith and Blair don't get along—someone is urging him to do a residency."

"Should he?"

"It wouldn't hurt, but he has a family to consider. He won't make much money for them doing a residency."

"This Beckers, or whatever . . ."

"Bechars." Fox spelled the name. "Well, he has a family too. At least, he has a wife and a baby. Bechars is due to go into the Air Force, and that will care for his residency. But he's got money-making on his mind, and the Air Force will be an irritation to his ambition."

"Is he a good doctor?"

"Very good. Maybe the best of the lot."

"And the one Dr. Smith doesn't get along with?"

Fox laughed, and Courtney gazed in fascination at the change it made in his face. His green eyes sparkled; the deep lines in his cheeks deepened further, and rounded, his straight-lipped mouth widened. He should laugh more often.

"Hank Blair," he said thoughtfully, the smile crinkles still deep about his eyes. "He is a loner . . ."

"Like you."

Fox's head lifted. "No," he said. "Not really like me. But he sets his own coúrse . . . and doesn't talk much about himself. Smith, with his racial hang-ups, thinks that is the cause for aloofness, and so dislikes Blair."

"I see."

"And Blair does nothing to correct the impression. He's a good doctor, a good man. A bit on the rough side, in speech and appearance. He had to scramble for his education, and that shows. I am hoping that he will go into primary medicine, he—"

Courtney's hand lifted. "Wait a minute! I'm new at this medical talk. Do you realize I've never even had my tonsils out? So—what is primary medicine?"

"You've heard of family doctors? And general practitioners? These are the modern version. They are men, in clinic or private practice, who first see the patient. Sick, injured, and so on. They are skilled in detecting symptoms, deciding on what treatment and examinations should follow."

They went out to the car, and started again along the highway.

"Were you," Fox asked, in the tone of a doctor taking a history, "are you, a native of Los Hermanos?"

"Yes. My father worked for the Clark Industries. He was an engineer."

"A friend of Uncle Stephen?"

"He knew him. When my mother died, he was worried about me, I was four—worried about what would happen to me if he should also die. There were no close relatives. So he asked Mr. Clark, his employer, if he could be named as my guardian. He told me about this, and Uncle Stephen told me. They both decided my dad was a big, healthy man, as he was. So Uncle Stephen laughed, and said of course he'd be my guardian.

"Then my dad was killed . . ." She was silent for a time, her eyes on the green signs across the highway.

"How was he killed?" asked Fox.

"In a plant accident. A crane caught him. It struck him with the big hook . . ."

"I see," said Fox, nodding his head. "Then of course Uncle Stephen cared for you."

"Yes. He did more than he really needed to. There was compensation money. But I was fourteen. He took me into his own home, and I think he became fond of me. I know that I dearly loved him."

Fox's lips quirked.

She looked up. "I mean it," she said in a quiet, sure voice. "I mean it when I say I love a person. I am old enough to know what love means."

Fox nodded, and said no more. She was old enough.

Eventually they reached town. Courtney leaned forward to look at things. Could they see the hospital, she asked.

"No. We don't pass it."

But she looked at all they did pass, at the skyline of office buildings and factories, at the parks painstakingly rescued from the desert, painstakingly maintained. Finally they reached the gate, the pines and the lawns of his home, the big house stretching its arms at the end of the drive. The red dogs came bounding to the man, and then greeted the girl politely.

Fox set the bags out on the ground. "Will you go inside

and introduce yourself to the Storys, Courtney?" he asked. "I want to go straight to the hospital."

Fred Story came out then, and Fox introduced the girl.

"We've given her the suite in our wing," Story told Fox.

"That's fine. I'm going on to the hospital, Fred."

"Yes, sir. Miss Courtney . . ."

She stepped forward. "I want to go to the hospital too," she said. "May I?" She looked up into Fox's face.

He hesitated, then shrugged. "If you really want to," he agreed.

She got back into the car. "I'll not be any trouble," she promised.

"Better not," he growled, his mind already completely on his hospital and what he might find there.

Courtney looked with rising excitement at the sprawling building; its wings seemed to reach out toward one. In the parking space behind the hospital, she waved Fox on, and she sat where she was for a time, looking at the lighted windows, at the people who passed before them. She saw two nurses come out, chattering. They got into a car and drove away, one of them looking over her shoulder as they passed Dr. Creighton's car, and saw the girl who was sitting there.

Then Courtney got out and walked to the door through which Fox had entered. Above it a sign said EMERGENCY in large letters. Inside—her experience with hospitals was only a matter of visits to friends, to her guardian in his last days —but she liked the way this place sparkled and shone. Being inexperienced, she noted each thing, smell, sound, and people.

Now and then someone would ask if she wanted something

"I'm waiting," she explained.

She walked through to a long hall, crossed it to a wide space where a desk said ADMISSIONS.

She looked about; she went out to the front porch and read the sign which would direct one down the curving drive to the CLINIC. Yes, across the street, there it was, a low, red-roof-tiled building.

She came back inside and walked down the length of one hall, returned, then went down another hall. People were sick here. There was a feeling of illness, and the sounds. A nurse behind a desk smiled at her. "Can I help?"

"I'm waiting," said Courtney.

She kept EMERGENCY always in sight, not wanting Fox to forget she was there, though he wouldn't. Would he?

She saw people come and go. A young man in white trousers, white shoes, a short jacket buttoned on the shoulder, got a Coke out of the machine. He smiled at Courtney. "Want one?" he asked.

She shook her head and smiled. Would he be one of the interns? If so, which one? Was he "rough" enough to be Dr. Blair?

"Did you know the Fox was back?" she heard the young man ask the nurse at the desk.

Courtney smiled again, and turned back. Twice she had passed the closed door which said DR. CREIGHTON. She doubted if Fox were in there, though he could be.

Finally, she went back to the car, and waited, letting the radio play softly. She looked up at the hospital, she looked up at the sky, the color of an opal, tender, deep blue laced with pink. A crescent moon was going down the western slope of it. Cars drove in, cars left.

And finally Fox came out, a bundle of papers in his hand. "I'm afraid I took too long," he said. "Good Lord, it's almost nine o'clock. You must dead."

"Are you?"

He looked sharply at her, then smiled. "I believe I am," he said. "I hope Story saved dinner . . ." He drove away.

"How were things at your hospital?" Courtney asked him.

"A mess," he said gruffly. "The wife of one of the doctors was killed last night—and—" He pushed some newspapers toward her. "We have troubles with our competition." Briefly he detailed the hospital situation in Carson.

Courtney read the headlines. "A bond issue would be bad?" she asked.

"Closing down this hospital to let a new one be built would be bad. Joining forces with Union and Dr. Hawthorne would blight the whole town." His face was stern.

"The minute you went in the door," she told him, "you were happy. You were home, where you belonged. And you seemed—oh—contented."

He said nothing, and she read the papers again. Dr. Hawthorne was announcing that Union Hospital was building a clinic. A vote had been scheduled for bond issues to build a new hospital . . .

"Hawthorne got the Board of Election Commissioners," Fox growled, seeing which paper she was reading. "That's the

way things got speeded up with me out of town. I don't
suppose Pat could do a thing."

"Who's Pat?" asked Courtney, folding the papers.

But they had reached home, and Fox did not answer her.
He was greatly troubled, she could see.

* * *

One of the homes which Courtney had seen as she drove
with Fox into Carson was that of Dr. Perry Hawthorne.
Perhaps she had even read his name at the gate. The grounds
were fenced with rough-hewn cedar poles, and they were
elaborately landscaped. Horses were to be seen in the fields
adjoining the house yard, and two clean-limbed dogs lay on
the porch tiles. Weimaraners, with strange amber eyes; Katharine Hawthorne said she was afraid of the dogs. She said it
again that night when the doctor, and their daughter, Christie,
came in from a ride.

They laughed at her, and Dr. Hawthorne went to the bar
to prepare a drink.

"Christie?" he asked without turning.

The girl had dropped into a deep chair; she looked tired.
"No, thanks," she said. "I'm going to bed in half a mo."

"Did you ride too far?" Katharine asked anxiously.

"Of course we didn't," said her husband, bringing her a
glass. "And guess what we saw?"

"I couldn't possibly guess."

"You could have seen it from our front windows. He
must have driven right past here."

"Oh, Dad . . ." Christie protested. She pushed her yellow
hair back from her face. "Why shouldn't he have a girl
with him?"

"Who?" asked Katharine.

"Dr. Creighton," said Christie. "Dad has a hang-up about
that man."

"It was Fox himself," the doctor agreed gleefully. "With
a *girl*, Kathy! Did you *ever*?"

"I'm with Christie. Why not? He's younger than you are,
and you like girls."

Dr. Hawthorne scowled at her, and looked meaningly at
Christie.

"I'm going to bed," the girl said, rising.

"Without dinner, dear?" asked her mother. Katharine was
thin to gauntness and would have been pretty as a girl, but
now, in her early forties, one saw the gauntness, the tension

. . . the heavy mass of her dark hair untidily drawn back into a bun.

Her husband sat down with his drink and the evening newspaper. "They've summarized the hospital situation," he said gleefully. "I wonder what Creighton thinks about that. He's been away for a couple of days, you know."

"You knew it," said Katharine.

"I certainly did, and I made a good deal of hay, too."

She came toward him. "You have no intention of building a clinic," she told her husband.

"Why not?"

'Because, for one thing, you are pressed for money just now. For another, what doctors would go in with you?"

"Oh, the hospital men."

"Like they do at Memorial?"

"Why not?"

"Dr. Creighton doesn't own their clinic."

Her husband said nothing. She was right.

"And you won't build a clinic, either," said Katharine again. "I'm going to fix a tray for Christie."

"She goes to bed to get away from our fighting. You know that."

"I know one thing," said his wife. "If you do build a clinic, I'll burn the thing down." She left the room.

Dr. Hawthorne sat with one of his heavy eyebrows elevated. Then he shrugged. She might, at that.

* * *

Up on the second floor of the hospital, Marion Clark sat at the floor desk with the supervisor of pediatric nursing and tried to figure out a way to get more patients and patients' beds into the space they had.

"I suppose Miss Tunstall and Dr. Creighton and I are going to have to have another huddle," Marion decided. "Though what new we can turn up . . . Last time we considered dropping our age limit, but that only puts the thirteen to fourteens into the adult wards, and they don't have any extra beds, either."

"Maybe we do need a new hospital," said the nurse hesitantly.

Marion looked up. "We need more beds here," she said quickly. "But I don't plan to vote for the new one that's being cooked up."

"I didn't know . . ."

"Maybe I don't know either, but Dr. Creighton is opposed to it, and that's enough for me."

"I suppose it should be. Has he got home?"

"He's expected." Marion bent over the charts and the nurse went down the hall. A small child was crying hard.

"I should have gone to Los Hermanos with Fox," Marion was telling herself. "I should have gone to Mr. Clark's funeral. I should have made George go, and we should have taken at least one of the girls. Maggie would have gone, and Nancy too, if I'd told her to go. They probably think it's strange that we didn't go, though they surely are familiar with the situation in our family. I haven't talked to them about it, but they must know."

She took up a new chart. Her pen checked the items, and then she thought, closing the cover, "Others at the funeral would have thought that we went because we expected something from the will. I could have said that we didn't, but how many would believe me? Anyway, George does expect quite a lot."

She opened the next chart, read it, and wrote her orders. "It would have been the decent thing to do," she said. "When I see Fox I'll tell him that I'm sorry."

She hoped he would indeed get home that evening. The hospital needed him. She did.

* * *

Alice Tunstall too hoped that Dr. Creighton would get home that evening. When she had checked her duties at the hospital, talked to a few people, picked up the back newspapers, she wondered how even Fox could ever make quiet and reason out of the chaos of death and destruction, and the sure promise of more.

She hoped she could get up to her apartment and not have to talk to anyone else. She had so many things to straighten out in her mind. It had been a bad time for Fox to be called away. Of course he hadn't known all that would happen. She wondered how much advantage that rascal Hawthorne had taken of the whole situation. The Forrest tragedy was just one terrible thing more.

Tunnie locked her car and went inside, up the stairs to her apartment. She would unpack, change into a housecoat, sit loose, read the papers, and think. The Lord and Carolyn Cotsworth willing. With her car parked out front, there was no hope that Carolyn would not know she was at home. Poor generous, well-meaning Carolyn.

She'd surely talk about the hospital. And being *tra-la* about everybody and everything, she wouldn't know or agree that Perry Hawthorne was the villain of the piece.

The apartment was quiet, there was Carolyn's salad in the frige, and her cookies. Tunnie could open her bag, take out her clothes. And she could think again about the trip. which she had made. Wisely or not, she had gone. She had seen the companions of her young years, though there were a few missing faces.

Clytie Cotsworth, for one. Among the prettiest of the nurses, and the most popular with the men, she was friendly to everyone, and almost everyone loved her.

Tunnie should go to see her. She lived in Los Hermanos, which wasn't too far, and Clytie was dreadfully ill. Or so Virginia said. Carolyn was sure she'd get better.

Tunnie carried her bag to the hall closet, stood on a stool to put it away on the top shelf. Now, to change her clothes, and get at the salad . . .

Clytie Cotsworth had not stayed with nursing. Home from the service, she had married—not one of the doting officers or men, but a civilian attorney, a successful man. Clytie had done well for herself.

And now, here was her commanding officer, Tunnie, living in the same apartment unit with Clytie's sisters.

Fate. Coincidence. "Small world."

* * *

On Wednesday night, the four interns who served at Creighton Memorial Hospital were late eating their dinner. They chose, without words about it, to eat together, an instinctive huddling together at a time of storm and crisis. This was unusual; ordinarily Ted Bechars would have gone home, if only for an hour. Blair would have snatched his meal, sitting at the counter in the kitchen, or making himself some sandwiches which, with a carton of milk, he would have taken to his quarters.

Tonight they sat together at the table, ate creamed fish and eggs on toast, french fried potatoes, and stared unseeing ahead of them. They knew that after the autopsy an undertaker had borne Mrs. Forrest's body away. They heard that there was to be no funeral, and interment would be private.

"Don't Dr. Forrest and Dr. Belze share an office over at the clinic?" Tommie asked unexpectedly.

Bechars and Blair looked at her, but no one answered her.

Minutes later . . . "What sort of clinic do you suppose Hawthorne plans to build?" Dr. Smith asked.

"He doesn't *plan* to build any kind," Hank Blair said this, gruffly.

"How do you know that?" Dr. Bechars asked him.

Hank shrugged. "I don't know. I just figure it was a move he made, to announce a clinic."

"He could build one. Or even use Union Hospital for one after the new county hospital gets built."

"When will that be?" Dr. Blair demanded blandly.

"I suppose it would take a year or so, even here where it never rains."

"It would take a favorable vote as well."

"Yes, but people seem favorable. Even people here in this hospital, patients, personnel . . ."

Dr. Bechars reached for a plate of pie. "This clinic of Hawthorne's," he said. "The staff men here have the place across the street pretty well sewed up. And they are older men, of course."

"Not as old as Hawthorne, some of them."

"No, they are not. But Crosby and Kayser are older. Anyway, I was thinking. If Hawthorne made plans for a really up-to-date clinic, maybe there would be a job for some of us."

"What happened to the Air Force?" asked Hank.

"I keep hoping it will go away. Which reminds me, why doesn't the military complex catch you fellows?"

"I'm a gurrul," said Tommie comically, and the men laughed.

"You sure are, babe," Hank told her. "And I didn't sign any papers, Dr. Bechars."

"Lucky you." Bechars ate his pie.

"Speaking of tests and stuff," said Dr. Smith. "I did some outpatient work today, and do you know? I had a woman come in for an EKG who was wearing stretch pants and pantyhose both!"

His companions laughed. "You sure learn a lot as an intern," said Bechars. "And I still mean to watch that clinic of Hawthorne's. He does things on a big scale. Rich."

"All doctors are rich," drawled Blair. "Haven't you heard?"

"Yes, I have heard that, and I hope it's true. I'd say it was true of Hawthorne."

"Our clinic is a good place," said Tommie. "I've seen it."

"Comfortable, convenient—but not really a clinic."

"They have a lab, and all the diagnostic equipment they need. But I wonder . . ." She broke off, and the three men looked up. "I wonder," she continued, "if Dr. Belze and Dr. Forrest will be able to go on sharing their offices. That terrible lawsuit . . ."

"That terrible *death!*" drawled Dr. Smith.

"Belze is one hell of a surgeon," Hank said. "And the autopsy showed that internal injury was too extensive for the woman to have lived."

"Forrest won't think so."

"He'll think; he'll have to. But he won't acknowledge it. You know? We may have to testify at that lawsuit if it ever comes to court."

"Especially you, as ambulance attendant."

"I'll be ready," said Hank, standing up. "I have my report down on paper, for Dr. Creighton to read along with all the other stuff he's going to have to handle."

"I hear the great and wonderful is home."

"Yes, he came in an hour ago. And he is great and wonderful; he'll handle things." Tommie sounded very sure.

"Did you see his girl?" asked Dr. Bechars. "I heard one came with him."

The others voiced astonished disbelief. "There was a girl," Dr. Blair confirmed. "I saw her. Just about the prettiest girl I ever did see. The way her eyes were set, her cheekbones . . ." He went out, and the ones left behind looked at each other in amazement.

"Do you get a picture of our Hank moving in on Creighton *and* his girl?" asked Dr. Bechars.

* * *

Having completed her arduous trip to the mailbox, with the help of her neighbor Clytie reached her apartment. She managed a courteous thank-you, and walked into the foyer. The sight of her familiar things strengthened her. She grasped the table; she made her way back to her bedroom and sank gratefully upon the chaise longue. She lay there for a time; she didn't remember how long. Had she gone to the mailbox? Yes, and mailed her letter. It would be picked up—and would be on its way. That was all that mattered.

She drowsed a bit, and wakened, drowsed again. "I am very ill," she said once, aloud. Long, long ago, she had been a nurse. But with one's self, it was hard to judge. She was

breathing too rapidly, that she knew. Her pulse was flutter-
ing. She had medicine . . . She could call Carolyn. Or her
closest friend here in Los Hermanos. She would think of
the number . . .

It was full dark when she roused again. "I wish I would
just die," said Clytie, alone, but no longer frightened. What
was it she should do? Oh, yes. Call Celine. Tell her . . .

Celine might have other things to do . . .

Finally, by a great exertion of will, Clytie turned on the
lamp; she dialed her friend's number. She hoped it was the
right one . . .

It was. Celine's throaty voice answered. Clytie could
scarcely speak. But she managed—enough—"I am—very
sick," she said, gasping. "I think—I think—"

She did not know it when Celine came, with her husband.
They had called Clytie's doctor, who said to bring her to
the hospital at once.

Clytie woke up in the hospital; she had been undressed;
there was a tube attached to her arm. Celine was in the
hall, and came in. Dear Celine, but she had let herself get
too thin, and she smoked too much.

The nurse said Mrs. Whiteside should not talk, so Celine
left. And Clytie, with a blue ribbon tying her hair away from
her face, lay upon the cool white bed, and was grateful
that she need struggle no more.

An hour or two after midnight, she slept, and the sleep
deepened . . .

"I would say her death was unexpected," her doctor told
Celine.

"She was dreadfully ill."

"Oh, yes. And she would have died within six months. But
just now . . . Well, if you will give the information we need
to the desk . . ."

"But, doctor, I don't know . . ."

"Mrs. Whiteside had a family, didn't she? Sisters, I think."

"Yes, Clytie did have sisters. Their names and addresses
would be in her desk at home. Didn't the hospital have her
next of kin?"

"Only an attorney's name. And his office address. They
could wait until morning, perhaps."

But Celine thought Clytie's family should know at once.
Two A.M. My God! Perhaps she should go home now and
wait, until daylight at least. She didn't have a key—and to

get the manager out at this hour . . . Yes, she would go home, set her alarm for six . . .

At six, she still did not have a key, and the manager was not happy about being routed out. What would he have said about two A.M.? Celine asked herself. She even giggled a little. Clytie would have laughed too. Poor Clytie.

"Mrs. Whiteside has died," she told the manager. "I need to find her sisters' address, to phone them . . ."

"Mrs. Whiteside dead?" the man asked stupidly.

"I told you! She died about one-thirty this morning. We took her to the hospital last night; we didn't take her purse and keys, and I need to get inside."

"Well, I don't know, Mrs. Huff . . ."

Celine leaned toward him. "You know me, don't you? You've seen me many times with Mrs. Whiteside. Look, you can stay right with me. I just have to look in her purse or her desk—maybe she had a telephone book with these names and addresses in it. I know her sisters' first names, but not their last ones . . ."

The manager finally agreed. He did know Mrs. Huff. She always drove her car over the edge of the drive and made a mess of the grass.

Celine found Clytie's purse, but no address. She went on to the big desk with its beautiful original brass. Clytie had promised the desk to her . . . She looked at the papers in the pigeon holes. She found the attorney's name, some scribbling on a pad of yellow papers—it looked like notes for a will—and—here! A Christmas card list, so headed. She read down—some names she knew, her own was among them. There was no Carolyn or Virginia—but there was one address in Carson. Just the street number. That could be it . . .

"I'm going to try to call this number," she told the manager.

"Look, Mrs. Huff—"

"I know. But why don't you go on, shave and have your breakfast? I won't steal anything, and I'll tell you when I leave."

She had a perfectly terrible time with the operator. That voice said they could not make a connection on a street number alone. But of course they could! Finally, through a supervisor, Celine got someone on the telephone line. A woman's voice—she was very nice. She said she was a doctor —a Dr. Clark. Oh, yes, she did know Mrs. Whiteside; her sisters lived upstairs in the same apartment, she would give Celine the number.

She was so friendly and nice that Celine talked to her, and told her about Clytie. "It was almost a coroner's case," she said solemnly.

"Those things are so distressing," said Marion. "You know —I don't believe I'd say that to Carolyn or Virginia." She gave Celine the number, offering herself to tell them.

No, Celine should talk to them.

She stopped long enough to make coffee, and to drink a cup.

All in all, it was past seven when she called Carson again and got Virginia. Carolyn had left for the hospital, a development she would never forget or forgive.

Virginia was quite capable of dealing with things like undertakers and burial plans. Really, she suggested that the lawyers be asked to make these immediate decisions. She did suggest that Celine—"I know that you two were great friends"—pick out clothing for poor Clytie. Here she wept a little. She would get in touch with her sister at once, she said, and probably she would call back. "But feel free to call us, and thank you so much for being kind to poor Clytie."

Poor Virginia, too. The first thing she did was to make some coffee for herself. Then Marion came upstairs, and Alice Tunstall came down—Alice offered to tell Carolyn.

No, Virginia thought she should do it.

"You'd better get dressed, then," suggested Miss Tunstall. "You can ride over with me. Twenty minutes?"

Virginia was ready. Miss Tunstall took her to her own office and suggested that she stay there. "I'll get Carolyn here," she said. "She's going to be upset."

Carolyn was all of that. Not so much about Clytie's death—they had been expecting something of the sort—but that Virginia had been the first to know. Why should she have been the one? Had she made any decisions . . . ?"

She went on about these things, but finally, with Alice's help, she was persuaded to go home. "Can you drive?" Alice asked Virginia.

"I will drive."

"I'll pass the word here in the hospital. Don't worry, Carolyn. I'll see you both this evening."

She watched Virginia drive away, and, sighing a little at the still-one-more complication, Alice went back into the hospital. She would tell Fox, and the administrator, that Miss Cotsworth . . .

* * *

The first one she met, and told, was Dr. Belze.

He greeted Miss Tunstall, seemingly preoccupied with the paper he held in his hand. She told him briefly of the death of Miss Cotsworth's sister. He looked up, frowning.

"Not the one who lives with her," Alice hastened to say. "This was a third sister who lived in Los Hermanos. They just got word."

"Oh," said Dr. Belze. "Regrettable." He walked toward the desk where he would sign in. He slapped the paper gently against his hand.

It was a subpoena. He, and Blair, the intern, had both been served subpoenas telling them they were being sued for a hundred thousand dollars for negligent and improper care, resulting in the death of Dorothy Forrest. They were to appear . . .

Blair had laughed. "Me and who else?" he had asked. "You got a hundred thousand, Dr. Belze?"

"I don't believe the suit is serious," the surgeon had answered him. "But, maybe, Blair, we should not talk to anyone except Dr. Creighton about this."

"He knows I don't have a hundred thousand cents."

"Yes, I know. But—keep still, will you?"

"I'll try. And we know we did all we could for that poor woman, don't we?"

They knew. Vil Belze knew an awful lot. That was the trouble. Too much knowledge was pushing at the bones of his skull.

He went up to the surgery floor; that morning he had no surgery scheduled, but he checked on his patients, and then went back along the hall outside of the operating rooms. There were wide windows that looked out across the basin of their valley; he looked out across the bright red soil and the brilliant green sage of their land. The sky was a blazing blue that morning, and ordinarily he would have rejoiced in it.

For a long time, the big man stood at the window; the subpoena crackled in his coat pocket, and he thought . . .

On Monday, Dorothy had warned him. On Tuesday she had called him and told him that Jane at that very minute was in a motel with her husband. Vil had said that he did not believe it.

"Well, I believe it!" Dorothy had cried. She had been weeping and her voice was shrill. "And I am going to do something about it!"

He had tried to talk to her. She was pregnant, and excitable. Even if what she said was true, there were ways to handle this thing.

"I know," she had broken in. "I know ways. Well, you be sensible, Vil. I can't be. Walter is my husband, and your wife—my best friend—I'm going to kill them both!"

Belze had not believed that either. Not for a few minutes. Then—yes, he believed that she might do something desperate and foolish. Certainly she had a grievance. Forrest was the biggest sort of heel if he were two-timing his pregnant wife . . .

The least Vil could do was to take the warning and prevent a greater tragedy. If he could . . .

Thinking back, Vil could not remember what his first feelings were concerning his own wife's involvement. He didn't believe Dorothy's story, so he had not needed to stir up any amount of protest or indignation. Even when he decided that he must try to stop Dorothy, she had been his focus of action. Of feeling. Not Jane, or Forrest.

As he finally began to move, he had not acted with a reasonable plan. He was shocked, rebellious that Dorothy would cook up this situation for him to handle; he was angry, first, at her. He had felt, as he recalled, almost like a tantrummy child, wanting to pound his fists against the wall, and scream. This could not be happening! He did not want it to happen!

But—if it had . . . Only then did he become angry as a man becomes angry. Fist-swinging angry at Forrest, sickeningly disgusted and angry at Jane. And at himself, too, if he had been so blind as not to know what was happening to his home, to him.

Jane—well the Belzes and the Forrests had been friends ever since the men had begun to work together at Memorial. They lived in the same neighborhood, they were together several times a week socially, sometimes at parties, sometimes in foursomes of bridge; the men played golf together— their wives did too.

Forrest was a lady's man, by his own declaration. This had become a running gag in their group of friends.

Jane . . .

Well, Jane was a cute girl. Pert, outrageous even at

times, and always friendly. Friendly with other women, and with men. All men. Never just one.

Except Vil, of course. She was Vil's wife, a good mother to the twins, a better-than-good housekeeper. Interested in her husband's profession, she had learned to be a good doctor's wife.

Dorothy Forrest . . . She was pregnant, so Forrest was being a husband to her.

If the story she was trying to tell to Vil was true, he at least had never guessed, and he would not readily believe it when Dorothy told it to him.

But, at the minute, the point was that Dorothy evidently did believe it, and if she really was out on the road with a gun, Vil was going to have to warn Forrest and Jane, whatever their being together implied.

If he could find them . . . Jane and her car were gone from Vil's home; their chicano girl was attending to the twins. Vil could go to Ravinia, and if he saw Jane's car— her beloved Jaguar, bought secondhand . . .

So Dr. Belze started out, first trying to call Dorothy to verify the name of the motel, but her phone didn't answer. He was sure she had said Ravinia, and he would prove, to himself at least, that Dorothy was crazy.

If he was wrong, if he found Jane and Forrest, he could save his wife, and his friend. Dorothy, too, of course.

Because of road construction and a long detour, that hour of driving, in his memory, became a horror of highway traffic, red lights, highway signs, cars passing and passed.

"I could have been killed, too," he muttered now. As Dorothy had been killed. He had missed her on the road, but he had found Jane, and Walter Forrest. Together.

Chapter Six

IT WAS early on Saturday afternoon. The Cotsworth sisters—"All that's left of us," Carolyn pointed out—had returned to their apartment from Clytie's funeral. It had been, really, only a committal service. At the same time, a memorial service was being held at her church in Los Hermanos. But Clytie's body had been brought to Carson the night before for burial beside her husband and parents.

"I am glad we had rain," said Carolyn. "It freshens the desert so." She carefully put her little hat in its box, and fluffed her white hair. "We'll have to stay dressed," she told Virginia. "One of us, anyway. People will be coming in."

"I am dressed," said Virginia, coming into her sister's bedroom. She still wore the black and white linen dress she had worn to the cemetery. It was plain, and cooler than a suit. Carolyn had not approved. "But I hope a lot of people will not come."

"They will," Carolyn assured her. "People from the church, the hospital, others here in the apartments. I am going to begin writing cards; so many have sent flowers, and food . . ." She went into the living room. On every available surface were pots of growing flowers and vases of cut ones.

"I wish we had gone back to Los Hermanos," she called back to her sister.

"But you were the one who said . . ." protested Virginia.

"I know, but now I think we should have gone."

"We'll see her friends. We'll have to go over there and empty her apartment. I dread that job. Clytie had so much stuff. Clothes enough for six women."

"And I suppose there will be legal matters," Carolyn agreed. "She made the law firm executors, you know. And

I'm glad. Though I don't suppose they have the will yet, not if it was at the bank."

"The lawyer could have got it out yesterday."

"Oh, Virginia. You don't know a thing about legal matters. Did you get the mail as we came in?"

"It's all on the desk. I think Alice fetched it. She's been very good to us."

"Yes, she has. Everyone has. They've called, brought in enough food to feed an army, and flowers . . ." She smiled tenderly. "Imagine even Dr. Hawthorne knowing about Clytie, and sending roses."

"Didn't Dr. Creighton?"

"Oh, yes. The hospital sent white flowers. Those white tulips and stock we took to the cemetery. But of course I work for Dr. Creighton. Dr. Hawthorne—well, I hope I'll be working for him, too, before long. He really is a wonderfully thoughtful man."

"You hope the single hospital will work out?" Virginia asked.

"Yes, I do. Of course I love Memorial. But the world moves, Virginia."

"So I've heard," said her sister. "I'm going to fix us a lunch tray. What do you want? Name anything. It's out in the kitchen. Sliced ham, roast beef, veal aspic . . . chocolate cake, coconut cake, caramel cake and angel food. Jello salad . . ." Her voice trailed away.

All afternoon the telephone rang, all afternoon people came to the apartment. Friends, church people—an endless stream, it began to seem. Carolyn got few cards written, and at five o'clock Virginia confessed she was tired "to a nub."

"We have so many friends," Carolyn rebuked her. "I am proud, for Clytie's sake. We . . ." Her head lifted.

The doorbell had rung again.

"I'll get it," said Virginia. "I still have my shoes on."

Carolyn frowned patiently. She did not think these humorous things Virginia said were funny. Or in good taste, just now.

Their visitor was a young man—twenty-six or so—nicely dressed. He carried a briefcase, and identified himself as Robert Ragsdale, a member of the law firm of . . .

"From Los Hermanos?" asked Carolyn, coming out of the living room.

She fluttered about. Could she offer Mr. Ragsdale a drink—something cold? Was he the son of . . .

He nodded. "Son and grandson," he agreed. He refused the drink. "I have to fly back in an hour or so."

The sisters had to say quite a bit about his flying—and the law firm he represented. Had he known Donald Whiteside?

Yes, he had. But that was before he had himself entered the firm. "I knew Mrs. Whiteside quite well," he said. "A lovely person. We all extend our sympathies."

The sisters smiled upon him tenderly. They both liked good manners in a young man. And to think he had *flown* . . .

"How did you get here from the airport?" asked Virginia.

"He used a taxi," said Carolyn in the kind tone which so aggravated her sister. "You didn't hold it, did you, Mr. Ragsdale?"

"Oh, no. I'll get another one. Now!"

"Oh, yes the legal matter." The sisters settled attentively, Virginia on the couch, Carolyn in one of the deep, square chairs.

"We are a little disturbed, said the young attorney. "We know that Mrs. Whiteside recently made a new will. But we know, too, that she did not take it to the bank, nor have we been able to locate it in her home. We searched rather thoroughly this morning—and we wondered . . . You knew, didn't you, that she had drawn a new will?"

He was looking at Carolyn. "No," she said primly. "No, I did not know."

"I did," Virginia spoke up.

Mr. Ragsdale turned to look at her hopefully. Carolyn's glance was annoyed. "How could you know?" she asked.

"Because she wrote to me about doing it."

"I didn't see any such letter."

"No. She wrote it especially to me."

"That is very strange," said Carolyn, plainly not believing her sister. "I was close to Clytie; she certainly would have told me . . ."

"We thought," said Mr. Ragsdale, "that there was a chance she had sent it to you."

"Oh, no!" cried Carolyn.

Virginia leaned forward, frowning. But she did not speak.

"All right," said Mr. Ragsdale. "Then we probably shall

have to probate the old one. Though we hope when we assess the household belongings that it will show up. Though there were some changes . . ." He took a blue-bound sheaf of papers from his briefcase. "This is a copy of the only will we do have," he said unhappily. He unfolded the pages, and Carolyn snapped on a lamp.

'In both wills," he said, "you are named the residuary legatee, Miss Cotsworth. There are specific gifts to friends, and relatives of her husband—a mahogany desk to her friend, Celine Huff, her ruby jewelry to you, Mrs. Shelton . . ." He glanced up and Virginia nodded. She still was deep in thought. "The estate is sizeable," said Mr. Ragsdale. "It should value out at about a hundred thousand."

Carolyn gasped. And fluttered. "My goodness, I had no idea . . ." she cried.

"Yes. Though taxes will take a part of it. There was a complicated trust fund structure at Mr. Whiteside's death on which taxes now must be paid. I'll explain it in detail when we finally settle the estate. Tell me, after we have assessed the personal property, do you plan, yourself, to come over . . ."

"Yes, I'll dispose of Clytie's things," said Carolyn. "Earlier today Virginia and I were discussing that sad task."

"Good. I'll be getting back then tonight. As I said to you, our firm will be the executor."

"I knew that you would be," said Carolyn.

"There will need to be stocks sold, various operations. The apartment lease extends until November, but we could save some money by subleasing before then. Mrs. Whiteside's car . . ."

"We'll come whenever you are ready," said Virginia. "Now, I'll drive you to the airport."

"I'll do it," said Carolyn firmly. "Could we offer you some supper first, Mr. Ragsdale?"

"No, thank you. I'll be home by seven-thirty, with luck." He held his hand out to Virginia. "Thank you," he said.

"I wish we could have told you that the new will was here," she said.

"How could it be?" asked Carolyn sharply. "If Clytie ever seriously meant to make one . . ."

"She did make one, Miss Cotsworth," said the lawyer. "And signed it. I was there."

"Well, then she must have—I knew nothing about it."

* * *

Even after being at home, and back at the hospital for three days, Fox Creighton still faced a mountain of work on his desk. Problems accumulated as fast as did unanswered mail. He had worked hard, and steadily, and still there were dozens of decisions for him to make. Letters to dictate, people to talk to—

He knew about the called vote on the bond issue, and about Hawthorne's announced clinic. He knew about the lawsuit arising from the death of Dr. Forrest's wife. He still had to talk to that man, and more particularly than he had already done to Dr. Belze and to Hank Blair.

He faced that task with dread, just as that Saturday morning he faced the paper work on his desk with dread. The weather did not especially help. The sandstorm when he was in Los Hermanos, a rain two days ago, and the heat since —everything added up to a feeling of impending doom. Which was ridiculous. Though with his uncle dead, Dorothy Forrest dead, and now Miss Cotsworth's sister—He glanced at his watch. He must be sure to go to the cemetery at noon. That service would be brief but it would offer no rescue from his idea that disaster was encompassing his small world.

He bent over his desk, pencil in hand.

Then he leaned back in his chair, and stretched his arms wide. He wished he could go home, perhaps ride with Courtney . . .

Courtney. He had just about decided that bringing her to his home had been a mistake. The Storys had taken her advent with their usual calm acceptance of everything Dr. Creighton did. The town, his friends, and especially his enemies, were not going to be so compliant. The town, even if no election were imminent, was going to make something of that young girl's living in his bachelor household. A phalanx of Mrs. Storys was not going to change that.

The girl herself was behaving well. Except for her telling him that she loved him, she had settled right down into living in his home. God knew, she was decorative. She was essentially a gay young person to have around; she could be heard laughing with the Storys in the kitchen, and what a picture she did make running across the grass with the two red dogs. But still—

He had heard nothing, and probably would not hear anything. But there were always those ready to sniff out gossip, to elaborate on it, to detect signs where no signs were evident, to make surmises where none was justified. And this added itself to his feeling of dread. What was going to happen?

He was, he admitted, superstitious about this sort of apprehension. He had felt it before, and subsequently, things had happened, a crash had come. One time, particularly; there had been another girl . . .

Abruptly he rose from his desk, put on a white coat and went out into the hospital. From basement to third floor, he covered the place, going to each segment and department. On a Saturday, few heads of these services were present, though all, he trusted, were available on call. He still was upset about Belze's disappearance on two nights at the beginning of the week. He faced a real showdown with the surgeon on that point.

His face betraying his preoccupation he strode through the halls, from lab to operating room. There was only one patient in intensive care. Emergency was busy, a precipitate o.b. had just come in; the kitchen crew was scurrying about with dinners an hour away.

Miss Cotsworth's office was empty, though he had seen her assistant busy in the diet kitchen. Carolyn would be back on Monday; he had stopped in to see her and Virginia briefly the night before, and he would attend their sister's committal service at noon. Miss Cotsworth was an excellent dietician, and she managed her part of the hospital's operation with both diligence and imagination.

By her own declaration, her aim was to make the patients happy while "guests" in the hospital, and to keep the personnel healthy and well fed. She was inclined to burble about all sorts of things, and the evening before she had so burbled. But knowing her as well as he did, Dr. Creighton still had been rather shocked to have her speak of Dr. Hawthorne's recent activities as "wonderful," and to hear her going into ecstasies about the man's charm.

She looked forward, she said, to a future in the big new hospital that would give her something she called radar ovens.

"Evidently you think we should join forces with Hawthorne and Union Hospital," Dr. Creighton had said to her dryly.

"Oh, but we are, aren't we?" she had asked.

And Fox had laughed shortly and departed. Sometimes, often, he wondered if he could at all judge the world and its ways. Perhaps he was alone in fighting this single hospital project. Could he, right or wrong, avoid its accomplishment? And if he could not avoid it, could he handle it?

Pat Kern and his very nice wife had been invited to dinner that evening. Pat had asked for a time when he could talk to Fox about the Hawthorne development which had "got away from me while you were gone." Even Fox was surprised to hear himself suggest the dinner engagement.

But it was all right. He wanted certain people to see Courtney in his home. Pat and Mary Kern were the first and best ones to assess the situation and to speak the proper word in the proper places. The Storys were pleased to be asked to serve dinner to guests.

"Don't let them give you an exalted idea of the mayor's visit," Fox warned Courtney. "He won't come wearing a chain of office. Incidentally, as a boy he knew Uncle Stephen."

The Kerns came—Mary a tall, erect woman, who played golf and gardened and liked to tell tales about her two children.

"Aren't you lucky to be Fox Creighton's ward?" she asked Courtney.

"I think so, considering we never saw one another before a week ago. He's been very kind and hospitable."

"Fox?" asked Mary. "Do you want me to tell you all about this man?"

"You do, and I'll clobber you," Fox promised. "Suppose we leave things at kind and hospitable."

Dinner was served at the round, glass-topped table out on the porch. It was cool, and the view across the lawns into the trees was restful. Late sunshine cast long, deep shadows. The table's centerpiece was a tall silver compote filled with polished black cherries, surrounded by three small, low bowls of pink roses.

The dinner was excellent—a delicate soup, breast of chicken—and Fox was amazed to hear himself talking about French cuisine.

"You go down the rue de Vaugirard to the Luxembourg Museum," he told. "You have sole and *fraises á la crème* at Foyot's. Or snails at L'Escargot. Absinthe at the Dôme."

"And a hangover the next day," drawled Pat.

Fox and Courtney laughed, but Mary protested to her husband.

Pat said he thought he had come out here to tell Fox he

couldn't stop Hawthorne from getting the vote scheduled. The man had the necessary petititons to present to the Board of Election commissioners; evidently he had been collecting them for some time.

As he talked, Fox listened. And as he listened, he gazed at the girl across from him; delighting in the movement of her thin wrists, the turn of her head as she talked to Mary, her voice light, with a lilt to it. He noted the hand with which she pushed the fold of dark blond hair off her forehead, and her smile which was young and candid.

He told Pat of his thinking earlier that day. "I wondered if I should have set myself to fight this thing so hard."

"What are you talking about?" demanded his friend.

"There are so many things involved," Fox explained. "So many things, and people, and circumstances." He looked at Courtney again and at Mary. "Do you girls have any idea of what we are talking about?" he asked.

"I do," said Mary. "Pat marches up and down and tells me. But perhaps Courtney . . ."

"I've found out about it," said the girl. "I even had this ogre Hawthorne pointed out to me."

"Who did that?" Fox asked her.

"Mrs. Story, when we went shopping yesterday morning. There was this big car, and a very handsome, villain-type man driving it . . ."

Fox laughed. "All right, all *right!*"

"Mrs. Story thinks you should fight any hospital where you and he would have to try to get along together," said Courtney.

"Then that is final. I'll fight it. But there still are an awful lot of people involved. Marion Clark should have a place for her sick children, and a crotchety old man with the gout should not have to inflict himself on a roommate. Cotsworth's radar ovens we can get along without, I suppose."

He had to explain that, and his guests were amused. "Did she really mean radar?" asked Pat.

"I don't know. There are infra-red, and micro-wave—why shouldn't there be radar ovens? Our Carolyn is completely charmed by Hawthorne, it would seem."

"Just what kind of man is he?" Courtney demanded. "I mean, really."

"He is tall and dark and handsome," Fox told her. "He makes lots of money, more than I do, or can, in medicine."

"But there are stories . . ." Pat put in.

"There are stories," Fox agreed. "Some of them probably are true. But we've had patients, brought to us on an emergency basis, who insist on transfer to his hospital."

"Is he the only doctor? Does he run the hospital alone?"

"Oh, no," said Fox. "There is a Board, and a medical staff; the place is licensed for operation, though you must realize, Courtney, it doesn't take much to get a hospital licensed. Medicare has made the situation quite a bit tighter, and that's where the shoe seems to be pinching Hawthorne. I believe some of his claims have been denied."

"There's a notice on his office door that says he does not treat Medicare patients."

Fox stared at the mayor. "How do you know that?" he demanded.

"I get around," simpered Pat.

"You seem to. But the facts still are, ladies, that Union Hospital *is* Dr. Hawthorne. He brings in the patients, he treats them. He used to do a lot of surgery, but I don't believe he does anymore. Though he is still top man."

"As you are at your hospital?" asked Courtney.

Pat and Mary looked up, their eyes shining. Much less could bring on one of the famous Fox Creighton explosions.

But not that night, not to Courtney. "It's not just the same," he answered, speaking slowly. "I own stock in Memorial, as I am sure he does in Union. I am Chief of Medical Services at Memorial, but I wouldn't venture to say that he carries that title at Union. I don't believe my red hair and winning ways have brought us any patients—but, yes, our positions are similar. We are both involved in our own operations. Similarly we would be involved in the reorganization that has been proposed. Everyone is and would be involved in that.

"The town is involved, and the surrounding territory. The kind of hospital service afforded them is a vital thing. This suggestion of Hawthorne's may have its merits, it may not. We do need more space, we do need more service. There are various forces that will determine the results of the election. I feel rather helpless when I contemplate all the forces at work here."

"I hope you are not helpless," said Pat dryly. "And you're not, of course. There is work being done. We need more hospital, if you say we do, but there are lots of us who don't want this particular move to succeed in giving us more."

They were still talking, and lingering over their dessert and coffee; the candles had been lighted, when Story whispered in the doctor's ear that he was wanted on the telephone.

Fox sighed and went into the house, then came back very quickly. "I'm afraid . . ." he began.

Pat was on his feet. "You and your excuses," he taunted. "Come on, Mary. We know when we are not wanted."

"Courtney will entertain you . . ."

"My mother taught me not to eat and run," said Pat, "but she didn't know how things would always be at your house."

The Kerns departed amid laughter, and Fox started toward his car. Courtney skipped to keep up with him. 'May I go with you?" she asked.

"Why on earth would you want to?"

"I like to see the people working in your hospital. I like to tag along and watch you."

"This case is that of a man who had his nose cut off." Fox watched her.

Courtney only gulped. "I still want to go," she insisted.

"All right. Get in."

She did, and they started, sand and gravel flying under his car's wheels. "Did you like the Kerns?" Fox asked her. He seemed curious about this young girl suddenly projected into his life's sphere. He often asked her questions and watched her.

"Oh, yes, I liked them," she said. "The mayor is a tennis player, isn't he?"

"Well, as a matter of fact he is. A good one. Did he talk to you about tennis?"

"Oh, no. But I noticed that one of his wrists was much thicker than the other, and sloping shoulders like his usually do mean tennis."

She saw the smile crinkles begin to web about Fox's eye. He seemed pleased. "That's very observant of you," he said.

"I notice things," she agreed. "Are you going to operate on the man—what would you do? Sew his nose back on?"

"Wait a minute . . ." Fox stopped her questions. "First, I shan't operate. I was called because a few days ago we had a little difficulty. The surgeon on call turned up missing. That happened on two nights, and I am sure there was a good reason. I had left word that if any surgical emergency came into the hospital I was to be called. I want to be on the scene if there are further problems."

"I see."

"Well, I'm glad you do. Because I am looking through the glass very, very darkly. Do you want to go into the bloody scene?" He pulled up in the hospital drive.

"Well—I would—" said Courtney. "Where was your surgeon, the one who . . . ?"

"I mean to ask him that, very soon," Fox told her, striding toward the hospital's lighted door. The ambulance still stood there, a police car behind it. "The fight took place in the city jail," he explained to Courtney.

"Haven't you asked him yet?" she persisted. "The surgeon . . ."

"Oh, Belze. No I haven't really got down to that yet. I've had things on my mind. But I'll do it quite soon. Now—can you find things to do?"

"I'll watch," she said, seeming quite happy to be where she was. He left her leaning against the corridor wall, watching the door of emergency. She was a strange girl . . .

Courtney did not think she was acting strangely. There was a red-hot current of life pulsing through that hospital corridor. People came and went busily. A nurse with a covered tray, a doctor, she supposed, shrugging into a white coat as he walked. The surgeon? He could be. Presently the emergency room door flew open and a younger doctor ran out—he glanced at Courtney. "I'm going after the nose," he told her. "Want to come along?"

"How far? Dr. Creighton . . ."

"He won't leave before we get back. Come on. Did you ever ride a bus?"

Not in a bus like this one! Dr. Blair introduced himself, and helped her into the ambulance. The siren sounded, and the "bus" rolled away.

Hank told Courtney about the accident. The man—José something-or-other—was in jail, in the tank. With a bunch of other drunks. There was a fight. "There's always a fight in the drunk tank."

Courtney clung to the bar at the side of the heavy ambulance which was going very fast, tipping as it rounded corners.

A well-aimed razor slash had cut off José's nose. "Clean as a whistle," said young Dr. Blair. "A tidy guard threw it in the garbage can. Dr. Belze wants it."

"Will he sew it back on?"

"Tonight? On his face? Probably not. Later, if he can keep it alive. For now he'll bed it in the abdomen, probably; stomach tissues are well nourished, and if there should be infection—as there can be, after the garbage can deal—it can be handled better away from the face and that cut."

"I'm glad Dr. Belze was available tonight," said Courtney.

The young doctor looked at her. "Yes," he agreed. "You heard about his playing hookey, did you?"

She did not answer him.

When they reached the jail, she was told to stay in the ambulance. "Virgilio, don't let her get out," Dr. Blair called back to the driver as he went inside.

While he was gone, Courtney talked to Virgilio. He said that Blair was an intern, but a damn fine doctor.

At the hospital, Dr. Belze waited, and Dr. Creighton was in and out of o.r., watching the surgeon dress the ghastly wound on the man's face. When Blair got back with the nose, wrapped in a bundle of paper towels, Belze muttered, "I should have sent a jar of saline."

The three doctors bent over the relic from the garbage can. Dr. Belze trimmed some tissue, and placed it in a pan of solution, then he busied himself making a circular incision in the man's abdomen. Dr. Blair went back downstairs, nodding his head. That was exactly what he'd promised Creighton's girl the surgeon would do.

The ambulance and the police car could withdraw, he said. They'd keep José at the hospital for a time. A policeman must be detailed to watch him.

Fox, having watched the surgery—"Not exactly routine," he agreed with Belze—went out into the hospital, and for the second time within hours, he made the rounds of it. Top to bottom, end to end. He even went into his office, and leafed through the mail brought to his desk that evening. There was nothing that couldn't wait. He might as well go home.

And he did go, out through the service door to his car.

He completely forgot Courtney, forgot that she had ridden to the hospital with him. Only when he went into the house did he remember—Good Lord! Was she still leaning against the wall outside emergency? She had not been, he was pretty sure, when they took the Mexican up to o.r. But—

He could call the hospital. But she was a resourceful

young woman; when she saw that his car was gone, she would call a taxi. Though, really, he was shocked that he had done such a thing. She was a guest in his house, and—

Of course he did call the hospital. The desk told him that Miss Armstrong had left a half hour ago. "I think someone drove her home, Dr. Creighton."

"Thank you," said Dr. Creighton. A half hour ago . . . She should be home by now, or she would come in very soon.

It was another hour before she did come. He heard the car come up to the house, he heard Courtney's clear voice, and a man's laughter. He opened the book on his knee.

She came into the house, her heels tapping. She came into the library, and he looked up. "I'm sorry that I forgot you, Courtney," he said. "It was rude of me. I—I just forgot."

"It's all right," she said. "When I realized that you had forgotten—I could have called here. Story would have fetched me."

Yes, he would have.

"But one of the interns—Dr. Blair?"

He nodded.

"Dr. Blair was going off duty, and he offered to take me home. He signed off roster—is that the term?"

Again Fox nodded. Her eyes were bright, and her cheeks were pink. Evidently she had enjoyed her ride with Blair.

"I'd never ridden in a jeep," she said. And laughed. "And I'd never drunk beer served in a pitcher, either. We stopped for a snack, you see."

Black cherries in a silver compote, beer in a pitcher . . . Dr. Creighton laughed. "You've had quite an evening," he said.

"Yes. Now I'm going to bed. Good night, Doctor."

"I would rather you'd call me Fox."

"O.K.," she said agreeably. "Good night." She was half-way down the hall to the wing.

Fox closed his book, and realized that he was still smiling. Courtney could definitely look after herself. And if she presented no problem, probably there were no problems at all. No crisis.

Though by the time he was ready for bed he knew that crisis indeed was there, and that it had many facets. He lay staring at the ceiling, turning the prism in his mind. The upcoming vote on the new hospital. Dorothy Forrest's death. Belze's absence . . . He was glad that Courtney was presenting no insoluble problem. That she was just a nice, intelligent girl, spending the summer in his home.

He jumped when the telephone rang sharply at his ear. He lifted the receiver. "Dr. Creighton." He listened. "Good God!" he said softly, and put the telephone back. He was on his feet with the same gesture, reaching for clothes—any clothes. Trousers, a shirt—his feet into canvas shoes—he fastened his belt as he ran down the stairs, and out to his car. A fire at the hospital—in the distance he could hear the sirens.

Talk about crisis! Here was one. He put on his emergency light, and leaned over the wheel.

The sprinkler system, the alarm at the fire station—his call had come from there—the personnel fire drills. If those things were all paying off, and they would be, already the patients should be taken care of.

There was a fire all right. Still blocks away, he could see the smoke and the flames. Good Lord! Was the whole place going up? He had to drive with some care because other cars were out, all streaming toward the hospital—but his hand on the horn ring, and his flasher lights let him get through. He parked away from the building—and ran.

There were lights still in some of the halls; the fire was in the center part—water sloshed about his ankles, the sprinklers had worked then—but the elevators? Stretchers were coming out, some ambulatories. A few beds were out into the corridors . . .

"It's in the elevator shaft, doctor," a man in a white helmet called to him. "We'll have to use the far elevators . . ."

And pray that the power did not go off. Fox was everywhere—up the stairs—thanking God for the "far elevators" and the fire doors at the stairwells, both put in since his coming. The sprinkler system had done its work, though he heard a patient fussing shrilly at having a hose turned on her bed . . .

The central core of the building was where the fire was, the big elevator there, the kitchens, the emergency and delivery rooms, the or.r's . . .

Good God, the oxygen!

He was down into the basement, turning valve wheels. Someone on duty should have been especially delegated to do that—he'd slipped up there. He went upstairs again. They'd had one patient in intensive, and perhaps he was still up there, but surely José's police guard . . .

His hair bouncing with his speed, he covered the whole scene. A fireman swore at him, and he swore back. He knew he was in danger; he counted on his staff to rescue the patients, they and the police and the firemen. "I want everyone out!" he shouted over and over.

He got thoroughly soaked by a firehose directed downward from the roof; the lights went out. On the parking lot a wire arced and sparked blue flame; a yellow-helmeted man climbed a pole and cut it.

Half the town was out there, a sea of faces. Nurses, orderlies, and patients on stretchers, beds, carts, sitting or lying on mattresses.

Would the whole place go?

No. "They have it under control, Fox," said Pat Kern.

The core of the hospital was hurt. Now came the problem, what to do about and for the patients? Those who possibly could be must be sent home. Fox began to go from one group to another.

"What a man," he heard someone say.

His mind kept telling him that a hospital fire was a terrible thing, but even now he still was feeling the stimulus of a crisis which he could handle, that he could fight with his muscle and strength.

Gradually the noise died, and the onlookers began to melt away. He would have sworn he saw Hawthorne's dark head among them, but he still was too busy to think about that.

He gathered the doctors about him, the staff men, the interns. They were to decide what to do with each of their patients, he said. Some could be taken into the hospital wings where there was only water and smoke damage. Auxiliary power was being arranged, but those who could be cared for at home should be taken there. "Of course be sure someone is there to receive them."

He and Pat Kern were carrying a stretcher and patient into the hospital when Tommie came up to them and said that telephone service was restored. "Not exactly full switchboard, but there's a call for you, Dr. Creighton."

"Where do I take it?"

"In your office. Where else?"

He laughed. He continued with the patient and saw her put into a dry bed. "Let's go see what that call was," he told Pat. As they walked along the littered corridor, he remembered and told about Courtney's deducing that he was a tennis player.

"She's a nice girl," said Pat.

He waited while his friend took the telephone call. As he listened, a dozen expressions crossed Fox's face, which was stained and deep-lined from the last hours' events. "I'll keep what you say in mind," he concluded the telephone conversation. "Thank you." He turned to Pat, his eyes half-amused, half-puzzled.

"That was a woman," he said, "telling me that Kathie Hawthorne has been saying that her husband would burn Memorial down if he couldn't get his merged hospital any other way."

"Mhmmmn," said the mayor.

"You don't believe he would?" Fox challenged.

"I don't know what I believe, Creighton. Personally, my own theory is that someone on your staff—some incredible someone—Mary put this into my mind—she said she believed Hawthorne would burrow from within. That he would seduce or otherwise pay various ones—oh, people like your mousey little dietician, for instance, to disrupt things here. A fire is pretty darn disruptive, sir."

"I never heard such nonsense!"

"Well, you'd better hear it, son. Hawthorne means business, and he'll stoop to anything to get that business done. Incidentally, I've been checking those petition lists he got together for the bond election. Your Miss Cotsworth's name was on one of them. Perhaps other personnel whom I don't know by name are there too. But she is the ruthlessly sweet type I do remember."

"Signing a petition is one thing but setting a fire . . ." Fox broke off. "Suppose we let the insurance people and the fire chief decide what caused this thing. And we'll go back and carry someone else inside." He did not want to think of Carolyn, or even Kathie Hawthorne's husband . . .

But by the time they had reached the front lawn again, the last patient was being transported. The power company was setting up two generators to give them electricity, and at the rear doors the Red Cross had a van from which they were serving coffee and sandwiches.

"Can't you find some place to sit down, Fox?" Marion Clark asked the Chief, bringing him a cup. "You look terrible!"

"I never learned to scrub tidily with my cuffs buttoned," he told her. "How are all your children?" He wiped a smudge from her nose.

"Mine here are doing fine," she said. "I sent ten of them home, you know. Some objected to going."

He laughed. "Nothing like a bit of excitement."

"That Peach—he carried nearly all of the kids out in his arms."

"He probably enjoyed it, too."

A volunteer brought them sandwiches and they sat on the steps to eat them, hungrily. "We've been working," Marion assured Fox.

"Yes. And now there's a fine big mess to clean up."

"Mrs. Rice will attend to a lot of that. Isn't that your ward helping at the canteen?"

Fox brushed his hair out of his eyes and leaned forward. It was Courtney, in blue jeans, her hair in pigtails. "How'd she get here?" he wondered aloud. "And she really isn't my ward, Marion. She was Uncle Stephen's, and had no place to go. At her age . . . He left her a small trust fund. Of course you know about his bequest to your three girls."

"What's more to the point," said Marion dryly, "George knows about that. How much do you think the girls will get, Fox? The lawyer's letter talked about sixteenths. That means nothing to me."

"I believe someone mentioned seventy thousand dollars. For the three of them, that is."

Marion sat frowning. "But—my goodness! Doesn't that mean . . . ?"

"Yes. The estate was well over a million. George really lost out."

"He really did."

"What would he have ever done with a million dollars?" Marion asked breathlessly. "For that matter . . ."

"The older girls can probably take care of their money. You've raised them sensibly. But Nancy will need her own guardian for a year or two."

"Yes, this will be a crisis for her. I suppose the money won't be available for a while, and when it is, the court would appoint a guardian, wouldn't it?"

"You, probably. The will's wording left no doubt that Uncle Stephen felt George unfit. He left him fifty dollars, having provided for him generously in the past."

"He had. And you got left his ward as *your* ward, Fox. You'll have to watch the girl, you know."

Fox lifted his head, startled. "What do you mean, watch her?"

"You'll find out. Just watch her, and you'll see."

"She's already nineteen, so she could be thought somewhat grown. However she isn't my ward, really. I am just giving her a home between school terms."

"But she was your uncle's . . ."

"Yes. And she truly loved him. She's an interesting girl —and self-sufficient." He was tempted to tell Marion that Courtney said she was in love with him, Fox. She might, or might not, laugh at that.

He wouldn't tell her that Pat Kern thought it possible that Carolyn Cotsworth had set the fire. He was still thinking about that when Marion told him that Carolyn had decided that the fire had settled all discussion. The two hospitals, she said, now would have to work together for the new institution "where all the dotors, together, would care for the sick of the district."

"She decided that, did she?" Fox asked, standing up, and extending his hand to Marion. One of the fire trucks was rolling down the drive to the street. He would go inside again, check on things—and perhaps get home for a hot bath, clean clothes, before he'd need to face the day. Sunday, wasnt it?

* * *

But the night was not yet over. The patients returned to beds in the two wings must be nursed and cared for. Day was breaking so the matter of lights had another fifteen hours in which to be solved. There was water—and food was a possibility through the diet kitchens, though the nurses must forget, as the doctors had to, what tasks were proper for nurses to do. Alice Tunstall had her hands full setting stations, defining duties, assigning nurses.

And in spite of being so busy, the fire, the damaged services, the shock to herself and to others—some of the girls had been in most unprofessional tizzies—in spite of all that, the mood of last weekend's trip lingered. Now the crisis was not war but a fire in peaceful southwestern America. No bomb could have been more unexpected, or have wreaked more havoc. Nor been as challenging to the supervising nurse. So many things had happened this past night, so many things must be faced this day.

For one thing, at the Red Cross Canteen, Tunnie had, for the first time, met the young woman whom Marion Clark called Fox Creighton's ward. Marion was surprised that Tunnie had not known about her.

She found the few minutes necessary to tell her about Courtney, and Fox's gesture of generosity.

"I am shocked," said Alice Tunstall.

"Well, so are a lot of people. But it all seems perfectly natural to Fox. The girl needed a home, he argues. He had a home, and plenty of space. I'd gladly help him with this ticklish situation, but he denies that help is needed."

"I'd help him too," said Alice. "In fact—" she broke off. Fox was coming down the hall.

"What are you girls plotting?" he asked. "If I ever saw guilty countenances . . ."

"Not guilty at all," Miss Tunstall assured him. "We are getting our services into shape. I've been through the wars before, you know, and Dr. Clark has raised a family, which amounts to the same thing. And now we both have enough strength left over to offer our help in solving the situation of your young ward."

Fox scratched his red head. "What situation is that, ladies?" he asked.

"Oh, Fox Creighton!" Alice protested. "Surely you realize that you are an eligible bachelor, with chances all about to change that status. For a man like you to take a girl of nineteen into his home . . ."

"It sets all the willing ladies on edge, doesn't it?" he asked, his green eyes sparking.

"Oh, Fox!" Alice cried in exasperation. "You *know* you shouldn't have done such a thing!"

"I know, as of this morning, I have much more important things on my mind than the sensitivity of the women in my life."

"Well, they're there," Alice assured him. "And they are sensitive. Up to and including the girl herself."

Fox ran his hand through his hair. "Ladies, I have to attend to first things first!" he cried in what probably was, not all pretended anguish. "And my first question to you has to be: would sending Courtney elsewhere solve my hospital crisis?"

"You mean the fire?" asked Miss Tunstall.

"Well, certainly not the girl herself," he assured his well-meaning friends. "This morning, I left Courtney at home digging a flower bed, you may be interested to know. She is going to plant something she calls pinks."

He saw Alice and Marion exchange glances.

"No!" he shouted. "I am not going to let you women

regulate my life and home. I don't care what you yourselves think, or what Carolyn Cotsworth tells you to think."

Miss Tunstall lifted her chin. "Now see here, Fox Creighton," she said coldly, "I have not talked to Carolyn about your ward. In fact, I learned about her only this morning, and it was Marion who told me."

Fox swung to face Marion. "It isn't like you to sound like Carolyn," he said.

"What makes you think I did sound like her?"

"The effect is the same; it is what I am judging. All right. You two go right on being virtuous, Courtney will go right on digging up the backyard, and I'll spend my time figuring out how much damage was done by the fire we had last night. Or did your concern for my reputation make you forget that we have had a fire!"

He strode away, and the nurse and the doctor looked at each other, unbelieving. "It would seem our Chief is upset," Miss Tunstall murmured.

"Only *seem?*" asked Dr. Clark.

* * *

The fire had gutted the center core of the hospital, but the fire fighters had confined it to that area. Dr. Creighton, the hospital board, the mayor of the city, had already commended the fire department for an excellent performance.

But the operating rooms were gone, and the intensive care area, the expensive, delicate cardiac monitoring instruments. The delivery room, the main kitchen—some post-surgical beds.

Offices and record rooms to the front of this part of the building were badly smoke- and water-damaged, but they could be salvaged. It was thought that the roof and the walls were not hurt. The diet kitchens and perhaps an outside catering service could manage meals. E.R. could be cleaned up and serve as an operating room; it was about to do so that first morning.

There had been a car wreck; one of the occupants needed surgery for a head injury; Dr. Belze was called at ten o'clock. "Business as usual, eh?" his wife twitted him.

Business, but not at all as usual. The doctor parked his car at the front door of the hospital, and went in that way. Ashes still were sifting down like fine gray snow, ridging softly against the window frames, blowing along the floor in feathered waves as he walked back to Emergency. He felt as if he passed through some horror movie, or some childhood dream. Where the impossible was accepted as normal, where the incredible was being believed. There had been a fire—last night he had worked along with everyone else, doing what he could to save life and property.

But it had not taken the fire to put him into this strange, dreamlike mood of the unreal and the unbelievable.

Now he scrubbed at the basin in e.r., and thought about the night—Tuesday night—when he had driven along the road until he had found Jane's Jaguar parked at a motel with Walter Forrest's bronze-green Cadillac brazenly beside it.

The motel was five miles out of town, but everyone knew those two cars. A few people might think that the two couples were having a late dinner out there, but Vil Belze did not search for his wife and his friend in the dining room. He did not bother asking for them at the desk. He went from one flat door to the next, pink door, turquoise, yellow, and green, routing out the tenants, until he found Walter Forrest.

Without speaking, Vil had pushed the man aside; he had gone through to the bath where his wife, wrapped in the bed's blanket, cowered behind the shower curtain. He had snatched the blanket from her and looked her up and down.

"Get dressed," he had told her, his voice hoarse and rasping in his throat.

"You'd better get back to Dorothy," he called to Forrest. "I think she is waiting for you with a gun."

He had not offered to touch either one of them. He had followed Jane's car to their home, but he had not gone inside. He could not go into his home, he could not go to the hospital, he could not go to any familiar place. For hours he had driven across country. That was where he had been when he was needed to save Forrest's wife. Where he was needed . . .

Forrest, when he went home, did not find Dorothy there, with or without a gun. He had been at home when the call came to notify her husband of the accident.

The hospital—Dr. Creighton—wanted to know where the chief surgeon had been that night. He needed to know, and if things had not been so wildly disorganized around the hospital, by now he would know.

Forrest knew. But he had dared to file a lawsuit for medical neglect, daring his friend to tell the sordid story, guessing that he knew Vil Belze better than Vil had known Walter Forrest, better than he had known his wife.

He had, over and over, wondered about Dorothy that night, about the wild ride she must have taken, her face white, her eyes staring, the gun on the car seat beside her. She had known where she was going; she had known about the detour, and had cut through a side road, but she did not reach the motel. Instead she had gone off the road at high speed, and had crashed into that pole. What terror had the poor soul known?

She had been found; the ambulance had been summoned; she was cut free from the wreckage and brought here to the hospital. Her husband came, but the surgeon was not to be found.

And when he did come in, there was nothing he could do. There never had been anything he could do . . .

Even now, as his mind went over and over the treadmill of that terrible night, the whole thing made no sense. That was why he had not believed Dorothy when she first had told him that Walter and Jane were having an affair. Yes, he knew that other men and women sought the excitement, the adventure and danger of such excursions into sex. He had read about them.

But he could not believe that such a thing could break into his marriage, or into his genuine freindship and professional association with Walter.

He could scarcely believe it now.

* * *

At one o'clock on Sunday, Courtney brought Dr. Creighton's lunch from his home. Told that she was in his office, with his lunch, he could not believe . . .

He was dirty again, disheveled. Belze had done some surgery earlier, then the two men and Peach had decided to go through the instruments which had been carried, helter-skelter, down from surgery the night before. Many of the items could be salvaged, cleaned and sterilized; it was fine that they had been saved.

Fox came plunging into his office. "What the hell are you doing here?" he demanded of Courtney.

She gestured to the covered tray. "You're here," she said simply, as if that covered the whole situation.

"I'm here and I am busy," said Dr. Creighton coldly. "I want you to go home and stay there. People are talking about you, and I would rather you would not add to their material."

She faced him, her expression only curious. "I think you'd better stop long enough to eat your lunch," she said quietly, then turned on the heel of her blue Grasshopper, and went out.

Chapter Seven

ALL OVER TOWN, all over the district, people talked about the fire to one another. Everyone had some comment, some theory as to cause, some sort of solution for what must soon be a community problem.

Everyone wondered what Memorial would *do*. About as many asked what Union Hospital would do now? They would take in Memorial's patients, wouldn't they? Why should they? Why shouldn't they? Well, for one thing, Memorial has not asked Union to do that.

But, surely . . .

Well, one thing you can count on. Perry Hawthorne will make the most of the disaster.

"But what can he do? I mean . . ."

"That man can and will think of something. I understand he just barely stays out of the law's reach with his medical practice."

"His wife seems a nice person. Why has she put up with him for so long?"

"Someone—a friend—asked her that, asked her why she stayed with the man."

"You mean now?"

"Yes, and over the years. And her answer was that she's known what the guy was, and is. But he earned good money, she's saving what she can—he provides her with a nice home—and then, there is their daughter.

"Christie."

"Yes, Christie."

* * *

About four o'clock that Sunday afternoon, Virginia Cotsworth Shelton came to the hospital. She drove the car which she and Carolyn owned jointly, and getting out of it, she looked in awe at the ravished building. Its white stucco walls were stained with smoke, the lawns were littered, and in places torn up by heavy equipment trucks. There were cars parked—but a large NO VISITORS sign had greeted her as she drove in. Still—

She wanted to talk to Alice Tunstall, she had waited all day to talk to her, while Carolyn went to church that morning, and again this afternoon—there was to be a Vespers service and tea at the church. Carolyn of course must be there, hospital fire, dead sister, or no. But Alice had been at the hospital all day, so Virginia would seek her there. This thing on her mind was too heavy a worry . . . She had not slept for three nights. Not since Clytie's death, and all the dreadful things that had happened since. She had to talk to someone, get some advice. And Alice was a sensible woman . . .

She went into the hospital by the wide propped-open doors of the ambulance entrance. The floors had been swept, but overall there was a feeling of destruction, of disaster. Signs were fastened to the elevator doors—OUT OF ORDER—a rope was stretched across the stairs.

"Can I help you?" someone asked, and Virginia turned quickly.

"I—" she began. "I guess I want to see Miss Tunstall. I thought she would be at home today, but—"

"Yes. With the fire, almost everyone came in this morning; there is so much to do."

Then why wasn't Carolyn there? She had a job at the hospital!

"I'll see if Miss Tunstall is free," offered the nurse. "May I have your name?"

Virginia stared at her. "My . . . ? Oh, yes, of course. I am Virginia Shelton. And maybe I shouldn't—bother—"

"Wait a minute, since you are here. I'll go see."

Virginia watched her walk down the corridor; there were other people moving about. She heard a telephone ring, she heard a man talking to someone, loudly and firmly. "There isn't any danger, Mrs. Bailey. But if there is someone at your home to care for you, we'll gladly send you home. Now, why don't you try to sleep?"

The nurse came back. "Miss Tunstall will see you, Mrs. Shelton," she said kindly, and pointed the way.

Alice was expecting her, and she offered Virginia a chair. "Sit down," she said. "Did you walk over?"

"Not today," said Virginia. "I had the car. First, I took Carolyn and some stuff to the church . . . Why isn't she here today?"

"The meals are coming in from a restaurant, Virginia. The kitchen help manages."

"I see. Well, I wanted to see you. I haven't been able to sleep for worrying about this thing."

Alice waited. Though she had a thousand things to do, she sat quietly and waited. "Why are you worried, Virginia?" she finally asked kindly.

Virginia jumped a little and looked up. "Oh!" she said. "I'm sorry. You are being patient with me, aren't you?"

Miss Tunstall smiled. "Tell me," she said.

"Yes. I mean to. And I'll do it quickly. You see, Alice, I don't know about such things, but I believe a crime may have been committed."

Now it was Miss Tunstall's turn to be startled. A *crime?* Could Virginia possibly mean . . . ? Oh, she couldn't! A dozen theories about the fire's origin were going around, but—

"Who do you think committed this crime, Virginia?" she said, speaking calmly. "And what crime was it?"

"Well," said Virginia, taking a white, crisp handkerchief from her purse, "I have been worried for three days. And yesterday—" She paused and thought. "Yes, it was yesterday," she confirmed. "Clytie died on Thursday, and we buried her yesterday noon—that was Saturday. So much has happened, Alice."

"It really has," Alice agreed.

"I know. And I felt bad enough about Clytie. I really loved her."

"Of course you did."

"Yes. And I'd want . . . Well, she wrote me about making a new will, you know. But when the lawyer came yesterday evening—such a nice young man. He flew his own plane to Carson, Alice!"

The nurse-supervisor waited.

"Well, he did," Virginia confirmed. "And he came especially to ask if, by any chance, we had or knew about Clytie's new will. And Carolyn said she didn't know a thing about any new will. But she did, Alice. I feel sure that she did. I think Clytie sent it to her. That morning—it was Thursday when Marion came up to tell us that Clytie was dead. Carolyn was awfully upset because *she* had been notified, not

her. And we were talking all around about Clytie and her
death and her funeral, when this special delivery letter came
for Carolyn; she signed for it, and took it into her room. I
am sure I remember that clearly, though things did get terribly confused afterward. She's never mentioned that letter
to me. It was in a long envelope and was thick. And when
I told the lawyer that I knew Clytie had made a new will,
Carolyn was very cross and upset. And do you know if destroying or even concealing a legal paper is a crime,
Alice?"

Miss Tunstall looked distressed, because of Virginia's ob-
vious distress. "Have you asked Carolyn what that special
delivery letter was?"

"Yes, I did, and she said I was imagining things. Carolyn
often acts as if I were a child, and not too bright for my
age."

Alice laughed.

"Well, she does," Virginia insisted. "I still have Clytie's
letter telling me about the changes in her will—she was still
leaving most of her estate to Carolyn, but she was putting
it in trust so I, or my kids, would get it. Carolyn couldn't
will it away from the family. Clytie thought she did some
foolish things."

"Oh, dear," said Alice. Abruptly she stood up. "Let's go
see if we can find Fox Creighton," she said.

"Oh, I wouldn't want to bother him."

"But that's what he's for. To be bothered. Come along.
Isn't our nice hospital in a mess today?"

"This hall looks pretty good. I mean . . ."

"Yes, we can use it, and the one above it, the two on the
other side as well. But of course there's the smoke smell
. . . Here we are. And Fox's office is really a mess! Water
damage, and all sorts of stuff piled into it."

She knocked on the half-open door and went in. Yes, the
place was a mess, all right, but Fox sat behind his desk and
looked up serenely at his visitors. "Come in, ladies," he said
cordially. "Can I offer you some chicken salad, and a piece
of chocolate cake?"

Alice stepped over a box, and went around a Gurney
cart. "Where did you get chicken salad?" she asked. "I had
beef stew for lunch."

"Mrs. Story sent me some food two hours ago. I suppose
she thought personnel and patients could rough it, but I'd
better be well fed."

"Like the lion in the zoo," Alice agreed. "To keep him calm." She looked around at Virginia. "Can you find a chair?" she asked.

Fox ripped paper towels from a roll, and wiped the chair which he set forward for Virginia. He offered one for Alice but she hitched herself up on the cart.

"Eat your salad," Alice told him. "I'll summarize what is on Virginia's mind."

"It would seem to be plenty," said Fox dryly.

"It is. You see . . ." And she did summarize the situation, Virginia watching and listening in admiration for her skill, Fox with growing concern. "And the thing we want advice on," Alice concluded, "is: what should Virginia do?"

Fox wiped his fingers on another towel. "You feel sure it was the will, Mrs. Shelton?" he asked.

"I can't prove it, but, yes, I feel sure it was. If not, why does Carolyn try to deny she got such a letter? She did!"

"And the Post Office would have a record of its delivery. Did she sign for it?"

"Yes, sir. Would it be a crime, Dr. Creighton? To destroy a will?"

"To destroy a legal instrument," he said thoughtfully. "Yes, I think—Oh, maybe not a *crime*. But listen to me, you girls—if we discover, if you discover, Mrs. Shelton, that a felony was committed, what are you prepared to do?"

"I'd want Clytie's wishes carried out. I've already asked Carolyn about the special delivery."

"I mean, would you confront your sister, at home, or even in court, and accuse her of this felony?"

Keenly he watched Virginia, and Alice watched her. The good woman was devastated. She sat there, thinking, her color changing, her hands worrying the white hankerchief. Then she began to shake her head from side to side. "No," she whispered. "No, I wouldn't."

But she's sure Carolyn did commit that felony, Fox decided. He watched Alice take the poor little woman away. And what a thing to have on her mind! What a thing for pious, self-righteous Carolyn to have done! Who would have dreamed . . . ? But, then, the night before, who would have suggested that the same Carolyn might have set fire to the hospital? Who had suggested that? Pat Kern, that was who. An insurance man, a sensible, reasonable person, usually.

Virginia had apologized to Dr. Creighton, she apologized to Alice Tunstall, for having bothered them at such a time. "How are you going to manage?" she asked. "Carolyn thought—hasn't Union Hospital offered to take your patients?"

Alice smiled at her. "I really don't know," she said. "Will you sleep tonight, Virginia?"

Virginia tried to smile. "I don't think so," she confessed.

* * *

Late that afternoon, Fox returned to his home, to get some clean clothes, he explained. He brought with him an armful of his own whites. Coats, long and short, a half dozen pairs of trousers, even some white buck shoes, all in a sodden heap.

Could they be salvaged? he asked Mrs. Story.

"I can wash the clothes, Dr. Creighton," she said confidently.

"Won't that be a lot of work?"

"Not the washing. The ironing, perhaps. But Courtney can help me; she takes very good care of her own clothes."

Fox glanced at her. "Do you?"

"Of course. Why not? I am not rich. I've just lived in rich men's houses."

He laughed. "See what can be done," he asked Mrs. Story. "The insurance men won't come around until tomorrow, but I don't believe my personal wardrobe will be an item with them. Now I'll go change. A fellow gets into a mess just walking through that place."

"You should take a warm bath, and relax. Eat a good dinner . . ."

"I plan to go back in an hour or two. The night shift may have difficulties."

"Yes, sir. But for an hour or two, rest."

"And relax," said Courtney softly. "How about a game of ping pong?"

Fox had started into the main part of the house, and he turned back to look at her. "Afraid not," he said. "Just clean clothes—maybe dinner—" he disappeared.

Courtney set the dinner table for Mrs. Story, not talking, but busily thinking. "If we can hold him," Rebecca told her, "I'll broil a sirloin steak."

"Get it out," said Courtney. "I'll get him to stay."

Mrs. Story looked dubious, but the girl was confident. She knew, she said, that the big man's mind needed relaxation more than his muscles. With the yard boy's help, she had the ping pong table moved out to the patio—the late sun shone there warmly. When Fox came downstairs in a white turtle-neck pull-over and gold-colored slacks, she suggested the sun, and once on the patio, she gave him a paddle. "If you don't know the game," she said, "I'll teach you."

He laughed. "I know enough to beat you," he promised.

They played, scarcely speaking. The balls peppered against the paddles, against the bricks; their shoe soles scraped and whispered.

"Hey!" cried Fox when Story brought him a cocktail and said the steaks would be ready in ten minutes. "That was a good game. We'll do it again."

"That we will," Courtney agreed, taking her glass of tomato juice.

"No cocktail?" Fox asked her.

She shook her head. "Not yet," she said. "I drink wine sometimes, or a little beer."

"Out of a pitcher."

She smiled, and gazed at the sky. "We do have magnificent sunsets," she murmured.

The sky was a blaze of orange and red, with great bands of purple clouds piling up in the west. "That sunset," Fox told her, "can mean a wicked storm in the mountains. Flash floods and all sorts of troubles.

The game, or something, had relieved his tension. He acknowledged that it had. He enjoyed his dinner and ate every bite of his large steak. "I ate your chicken salad about three o'clock," he told Courtney.

She nodded. This man—his brusqueness fascinated her. Yet she knew him to be kind, thoughtful. She had never known anyone like him. Well, of course she had not! She prayed that the telephone would not ring—but inevitably it did.

And Fox said that he must get back to the hospital, *pronto!*

"Something's happened?" Courtney asked, following him.

"Sure, something's happened. Oh, not a fire again. An accident is being brought in—if it's bad we'll need to improvise a lot of things." He got into his car.

Courtney was standing at the other side. "I want to go with you," she said. "May I?" She got into that seat.

He started the car and drove it away. She clutched at the window ledge. "Was this an ambulance case?" she asked.

Fox nodded. "Rancher kicked by a horse. I hope to hell Belze is around."

"He's the one . . ."

"He's a grand surgeon. Just now he seems to have personal troubles. I only hope they won't interfere . . ."

At the hospital drive they had to wait on the ambulance which was coming fast from the other direction. "That Almandarez," Fox muttered. "I only hope he saves more lives than he risks."

Courtney smiled at him. He was praising the driver.

She watched the stretcher being very carefully taken out of the ambulance. "What do you have, Blair?" Dr. Creighton called.

"Subject to a better opinion," said the young doctor, "I think we have a pneumo-thorax."

The doctor whistled soundlessly.

Hank threw Courtney a smile. "How you doin'?" he asked as he passed her.

"Fine," she answered. "I'm a lucky girl."

"We're all lucky. Learning that we can get along without sleep . . . Watch it, Virgilio!"

"You watch your end, I take care of mine," said the driver.

Courtney followed the procession inside where the surgeon —she hoped—met the stretcher. The man on the cart was in great distress.

She touched Fox's arm. "Could I watch?" she asked.

"Think you can take it?"

"I'll take it."

"All right. I'm going to scrub in case I'm needed. Oh, Blair!"

Hank was bring the stretcher out. "Yes, sir?"

"Miss Armstrong wants to watch. If you're planning . . ."

"Sure," he said. "Wait just a minute, sister."

She watched him help the driver put clean sheets and blanket on the stretcher. She herself folded the red one, and followed the men outside. Hank did not get into the ambulance. "Where does it go now?" she asked.

"Basement garage. Until the next call."

"Does the driver stay with it?"

"He has a room. Now. You still think you want to watch that pneumo?"

"I know I do."

"Then let's go! They won't waste time."

He brought her a gown, and put on one of his own. He fetched two stools, high ones, and took her with him into the emergency room where several shrouded women moved about the man on the table, cutting him free of his clothing, trying to ease his great discomfort.

"A horse kicked him," Dr. Blair murmured to Courtney, putting the stools against the wall. "His chest is caved in."

"Do you wish you were a surgeon?" she asked him. She was gathering her thick hair into one hand, twisting it. She pulled the red scarf from her throat and tied it about her head.

"I'm learning something about surgery," the intern told her.

"I know—you like primary medicine. That's what you did for this man tonight, wasn't it?"

"Well, an ambulance attendant becomes a primary physician, whether he wants to be one or not. We see the patient first, diagnose the trouble, and refer the case to a specialist." He laughed at his own whimsy.

"General practitioners . . ." Courtney murmured.

He nodded. "And pediatricians, internists, they all practice primary medicine."

The doctors came in, gowned, masked, and gloved.

"Is that Dr. Belze?" Courtney asked Hank Blair.

"No, it's Forrest. He's a chest surgeon."

"He's good-looking," said Courtney, settling on the stool. "Tell me what's being done, doctor."

At first, Dr. Blair was embarrassed and he kept his voice to a low monotone. "This sort of lung injury," he said, "doesn't need a kicking horse. I did some time in a t.b. hospital during med school. They kept a surgical tray ready for emergencies much like this—lung collapse. They'd set it up beside the bed, with a sterile gown and cap for the surgeon, a scrubbing basin with white soap and alcohol ready. The patient, just like our man here, would be gasping for breath, pale as a grubworm, his eyes popping—notice his fingers, Courtney—".

"Speak up louder, Dr. Blair," said Dr. Creighton. He stood across the table from Dr. Forrest. "We want to notice things too."

Dr. Blair looked unhappy. Every eye in the room was upon him. "She asked," he began.

"I know she did. She's as curious as a cat. But—speak

up." He accepted a shining instrument and used it. Dr. Forrest's shoulder and back hid what he did from Courtney, but now he turned his head to look at her. His eyes were wide-set, heavy-lidded.

"Well," said Hank Blair, "I was going to point out the cyanosis evident in the patient's fingers. That's the loss of circulation, Courtney. The man isn't getting the air he needs. He's suffocating, he knows it, and he is terrified. See the way his throat and abdominal muscles are straining . . ."

The door opened and Peach wheeled in an oxygen tank, set it close to the table.

"The central supply hasn't been reconnected," Hank explained. "Because of the fire, you know. I didn't know we had oxygen in tanks . . ."

"A supply came in today," growled Fox Creighton.

"In an accident like this," Dr. Blair resumed, "there are at least two broken ribs, and the sudden collapse." He leaned forward. "That's a morphine needle he's going to use," he told Courtney, "and a swab. He'll inject morphine . . ."

"One half grain," said Dr. Creighton's voice.

"That's right," said Hank Blair, and ignored Dr. Forrest's hoot of laughter. "He's preparing the area between the seventh and eighth ribs under the left scapula."

The patient's loud breathing filled the room, seeming to echo. It was a frightening sound. A nurse went around the table, she carried a glass jar and a rubber tube; she set the jar carefully on the floor.

Dr. Forrest held out his flattened, gloved hand.

"That's a bayonet-tipped trocar," said Dr. Blair. "He's thrusting it in, now he's drawing it out—he'll keep his fingertip on the canula while he takes the collector and inserts it. See, he's fixing the end of the tube into that jar of water under the table . . ." He broke off.

There was the gurgle of escaping air; the patient gasped loudly, and gasped no more.

"That must be a wonderful relief," said Hank, "to be freed of the pressure on his collapsed lung."

Everyone waited. Tension built, then the man on the table relaxed, and sighed.

"We've done it," said Dr. Forrest.

Dr. Creighton looked across at Courtney and Hank. "You've both done a wonderful job of observing and lecturing," he said. "I'm proud of you."

Hank touched Courtney's arm. "He wants us to get the hell out," he said.

* * *

She was no longer in the hospital when Fox was ready to leave. This time he checked. He supposed Blair had taken her home in his jeep. He remembered the pitcher of beer and went past the restaurant-tavern which he had decided was the place where they might stop again.

Courtney was there. He remembered the red scarf with which she had tied her hair in e.r. She was sitting in a booth, but the man across from her was not Hank Blair.

Dr. Creighton left, fast, before he would be seen. And he drove homeward fast, his face flushed with anger, his eyes shining.

Why? he asked himself. Why would she be sitting in a tavern with Perry Hawthorne? How had she got to know that man? Had Hank Blair . . .?

He was prepared for some disloyalty in the hospital ranks. Carolyn Cotsworth said openly that Dr. Hawthorne was wonderful, and that the two hospitals should merge.

But Blair? Fox should have checked to see if the jeep were still at the tavern. He could now go back and see, or he could check the hospital, ask if Dr. Blair was on roster . . .

He'd do nothing of the sort. He didn't care . . .

Well, he did care what might happen to Courtney, because he had taken on that responsibility. Taken it on without knowing much of anything about her, her character, her tastes. A crazy thing for him to do. Everybody thought so, and he was now ready to agree with everybody.

He went up to his room and to bed. When he heard a car drive in he held himself rigid. He would *not* spy on Courtney!

But—if she had been with Hawthorne—and she had been —for a short time, or a couple of hours—how would he handle *that* problem? *That* crisis?

Because of his assumed responsibility, he was going to have to do some fighting there. He must, at the least, tell Courtney about Hawthrone's reputation with women. She should know what kind of doctor the man was . . .

Oh, dear Lord Jehosaphat! How was he going to tell her such things, and not make himself to be a crabbed old man, a jealous doctor . . .

He turned his pillow, and punched it. Last night he'd had a fire to fight. Tonight—

He'd take the fire, anytime.

The next morning he was up and gone to the hospital before Courtney could appear for breakfast or any sort of conversation. He didn't give much talk to the Storys either. Yes, he thought they might have rain. Yes, he was early. He'd have insurance men all over the hospital that day.

And he departed with his last sip of coffee still hot in his throat, a piece of cinnamon toast in his left hand.

He was busy all day, trying to decide medical problems only. He would let the Administrator deal with the fire chief and the insurance adjustors—but there were inevitably problems which included both sides of the situation.

He did say they should take in only emergency cases, and empty beds as soon as patients got well enough.

Yes, the o.b. cases were acceptable emergencies, but elective surgery could be postponed, and extensive tests would have to be done at the clinic.

And every doctor's patient immediately became an exceptional case.

He was tired, and wild-eyed, when he decided, at six-thirty, that he was going home and would stay there!

He showered and changed, and came downstairs for dinner. Courtney was sitting in the living room, nicely dressed in light blue, her hair tied up and back with ribbons.

"You look very nice," Fox told her. "Is dinner ready?"

"I think Mrs. Story is waiting for you. I have a date."

It took him a minute to comprehend what she had said. "A date?" he repeated stupidly. Then he remembered the night before—Hawthorne! And his face stiffened, his eyes hardened.

"Dr. Blair," said Courtney softly. "He asked me last night."

"Oh," said Fox. "He asked you when he brought you home from the hospital."

"Yes, he did," said Courtney. "I'll go tell Mrs. Story you are ready for your dinner."

Fox made no reply. He picked up the evening paper, and sat down. He still thought Courtney was the prettiest girl he had ever seen. The way her dark eyes were set, the curve of her cheek, her exquisite skin . . .

The front door bell rang, and he jerked to his feet. He could attend to Courtney's date.

Dr. Blair was not at all upset to be admitted by the Chief. He came in with the cheerful announcement that it was raining. Since it had been for two hours, Fox considered no comment necessary.

"Courtney said you had a date," he growled.

"Yes, sir, we do. It's my twelve hours."

Fox picked up the newspaper again. "Sit down, Blair," he said gruffly. Surreptitiously he examined the young man whom he saw every day, many times a day. Thick hair, worn long. Too long, Fox thought. It more than curled up from the collar of his blue shirt. He wore a dark blue blazer, and brown slacks that certainly were Levi's.

Were these date clothes? For a girl as pretty as Courtney, dressed daintily in blue—linen, or something—with fragile white slippers on her feet, blue ribbons in her hair?

Of course Levi's were probably all that Blair had in the way of clothes. He—Fox rubbed his hand down across his face, recognizing his feeling of superiority. A hateful feeling, a hateful man to feel so.

Was he actually jealous of the boy? He felt as if he might be. He knew that he was annoyed. Why should Courtney involve herself with a chap like Blair, one of Fox's interns?

He himself was often bothered—even annoyed—that Courtney should be living in his home. Last night had been one of those times. At others he must have shown his annoyance, and if she ever got around to coming back from the kitchen, he probably would show it tonight.

And he should not. Of course a lovely young girl had dates. Having her in his home was entirely his idea. Blair was not so bad. Irritating at times, but he was going to make a good doctor. Fox could certainly afford to be decent to him, a guest, however briefly, in his home.

"Would you care for a drink, Blair?" he asked. "I thought Courtney was ready . . ."

"I've been here only a couple of minutes, sir," Hank pointed out. "And no, thank you. I don't want a drink."

"I'll go see what's holding her up. She was here just before you came."

"Don't bother, sir." Dr. Blair rubbed his hands down his trouser legs. At ease when he first arrived, and when Fox had sat glowering at him, now the boy seemed upset. Probably due to the Chief's cordiality. But, damn it, Fox had no experience with this sort of thing. Both men were visibly relieved when Courtney came down the hall, as blithe as a bird. "Oh, Hank," she said. "Have you been waiting long?"

He went toward her. "Not long," he said. "Shall we go? You'd better get a raincoat. You look very nice, Courtney."

She did look very nice. Even bundled into a white raincoat with a plastic thing over her hair, Fox still thought she was the prettiest girl . . .

He was not at all prepared for her to come to him, stand on tiptoes and kiss his cheek. "Don't worry," she said. "I love you but Hank and I have things to do tonight."

And she went out the door, across the deep porch, and let Blair tuck her into the jeep's seat. He had sense enough to have the curtains buttoned down.

What things did they have to do? What could they possibly . . .? Now Fox would worry.

For a minute after the kids had driven down the drive and disappeared, he stood on the steps and worried. About the weather, for one thing. They were having a nasty storm up in the mountains, and flash floods were no joke in the desert.

He even asked Story if he knew where Courtney was going.

"She said that she and the young doctor were going downtown, Dr. Creighton."

Downtown. Well, of course, there were restaurants, movies, bowling alleys, downtown.

And flash floods would be no problem.

* * *

Stephen Clark had been dead for a week. A long week, certainly, what with Mrs. Whiteside's death and the hospital fire, but George Clark must wait until that rainy Monday evening to come to the apartment and wave in his wife's face the letter he'd had from the lawyers. The girls were there. Nancy was, and Laura Ann, but they both quickly found reasons to go elsewhere.

"They could be a little friendly with me," George complained to his wife.

"You come here in a mood . . ."

"A *mood?* You call the way I feel a mood? To be written out of my own father's will?"

"How long have you known that, George?" Marion asked. She decided she might as well sit down and get this situation talked out. Though, really, she had other things . . .

"Oh, the damn lawyer wrote to me. Right away, I guess."

"If you had gone to the funeral . . ."

"You didn't go!"

"I was only a daughter-in-law. You were his son."

"That wouldn't have changed a damn thing. I'd have just been there for the people to look at and know that I'd been disinherited."

In his mid-forties, George Clark was still a handsome man, his face soft, and his eyes burning. "Did you know about the will?" Marion asked him. "Before your father died, I mean."

"Oh, he said he wouldn't leave me a red cent, but I never believed him. I thought he had too much family conscience."

While George had had none.

He slumped into a deep chair, then he got to his feet and prowled about the room, taking a handful of mints from a dish, eating two or three, dropping the rest to the tabletop.

"What happens to me now?" he cried. "I'm in debt up to my ears. I can't even hire a decent lawyer. They all want a retainer."

"Why do you want a lawyer, George?"

"To break the damn will, dum-dum. To break it wide open."

Marion rubbed her fingers. "Can you do that?" she asked.

"I can sure as hell try."

At nine o'clock he finally left; Laura Ann returned and she and Nancy went to bed. But Marion, upset as she always was after a scene with George, said she believed she'd go up to Tunnie's.

"Don't tell her all our troubles, Mum," said Laura Ann.

"Nothing she doesn't already know, dear," replied her mother. Laura Ann was not always easy to live with.

Before she went upstairs, she called Tunnie. "If you're not ready for bed . . ."

"Oh, no," said Alice. "Not by an hour. Come on up."

So Marion went, finding herself tiptoeing past the Cotsworth landing. She was still smiling about that when she went into Miss Tunstall's open door.

Tunnie nodded. "Carolyn can be a little much," she agreed. "Well-meaning, as I am sure she is. Sit down, Marion. Would you like coffee, cocoa, or something cold?"

Marion shook her head. "Just to talk to someone I consider sane and sensible." She brushed her dark hair back from her face. "But I do not mean to talk about the fact that my husband just paid us a visit."

"Oh? Did he want . . .?"

"I think he wanted me to finance his legal fight to break his father's will, but he never actually came out and asked. You must know by now what my position is with and about George."

"Though you've never divorced him."

Marion shrugged. "I would if I wanted some other man. To date, I don't. I haven't."

"You're a young woman."

"I'm forty-five."

"And very handsome."

"Thank you. My red blouse lends a glow. So—let's talk about the hospital fire, and worry together about what comes next in that situation."

"I heard Fox Creighton today advising Peach to let him and the Board do the worrying."

"Well, it's good advice. For Peach, at least. Wasn't he magnificent last night?"

"Saturday night, dear."

Marion brushed her hair back again. "Yes, of course it was. But Peach—I never guessed, Tunnie, how terrible a hospital fire could be. Terrible especially for Fox Creighton. You know? He told me that actually the fire was a relief. He said that it was something he could put his muscles into and fight. All his other problems—Did you know, Alice, that our dear, sweet Carolyn signed one of the petitions that got the bond issue election for the new hospital?"

"She is a very silly woman."

"Oh, of course she is. And you could not persuade her that a joint hospital would be anything but fine. She cannot see Union Hospital as a threat, and that our fire increases that threat."

"Unfotunately she has a lot of people for company in her thinking. I've made no survey, but I am afraid the town as a whole is saying that the fire shows that the town needs this big new hospital."

"I wish Fox would speak out."

"I do too, except that I am afraid he would say, 'Have your hospital, but you won't have me.' "

"Would it make a difference?"

"To the voters? I don't know. Many people remember his

father and his grandfather. Many have known good hospital service from him."

"But often they don't know it's from him. He runs things, but no bedside manner is in evidence."

"The patients must see him all over the place."

"But he's a quiet man."

"Not when he's mad."

"Even when he's mad," Alice insisted. "He's quiet about himself. Why, Marion, I doubt if even you know the inner Fox Creighton."

"Oh, he has his reserves all right."

"He certainly does. But I can remember—You know, I have known Fox since he was a resident in the hospital where I trained and worked. Oh, Marion, he was such a fine young doctor! Red-headed, brash, but so *good* medically!

"And that was where he began his research work against the pneumonia germs in the blood stream. Of course we had penicillin and sulfa by then and he worked on further white cell research. How to combat fever, especially. He was given awards—the highest the medical profession can give. He could have worked anywhere. But when he came here to the hospital, I came with him. He was a gay young man, Marion."

"I can't believe it."

"I know he was. And Pat Kern could tell you. Not wild, but just a big young man with a strong healthy body, and a super-fine mind. He should have—he could have—gone anywhere. But—" Alice Tunstall fell silent, and Marion saw tears gathered in her eyes.

"There was a girl," she said finally. "Maybe you can't believe that, either. But there was one. She was a pretty little thing. Dark, with eyes that seemed to be set aslant, long, thick black hair, and a voice that throbbed when she talked. Fox was crazy about that girl. All the other men were too, but she loved Fox. They planned to be married. She was a lab technologist, and by the time their wedding day came around, she was dead of anthrax germs in a lab explosion. All of Fox's research, and that of his colleagues, could not save her. He was entirely crushed. He continued his work but he was no longer gay. And then—this was five years ago—you remember that tragedy—his parents were killed in that plane crash. He was needed here to carry on his father's work; his research was set aside. And he came here where he has worked for our hospital with all the skill and intelligence he had put into his antigen research. He built it up, reorganized it. I know that because I've been right here with him, and I've seen what he did. You saw it. I only hope, I truly hope, that the man won't have to endure another crushing hurt."

She's in love with him, Marion Clark told herself. Deeply, helplessly in love with him.

* * *

By ten o'clock that night, the storm had moved from the mountains to the valley; rain washed along the streets, streamed down the windows, soaked the ashes of the fire at the hospital into black ink.

It would stop as suddenly as it had begun, and the people of the valley were grateful for the rain. It might be the largest part of their year's water supply.

It had been noon when the Jimmie Newell family car headed out of the barnyard on its way to Carson and the hospital there. In the back seat, Mrs. James Newell, Jr., twenty-one, braced herself against the sharpening labor pains, and reached out now and then to steady her three-year-old daughter, Sandra, who, she hoped, would nap there beside her. She had brought a blanket in which to wrap the child.

Her father-in-law had agreed to drive her to the hospital. "It's raining anyway," he said. His wife could take the child into town and do some trading while Joyce was having the baby. He only hoped the road wasn't washed out anywhere. The little creeks had turned into rivers, and some of the bridges made for tricky driving. Anyway, it was black as night, with the clouds right down on top of the mountain passes. Maybe they should have stayed at home. Babies had always used to get themselves borned at home. Too bad young Jim was off seeing about a ram . . .

Talking so, he drove as carefully as he could, holding the wheel as if it were a menacing weapon, but even so, as they were approaching the little settlement of Monterey, the car went out of control, crashed through the guard rail of the bridge over the Gila River, landing upside down in the swirling, red-muddied water. Neither the driver nor his wife survived; their daughter-in-law was knocked unconscious.

When she revived, the first thing young Mrs. Newell knew was that Sandra was crying. The top of the car had caved in and the water had risen two or three feet inside the car, leaving little more than a foot of air space between them and the water and the car floor, now their prison roof. Joyce Newell made Sandra comfortable in the air space, then she sat, neck deep in the water, worried about her parents-in-law who were certainly dead, but more concerned about her pains, though she was afraid to try to get out of the car because the river might be too deep. It was very dark there in the bottom of the steep-walled, tree-covered canyon, and she had no idea how long she had been unconscious.

A full five hours passed, there in the gloom, with the sound of the river about the car—and then the sun came out. She thought. Anyway, it grew lighter, and she could see that the water was not so deep, that it was indeed shallow enough for her to wade. With this promise, she kicked and shoved —and shouted—until she got one of the doors open for about eighteen inches. Not enough for her bulk, but she squeezed through anyway, reached in and pulled Sandra out, carried her through the waist-deep water to the river bank and up its slippery side. She started walking.

It was almost eight o'clock when, dripping wet and covered with mud, she reached rancher Jerrell East's dooryard. Mrs. East offered to care for Sandra, and to call the sheriff about the car and the two dead people in the river while her husband would drive Mrs. Newell on to Carson and the hospital.

He drove at top speed, and they reached the emergency room door, with Joyce too near her time for Dr. Kayser and Dr. Belze to get her ready for the delivery room, if they still had had one. At nine o'clock, still mud-spattered, she was delivered of a healthy six-pound son.

They had not really needed a surgeon. Dr. Belze examined her and found that her only injuries were minor cuts. Normally the shock of the noontime crash would have been expected to hasten labor, but Dr. Kayser thought the cold water, in which Mrs. Newell had sat for hours with death beside her, must have prevented an earlier birth by contracting her muscles.

The doctors discussed the matter, Dr. Creighton with them. And, when told that the mother was comfortably in bed, he went with Dr. Kayser to see her. She looked up at the men, weary, yet smiling. She was grateful, she said. "What would I have done without this hospital at the end of all that terrible trip?"

The doctors nodded and advised her to sleep.

But leaving her room, leaving the hospital, her words

echoed and re-echoed in Fox's mind. *What would one do? What would one do without the hospital?*

* * *

On that rainy Monday night, there was a meeting of the City Council of Carson. Pat Kern, the mayor, presided, and almost at once it was decided that the meeting must be moved into the rotunda of the City Hall. The Council room was much too small for all the people who seemed ready to attend, as, by law, they were privileged to do.

The move was made, and in the shuffle Pat found himself walking beside a pretty young girl in a white raincoat. "Courtney?" he asked in surprise.

The girl turned and smiled. "Oh, yes!" she said. "You're —how does one address the mayor?"

"Just as one does any mortal man," said Pat. "What on earth are you doing here?"

"Civic interest. Do you know Dr. Blair?"

Pat looked at the big young man and shook his head. "From . . .?"

"I'm an intern at Creighton Memorial," said Hank quickly. "I heard about the petitions, Mr. Mayor, and I wanted to see which way things were going."

"They can't effect anything tonight," said Pat. "Not with the election already set."

"I guessed that, but isn't it important to know about trends?"

"So I've heard," said the mayor, leaving them and managing to skirt the crowd to get to the table which would serve the Council.

The officials were seated, and the visitors—close to a hundred of them, of all sorts—and the Mayor brought the meeting to order. Courtney and Hank sat close to a wall, as unconspicuously as they could. "I don't think we're among friends," Hank told the girl. They listened to the routine reports, to the business on the agenda—the paying of salaries, the change of a zoning ordinance, the plea of someone to close some alley—the usual business of a small city's governing body—and then one of the men in the audience was recognized. He was a poultry dealer, he said.

"Yes, I know you, Mr. McConville," said Pat Kern courteously.

"Yes, sir. Well—"

Beside him rose a determined woman. She wore a shaggy coat, shiny turquoise, knee-length boots; her hair was cropped close to her head. "Since the fire," she said brightly, "We think we can't wait to get this hospital business settled."

"I'd kill a wife for interrupting that way," Hank Blair told Courtney.

"I hate it too."

"Mr. McConville?" the mayor was asking, still courteously.

"Yes, sir. Well, we are vitally interested in what goes on in this town. A lot of people are.' '

"We have twelve hundred and fifty names," asserted his wife.

Mr. McConville sat down. "Let her talk," he said.

"She will anyway," said a voice from the back of the hall, and laughter rolled across the room.

Mrs. McConville was not perturbed. She said she believed in getting things said and done, the quickest way possible.

Even then it took a time for her to present her roll of petitions.

"Toward what, precisely, Mrs. McConville?" asked the mayor.

"Why—to consolidate the two hospitals here in town. Union and Memorial. Of course!"

Pat mentioned the upcoming vote.

She mentioned the fire. "I'd be afraid to be sick there in that building," she declared.

"She can always go to Union," murmured Hank.

In short, she and her petitioners wanted the Council immediately to effect the combination of the two hospitals. Oh, she didn't know how. Maybe use some present building— Union wasn't big enough, and the fire made Memorial unsafe . . .

"It's not," said Hank to Courtney.

"Speak up!" she urged.

He laughed.

After a half hour, the meeting was adjourned, with Mrs. McConville ready to tell anyone that they could too get a joint hospital in operation right away. There were schools, the hotel—the Armory—oh, any number of places.

There was an account of the Council meeting on the ten o'clock news. The newspapers would detail it the next day. And someone told Dr. Creighton that Hank and Courtney had attended.

* * *

The next day, with a clean-up crew busy in the burned-out areas of the hospital, Dr. Creighton called one of his regular meetings of the interns. Among other things, he brought up the matter of crises, as they could and did happen "Now perhaps I need not say to you that any crisis in lives of you four should be the first order of business, either in these regular meetings or with me in privacy. If you have an individual problem, if I can help in its solution, I am always ready and glad to confer. Just now, the hospital has had, and is having, problems. I need not detail them to you because you are here, you know them. And if you, individually, have a problem concerning this hospital and because of our present situation, our delicate condition, I would be glad to discuss it here, or to confer privately.

"But—" His right hand extended toward them and began to slash up and down. His green eyes blazed. "Problems solved or unsolved, the hospital work must go on, my work must, and yours certainly must. Burned hospital and private interests notwithstanding. The *Board* will make the decision of the future of Memorial Hospital and its services. *I* shall continue to make the decisions on what we do and do not do under the present conditions. Those two decisions are not your concern, or your worry. Under the structure of Memorial Hospital and your intern service, nothing has changed. When it is about to change, I shall tell you. I—" He looked up.

Dr. Blair had risen to his feet. "Yes?" he said.

"I only wanted to ask—You've heard perhaps that I attended the Council meeting last night?"

Dr. Creighton puckered his lips and rubbed his hand back over his hair. "I know that you were off duty for twelve hours last night, Dr. Blair."

Hank's colleagues were staring at him, their faces amazed, concerned, even amused. He ignored them. "Had you also heard that Miss Armstrong went with me, sir?"

Now Dr. Creighton's face settled into its petrified-wood expression, which anyone in the hospital knew, dreaded and feared. "What Miss Armstrong does, where she goes," he said icily, "is not my affair. Just as where you go and what you do, is not mine. Provided, of course, that you do nothing to compromise my home, or the hospital. Your life, Miss Armstrong's life, are things of your own. As my life is mine.

"But—" His finger jabbed. "But—" he said again. "For me, as for you, the hospital must come first. Our families and friends know this, or should. You know this, or should. Your first attention must be on your hospital duties, and its interests."

Dr. Blair did not sit down. Pamela Thomas wrung her hands together in anguish for him.

"You think that?" he asked the Chief.

"I think that," said Dr. Creighton. "Do you?"

"Do *you?*" Hank asked again.

Fox nodded. "For this time, yes," he said quietly. "For this hard time, yes. That is our first duty. Other things will build around that sense of duty. You'll see. There is honor involved here, Dr. Blair."

Hank had never once flushed, now he did not blink. "There is honor in other places," he said quietly. "In other relationships."

For what seemed like a long time, the two men gazed at each other. They're alike, Bechars thought grudgingly. Blair is exactly what Creighton must have been a dozen years ago.

Hank was thinking of Courtney, that clear-eyed, honest girl. Fox too had her in his mind, blue ribbons, floating soft hair—but he did not think of her as loyal to him, though, yes, she had said that she was in love with him.

He pressed his lips together in a thin, hard line.

Hank Blair turned to look at the other interns. Bechars had a strange expression, Tommie just looked frightened; her cheeks were red. Smith lounged in his chair. His face said, "There goes the ball game."

"The Old Man has a point," Hank told them, speaking clearly. "Our first interest and duty is here, with the hospital and for it." He glanced at Dr. Creighton, who waved his hand to the door.

The others rose; they all filed out of the room.

"You *talked* to him," said Dr. Thomas in awe.

Hank shrugged. "You can talk to him," he said, and he walked swiftly down the hall.

Dr. Creighton, ruggedly handsome, immaculate in his white garments, went directly from the interns' meeting to one with the Hospital Board and the Chiefs of the Hospital Services. He had, that early morning, conferred with Carolyn Cotsworth, and asked her to see if their present catering service could provide an appropriate luncheon for the meeting. "Nothing exotic or elaborate," he cautioned. "After all, the Board will be here to assess the damage done to us by the fire. We don't want it to appear that we can get along with a hole burned in our center structure. Could you manage something?"

"I think so, doctor," she said confidently. "I think we can serve a fairly decent meal in the first floor east sunroom. I can get it together in the first floor diet kitchen?"

She did indeed manage the luncheon. Paper place mats on the long, oblong tables, icy-cold tomato juice to start. A coffee urn bubbling fragrantly, platters of baked ham, bowls of green peas and new potatoes in a cream sauce, a tossed salad that was crisp and nicely dressed, a dessert of vanilla custard and really good canned peaches. More than an adequate meal, quietly served.

At its conclusion, when complimented, Fox sent for Carolyn and gave her full credit. She flushed, she smiled self-consciously, then she got a little teary. "I was happy to do it," she said. "After all, it may be the last time—our poor hospital—it does seem to be *done*."

"Er-yes," said the Chief of Servies. "But let us determine death before we bury the patient. Thank you very much, Miss Cotsworth." He saw Marion Clark and Alice Tunstall struggling to control their laughter. They could have told him—

"Suppose we get about the tour," he said loudly. "Anyone who would like to make notes will find paper at the door."

So the group started, a score of men and women. They went over the whole hospital, basement and the damaged services there, the oxygen supply, the laundry, the furnaces, the air conditioning, the first floor wards and kitchens, the second floor corridors and wards, the elevators that worked, the main one that did not—the shaft was a smoke and fire-blackened horror. The delivery room. Up on third, the operating rooms, intensive care, the cardiac unit—all out of commission. Everywhere was the smell of smoke, the evidence of water damage.

They, in groups of Board members, entered the rooms, the wards, and talked to the patients.

"Their morale seems high," said the Chairman of the Board, "but I wonder about the morale of possibly future patients."

"We are limiting admissions," said Dr. Creighton.

The tour continued, with the Board members doing a lot of chatting among themselves. The staff began to look at each other in rising dismay. Even some of the patients had said things—and the personnel too. One Board member talked to the man who was cleaning light fixtures, another, a woman, gossiped amiably with a Gray Lady at the downstairs desk.

The staff overhead the talk, the gossip. "Who told you that?" asked Miss Tunstall.

"Where did you get such a story?" asked Dr. Clark.

"Hawthorne's been at work," she reported breathlessly to Fox.

"Hold it until we get together again," he advised.

She did, but once the Board and the staff were seated again in the sunroom—Dr. Kayser had been called away—Dr. Clark spoke eloquently and specifically.

"Dr. Hawthorne," she declared, "seems to have been spreading some highly exaggerated stories about the damage done here! We have not been turning away emergencies. We do not feed the patients bologna sandwiches and baked beans! We do change the bed linen every day—"

"That patient said you did," said the Board member soothingly.

"Yes, but she had heard that we didn't. And she heard it through Dr. Hawthorne."

The Board member shrugged. "Yes," she agreed. "He seems to have been at work."

"Gossip and tall tales," cried Marion. "We had a fire, we were hurt—but nobody got thrown out of any window during the hottest part of the fire . . ."

"I heard that at church, Sunday," said an elderly gentleman. "That the children had been dropped out of the windows. I didn't believe it, but the person speaking said Dr. Hawthorne had been here and had seen it happening."

"Did he say that he had offered to come in and carry the children down the stairs and out?" Marion demanded. "He was here—I saw him. But he was not helping."

"Did you also hear," asked Fox, "the gossip that says Hawthorne was responsible for the fire?" He was very angry.

"Now, Fox . . ." protested the old gentleman.

"No, I don't believe it," Fox admitted. "But I am sure some or all of you have been listening to the talk, and have believed some of it. And that *some* implies other terrible things. The building is unsafe, unusable. The patients cannot expect anything like safety from the personnel. And if you believe even one of the stories, then, I say, we should go out of business, shut the thing down!"

His startled listeners looked at each other.

"Close the physical plant, you mean?" asked Dr. Belze, not believing what he heard.

"What else?" Fox challenged.

"A lot else!" cried the Chairman of the Board. "This hospital—Why, Fox Creighton, this is a living thing! It breathes and nourishes, and gives life in its turn. No matter what the gossips and its enemies say, Memorial Hospital is not dead, and it need not be. Its spirit . . ." He was drowned out by a splatter of applause around the table.

"Suppose," said Fox Creighton, "we stick with the physical plant." But his voice husked, and his green eyes shone.

"He's excited," Tunnie whispered to Marion, who nodded.

"I think," said a gentleman at the far end of the table. He was a large man, well dressed—all during the tour, and listening to the talk after their return, he had made notes. Now he riffled the pages of his tablet. "I think," he said again, "that it is time to consider, constructively, what has happened, what we have to work with. Not paying attention to gossip, we should discuss what we should do about the hospital, and how we should do it." Since he was the president of a bank, his voice bore weight. "Not for just now," he continued, "but long-range. Let us, for instance, get figures on how much insurance will be paid on reconstruction. Get estimates for rebuilding and replacement. Things like operating room equipment, you know. And, in addition, let us consider means by which we could, if we rebuild, add to the hospital, to expand our services."

"How you goin' to find the money?" asked someone.

"There are ways," said the banker. "Subscription, indorsements from private individuals that will express themselves in money, perhaps endowments, even investments. We could borrow on prospects as well as possessions, you know." He glanced at Dr. Creighton.

"I still think we should close out, shut down," he said.

"That's for now. For the future, doctor—couldn't we rebuild?"

Somebody said, "Bond issue."

"Not as a public hospital," said Fox loudly.

"Why not?" This from one of the women.

"Because," said Fox, "a hospital, run by this town, would be a hospital run by Dr. Hawthorne and the staff at Union."

"Not if we merged. Don't you think we could do that?"

"Oh, yes, you could," said Fox. "But not with me as Chief of Services. Not with me even on the staff."

"But you are the *hospital,* Fox!" said the Chairman.

"Yes," said Fox, "I am."

* * *

The meeting lasted for another hour, and when it was over, the hospital personnel hurried about their tasks, trying to catch up. Alice Tunstall checked the duty roster, she made a partial inspection of the hospital wards, she studied some requisition lists with her usual efficiency and attention to detail, but there were brief moments—as she walked from floor desk to floor desk, or closed one chart and opened another—when her thoughts went swiftly to the noontime meeting and to the big, virile man who had presided at it. He was having a hard time these days. Harder than it was right or fair for him to have. Tunnie had never thought it just for a doctor's performance of his profession to be hampered by gossip. The tales about the damage done to Memorial by the fire would indeed affect the attitude of future patients. The hospital's efficient service to the community would be impaired.

Then—one of the women on the Board had asked her, frankly, if the stories about Dr. Creighton's having a young girl living with him were true.

Alice had been tempted to ask her what difference it would make. But she restrained herself and quietly explained what the situation was, mentioning the Storys. "I happen to know that Fox often forgets Courtney is in his home."

The woman had said, "I see," but Miss Tunstall had accomplished little. Fox Creighton was a young man, and—

Alice thought about him as she had known him when he was a still younger man. There had been a girl then, too, and tragedy.

Now, still certainly young enough, and again with a girl in the picture, he must handle the tragedy of the fire, a tragedy that seemed to be all about him, to encompass him.

It seemed that she was giving her every spare moment to thinking about this sitution, trying to find ways in which she could help. And there did seem to be one way.

But knowing Fox as she did, should she, could she take this chance which seemed open for her?

She would do it for his sake. She would do almost anything for Fox. She knew that running a hospital was not
enough for a young man. For any man.

Or woman. It had not been enough for Alice Tunstall.
Though she probably should keep hands off, let things
alone . . .

                        *   *   *

It was eight o'clock that night. The storm had dissi-
pated; a blazing sunset glowed in the cobalt sky. Fox went
home for dinner. Courtney came in late, a little breathless;
she expected Fox to ask where she had been, but he did
not. And she didn't tell.

He glanced at her now and then, as he would have to do
across the round table. She was wearing a white dress, with
a jacket. A small yellow leaf had fallen on her shoulder,
and it clung there against the red flannel. There was a certain
intimacy to that golden leaf; when she first came in Fox
had raised his hand to lift it off. He wanted to do that, more
than he had ever wanted to do anything! But he could not.
He must not . . . But—

He ate his dinner, and said, abruptly, that he was going
back to the hospital.

This time she did not ask to go with him. And he knew
that he was sorry.

He drove very fast, whirling his car into the hospital drive.
He would have disciplined anyone else driving so—he knew
that. And was angry at himself. But . . .

He was deep in paper work at his desk, the dictaphone
speaker in his hand, when the telephone rang.

He made a short sound of annoyance and snapped the
switch, then reached for the telephone. "Dr. Creighton," he
said brusquely.

"Sir," said the switchboard girl, "Dr. Hawthorne would
like to speak to you."

"No way," said Fox, ready to hang up.

"He says it is urgent, sir. An emergency."

Fox ran his hand through his shaggy red hair. "Miss
Burgess . . ."

Then Hawthorne's voice came through. The girl, on her
own, had made the connection.

"Creighton," said the other doctor, "you've got to help
me. My daughter—she's seventeen—and she's—she's—" His
voice broke and the anger in Fox's eyes melted to concern.
"She's sick," Hawthorne told him. "She—she is violently ill.

Nauseated. I can't stop it; she is pale, cold." His voice broke again. "Blood is gushing from her mouth. Can I bring her to Memorial for care? *Can I?*"

The man sounded anguished, but he could be acting. Fox had no reason to trust him. This could be a trick . . .

"I'm sorry, Dr. Hawthorne," he said coldly, "but Memorial Hospital is taking no additional patients."

"But you can't refuse!" cried Dr. Hawthorne, his voice high. "You can't! You can't possibly!"

"I thought closing us down was what you wanted," Fox broke in.

"Look, man. Listen to me! My little girl—she's lying here —unconscious. I'm sure there is a massive hemorrhage. You can't just let her *die,* doctor!"

No, Fox could not let her die. Not anyone. And certainly not a young girl—seventeen—

"We don't have the facilities," Hawthorne was babbling. "She wouldn't survive a plane trip to Los Hermanos . . ."

Not if he were honestly reporting the symptoms. If his daughter did have an aneurysm—and it had ruptured— "You would have to sign a release," Fox said, his tone of voice completely professional, even businesslike.

"Creighton," said the anguished father, "you are making this a personal thing! I mean . . ."

"I have no choice," said Dr. Creighton. "You have put me in a position . . ."

"All right, all right!" said Dr. Hawthorne wearily. "Christie is all that matters. Yes, I will sign your damned release."

"Then," said Dr. Creighton, "bring her in."

He pushed buttons and talked to the operator again. He would need Dr. Belze—an o.r. crew—wait, let him talk to Dr. Belze.

He breathed a sigh of relief to find Belze immediately on the phone. He crisply detailed the situation, and said that he suspected an aneurysm. Would Dr. Belze come?

"For Hawthorne's daughter?" Dr. Belze repeated in amazement. "Can we do that, Fox?"

"Can we refuse to do it?"

"Well, I don't know. The way things have been in the town lately . . ."

"And the way they have been in our hospital," Fox agreed. "Perhaps there has been too much talk, too much concern with things that should be considered only a medical problem, the problem of serving the public."

"Yes, sir."

"So this, tonight, is a medical problem, and I am afraid a tough one. I should like to think . . ."

"I'll be there, sir."

And the two men were right where they had been for a week. Ethical, courteous. Ever since "that night" . . . The time would come, and certainly soon, when Vil Belze and Fox Creighton would have to talk about that night.

The case came in, the girl on the stretcher, so thin, so small as almost not to lift the sheet. She was in dire condition, her color gray-white, her pulse thready. Dr. Hawthorne was told that he could remain in the emergency-operating room. He decided not to, but after a few minutes he did come in, and stood hunched against the wall. His wife waited in the front hall.

Dr. Belze was in scrub, and Dr. Crosby came in. Fox too would scrub, just in case . . .

Belze was entirely silent; he had not liked what his preliminary examination had shown him. There was a definite mass . . .

Crosby was talkative. He even asked if doing this surgery on Hawthorne's daughter wouldn't influence the town's vote on the bond issue.

"The cat can jump any way," said Fox. "I believe this job may even prove to people—to some people—that we are already working together." He had pinned the signed release on the bulletin board.

The surgeons went to work, not liking to work *in extremis,* but miracles sometimes happened. The tension in the room was almost unbearable. Dr. Belze made his incision, Crosby placed retractors and haemostats, and both men looked up at Fox Creighton. Before he could ask for a suction apparatus, the thin artery wall ruptured, and blood welled out, covering the surgeon's hands, the drapes, filling a basin, and another . . .

"You would not think . . . a girl so small . . ." gasped Dr. Crosby.

Fox went over to Hawthorne and led him, almost by force, out of the room. This had indeed become a personal thing. He took the stricken man to Kathie, and then out to Kathie's car. Very little was said.

He went inside, to his office, and began to fill out the death forms. Thinking of the blond young girl, it struck him that, instead of Christine Hawthorne, he could have been writing *Courtney Armstrong* on the top line. A young girl with life before her. And now . . . This *could* have been Courtney. He felt a great personal loss.

The fine blond hair, the young body . . .

He completed the form and took it out to the office. He would go home. The surgeons had already left.

He heard someone talking about the case, and the replies . . . "the weirdest thing . . ." ". . . . just buckets of blood . . ."

He went out to his car. He was going to talk to Courtney, really talk to her. Or perhaps he would talk with her. There were many ways to cut off a young life. That had been, subconsciously, the reason he had taken Courtney into his home. He did have a responsibility, a great one.

He went into the house, almost eagerly. But Courtney had gone out. "She said she would be home before ten," Story reported.

Fox nodded, and went upstairs. Loneliness filled the house like mist.

* * *

Next day, of course, the town was talking, faster, louder, more universally, than ever. The subject: the death of Christie Hawthorne on an operating table at Creighton Memorial Hospital. How could such a thing come to be? Who had failed to save the girl's life? She had not been sick, had she? Well, of course she was a wispy thing, but—

"This will kill the hospital." Even personnel at Creighton Memorial decided that it could.

There were those—perhaps as many—in Union Hospital, and around town, who said that the event would kill Union.

There was so much to be heard—even the Storys discussed it—that Courtney came to the hospital at noon, bringing freshly made sandwiches, cupcakes, grapes and iced coffee, and asked Fox if he would eat lunch with her and talk to her about what had happened.

"You've heard talk," he said, clearing the desktop.

"Yes. A lot of talk. I knew—you can tell me what did happen."

Last night he had wanted to talk to her. He would talk to her now, even on her terms. "I am angry," he warned Courtney.

"All right," she agreed. "Are you angry because that girl died here?"

"I'll tell you what happened," he said. "Do you know what an aneurysm is?"

"I looked it up in the dictionary."

"Yes. It is a swelling in an artery, forming a thin place in the bulged-out wall. Blood gathers, backs up—there is more swelling. And distress because of pressure, interfered circulation . . ." He sketched on a pad of yellow paper, Courtney leaned close to see. Her yellow hair fell across Fox's hand, and he straightened, sat back.

"Well—sometimes we can tie off the artery," he said, "do a bypass, things like that—patching. Last night, we could not. The thing had already begun to leak, and it ruptured.

"The reason she died here . . ." He told of Hawthorne's plea, of the signed release, and finally of the man's anguish.

"He loved his daughter, he tried to save her. And, trying, he did perhaps the one decent thing he has ever done in his life. Now, from what I hear, he is being condemned for doing it."

Courtney looked up, her eyes troubled. "But . . ." she said. "They condemn you too. Or seem to."

Fox laughed, and took another sandwich. "Has anyone said I kidnapped the girl and brought her here?" he asked.

"No." She sat thoughtful, then looked up. "I think, really, they resent your being a better doctor, having better surgeons, even a better hospital."

"Good girl. That is what they resent. Forgetting always that Memorial, like Union, has been offering medical service. It is available, if the patient wants it, and asks for it. Neither of us kidnaps anybody."

"Of course not. The town knows what sort of service is available. They choose. But—I am puzzled about other things, Fox. One other thing especially. And that has to do with another death. It happened just before I came here. The wife of one of your doctors, the man who did what Hank Blair called a pneumo-thorax?"

"Yes," Fox agreed. "Dr. Forrest, our chest specialist and surgeon. A good man."

"I know that. But isn't Dr. Belze a good surgeon too?"

"The best." Fox was watching her keenly.

"All right. Evidently Dr. Belze had to operate on Mrs. Forrest—she'd been hurt in an automobile accident—I don't know the whole story . . ."

Nor anyone else, thought Fox wryly.

"But Dr. Forrest is suing Dr. Belze, isn't he?"

"Yes. He filed a suit for damages. He thought there had been unwarranted delay in getting to the surgery."

"Had there been?"

"I was in Los Hermanos. Some day I'll get around to sifting down through the various claims and reports."

"What will you do about it?" Her dark eyes were wide upon his face.

"What makes you think I can do anything?"

She smiled at him.

And Fox . . . He rose from his chair. "I have to go to work," he said abruptly. "Pack up your lunch wagon, Courtney. I have a lot of paper work to get through."

She nodded, and she still smiled.

* * *

Courtney left the small bowl of green grapes on Fox's desk, and when Miss Tunstall came into the office that afternoon she helped herself to a cluster of them. She had brought papers with her, and for ten minutes she discussed hospital matters with the Chief. Then she sat down in the chair beside his desk, and began to eat the grapes.

He looked at her, his eyebrows up.

"Yes," she said. "I do have something else on my mind. I don't know how important you'll think it is, but I'd like to talk about it a little."

"All right," Fox agreed. "Let's have it."

"Yes. I want to talk to you about Clytie Cotsworth's will."

"Oh, now look, Tunnie," he protested. "I have problems on problems, and you come in here to offer me another one? Why, in God's name, should I concern myself . . ."

"I think," Tunnie said, "that your mind should be diverted. Another sort of problem just might do it."

He laughed, but more as if in pain than to express amusement. "You brought this thing to me before, Tunnie," he reminded his old friend who was still a damned good-looking nurse.

"Yes, I did," Alice agreed. "And you told Virginia she should force Carolyn to produce that will."

"I doubt if she could produce it. But I did think—I do think she should tell Carolyn that she knows she destroyed the will."

"Would that do any good?"

"Maybe not. Other than giving her a club to hold over her sister. A threat of exposure."

"She'd still have to listen to people telling her how wonderful Carolyn is with her flower arrangements, her decorated cookies . . ." Miss Tunstall sat up straight. "Do you think she set fire to the hospital, Fox?"

That was what she had really wanted to ask him.

"They haven't put her in jail for it, have they?" Fox asked quietly.

Alice made a gesture and sound of disgust about the whole situation. And Fox's refusal to express himself on the subject. She reached for more grapes, and he pushed the bowl toward her. "Courtney brought them," he told her.

"They're good. How are you getting along with your orphan?"

"Tunnie," he said, "I don't need sunshine to see right through you. But I'll answer that question too. And tell you that I find myself enjoying Courtney. She's decorative. She has a good, alert mind. She is a gay, laughing creature. My house has lacked that. She runs with the dogs, and it is a sight to see. She digs and snips and sprinkles in the flower beds, and twice she has made me play ping pong with her. Once we got out on the lawn, and played catch." He knew that Tunnie was watching him as she listened.

Alice wiped her fingers with the handkerchief which she took from her pocket. "Did you know," she asked blandly, "what the oldest Clark girl is planning to do with the money her grandfather left her?"

Fox sighed. "My life," he complained, "these days does seem to be made up exclusively of deaths and wills."

Alice smiled at him. "Not unusually so," she assured him. "Doctors deal with death, and wills follow death."

"I suppose. All right. What is Laura Ann planning?"

"I'm surprised you remember her name."

"She's a second cousin, or a first one once removed. Something of the sort. Isn't she the one . . .?"

"Yes, she is. She got into trouble—it's still called that —and had to marry a boy while she was in high school. The baby died, and she divorced the fellow. She is working, but she lives with Marion and Nancy."

"Mhmmmn. So tell me what she is going to do with the money."

"Why, she is going to give it to her father, to George Clark."

Fox whistled soundlessly.

"Marion—you can't believe how shocked she is."

"Me too," said Fox. "I am deeply shocked. Doesn't Laura Ann know what her father is, and has been?"

"That he earns what income he has by gambling? Maybe she does know, maybe she doesn't know or believe it. Maybe, Fox, she even blames her mother. For her father's not living with them, for not supporting them."

Fox nodded. "That's a possibility," he agreed. "Young people—well, anybody, I suppose—judge from the facts they know. Marion has kept working, and has established what is called a career. She must run the family and home efficiently. And the father seems to have been excluded, left out, maybe even pushed out. His father rejected him. Marion raised her daughters without him. Yes, all those things could be established as facts. I suppose one could tell almost any story two ways, Tunnie."

She stood up. "Mine, and yours too," she said.

"Oh, yes. If anyone would bother to tell those stories at all."

Chapter Eight

ON THURSDAY, Creighton Memorial Hospital announced its immediate closing. Dr. Creighton sent out the word, in letters to the City Council, in an article for the newspaper, on the town's radio, and by a personal appearance on TV. He looked very well on TV. His rugged strength, his intensity, his honesty, all came through. His green eyes were steady, his voice rang true.

"We have been sorely pushed for room," he explained. "We could not, we felt, burden the people, the community, with outrageous hospital costs, though we did hope to find means to expand our facilities, to add more rooms, and more services. More doctors, and additional personnel. Since the damaging fire of several days ago, the situation has become critical, but we still hoped to find a way to continue, to rebuild and to grow. However"—and his big, clean hand slashed at the viewer, the listener—"Creighton Memorial has no wish to be part of any dual hospital, or one financed and directed by the Federal Government."

Asked about his own individual plans, he replied that they were indefinite.

He was asked what the town of Carson would do? And its industries which had depended on the hospital for care and service in a time of disaster or emergency?

"What will they do?" Fox repeated the question. "What does the individual man do? The little man when he becomes ill, or his aging mother breaks her hip? He, or she, is taken to the city, to Los Hermanos, or to one of the hospitals in towns a hundred miles away. Yes, it does mean a costly ambulance ride. The whole project becomes very expensive.

"Of course," he pointed out. "Our town will still have doctors. There is a fine clinic across the street from Memorial

158

Hospital, most of our staff doctors have offices there, and they have means available for diagnosis, X-ray, a laboratory. They can conduct tests ...

"But in a clinic they are not able to offer bed care; there is no operating room to permit surgery of any dimensions. Years ago, deliveries were made in homes. I suppose they could be again, but the clinic could care for this only as an emergency measure. There would be no nursery, and no incubator care for infants."

He agreed that he was concerned for the patients who must be moved elsewhere, and especially he was concerned for the three hundred citizens of Carson who were—who had been—employed at the hospital. He would endeavor to secure care for such patients as needed it in other towns, or in Los Hermanos. He would try to find employment for the personnel, though it would mean dislocation of many families. He said again that he was sorry things had turned out this way. Of course the fire was somewhat to blame, though that damage could have been rebuilt. The main cause for the closing was the town's seeming wish to change the hospital picture and service in Carson. These things said, he would say no more.

All over the town the reaction was, at first, that of stunned disbelief. And then protest, dismay—questions. In the hospital, and out.

"They done cut the ground out from under our feet," said Peach.

"What have we been working for all these years?" asked Carolyn Cotsworth.

What are we going to do? Everyone asked that. Literally everyone.

Dr. Belze, Dr. Creighton himself—people asked him and he said, "I don't know. What are we going to do?" The patients asked the question and were soothed by nurses and their families. They would be taken care of.

The interns asked it. Dr. Bechars looked askance at his prospects with Hawthorne. The Air Force began to look like a haven. Dr. Smith would go back to Alabama, "a few weeks early, seemed like." Tommie would make plans for her marriage in June, then consider a residency. Hank Blair, who had expected a second year at Memorial, said he'd wait and see. He'd get something. Meanwhile he'd watch this thing. He could always hire on as rough labor, cleaning and boarding up the burned part of the hospital.

He and Peach could stow gear in mothballs . . . He talked that way. No, he wasn't angry. What else could the Fox do? The town had given him no option.

The townspeople were really the puzzled ones, the silent and frightened ones, the angry ones. They must face the realization that they were without a good hospital. They called Memorial that.

They were reminded that the vote on the new hospital was coming up. The bond issue would surely pass now.

Yeah. Yes, but—

* * *

Fox Creighton, swamped with all the details of closing down, all the mechanics of it, still had a tremendous sense of loss. There was nothing to build toward, nothing to plan in a large sense.

He was like a man loose in a boat without steerage. Eventually he would drift somewhere, he might even rig something—but right now, he was lost.

That first evening he went home, glad to get away from his hospital, wanting companionship other than people with anxious faces and brave smiles.

Courtney was not in the house. And, golly, he missed the girl when she was not around!

Where was she? Didn't she guess that he'd be low? She had said, at various times, that she loved him. He had laughed at her, though maybe she meant what she said. He might be ready to believe her, but now . . .

Her absence angered him, though he could not have told if he was angry at himself, or at Courtney.

Fred Story brought him a drink; he and Mrs. Story together served his dinner, and they asked him about the town's need for a hospital.

"They'll have one," he assured these sympathetic, friendly people. "There's that bond issue vote coming up, remember."

"Just what does that mean, sir?" asked Mrs. Story, her eyes troubled.

"Well," said Fox, looking at the juicy slice of meat loaf on his plate, the rim of which was dark blue, bordered in gold. A handsome plate. "If the vote is favorable, Carson will have its public hospital, probably a large one."

"When will we have it?"

"Oh, it would take over a year, certainly, to build. Another year perhaps to equip and staff it."

"Would it be a good hospital?"

"I'd hope so. Union, and Dr. Hawthorne, would certainly be a part of it."

"But, Dr. Fox . . ."

"This vote gives the town a chance to decide what it wants, Becca."

"They don't know what they want! We can't have that kind of hospital instead of Memorial. Will you work against it?"

Fox laughed, and picked up his fork. "I've been working against it," he said, "for the past five years."

* * *

With the town in a turmoil over Memorial's closing a large part of the protest and discussion centered upon the mayor of the city, upon Pat Kern. He had expected that the situation would come to roost on his shoulders, but he had foregone his temptation to leave town, or to refuse to answer the telephone.

He even went to the drugstore that late afternoon, and talked to those who wanted to talk to him. Mainly, he listened. He didn't really know what Fox Creighton was up to. If he said the hospital was closing, he meant that the hospital was closing.

"It just isn't right!"

"Whose right?" asked Pat. "Fox's? His grandfather opened the hospital, his father and he have kept it open, why haven't they the right to close?"

"This—those doctors won't stay without a hospital. This leaves us with only Hawthorne and Union."

"Don't you want that?"

"He can't even handle Medicare. The Government says he can't."

"Then maybe the Government isn't right." Pat was beginning to enjoy this debate.

One man said it would be no loss. He wasn't surprised. Things had been going from bad to worse out at Memorial. Right now there were two lawsuits on the docket. "You don't have that happen in a good hospital."

"What makes a good hospital?" the mayor asked the counter, full of coffee drinkers. "And what makes a bad one? Do you know?"

* * *

Now things really were strange for Vil Belze. He had not thought there was any way for him but up; he had ex-

pected—he thought he had expected—almost any development at the hospital. But the actual notice of the hospital's closing was able to shake him hard.

For one thing, Jane kept asking him questions. Why?
When? What would he do? Where would he go? When he answered her only briefly, if at all, she became angry. After all,
she claimed, she had a right to know where they stood, what
lay ahead for her and her children.

"Whose children?" Vil asked coldly.

"Oh, now!" cried Jane. "Really!"

"Yes. Really."

He didn't want to get into a charge and recrimination
session with Jane. One day, and soon, there must be a showdown, but first . . .

Yes, first. He must get relief from the days of torment
which he had been passing, the nights, the hours, the minutes. He was weary, weary of knowing the things he did
know and not being able to speak of his torment, not able
to make others know too.

He was going to have to live with the shambles of his
life, perhaps with Jane, perhaps not. But certainly he must
work, honorably, and he must raise his children to know
that their father had always so worked. He believed sincerely
in precept and example. He was a good doctor. And he
wanted to be known as one, always.

Lawsuits, won or lost, had no part in such a picture. The
delayed arrival of the surgeon had not caused Dorothy
Forrest's death, but Belze wanted his record clear with the
Chief of Medical Services. He wanted Fox Creighton to
know where he had been on that Tuesday night, and to believe the story when it was told to him.

So that evening he drove out to the Golf Club, where he
had located Dr. Forrest as present. He was calm, he was
quiet—he noted the things he passed and saw, the wide
road, the little adobe houses, the large ranch homes, and,
against the sky, the rising escarpments of the mountains,
washed in gold by the late sun.

Himself a member, the club was a familiar place of
wide green lawns, snow-white buildings with awnings striped
in red and white, carefully nourished trees. Dr. Forrest, he
was told, was having dinner on the terrace. Dr. Belze went
across the wide lobby, and out through the glass doors. The
terrace served the pool, and there were a dozen tables, many
lounges and chairs, a score of decorative people. Forrest sat

alone at a small table; he seemed to have had a swim, but had pulled on a yellow terry shirt.

Followed by the incredulous stares and murmurs of the people on the terrace, Dr. Belze made his way swiftly between the tables. Forrest saw him coming and made a jerking movement to rise, to leave, then he settled back into his chair, and waited for his onetime friend.

"Vil?" he said, when Dr. Belze pulled a second chair up to the table.

"Weren't you expecting me?" Vil asked; he shook his head impatiently at the waiter solicitously at his shoulder.

"I see you every day."

"In the hospital, at the clinic, yes. But you've been avoiding me everywhere else."

Dr. Forrest was a tall, bony man with large, pale eyes, a thin face in which his cheekbones and jaw were prominent. His thick brown hair lay in a brush across his forehead. Some people considered him handsome; he had cultivated a manner of speaking bluntly, and roughly. Some people admired this as honesty, and quoted him freely. Women found his roughness fascinating. Men respected him as a talented doctor, but often disliked him as a person. Vil Belze had, for years, been this man's friend. Partly, he had always known, because they were so different. Belze was a quiet man, a courteous and thoughtful man. The two were—different.

Tonight—

"I had to see you, Wally," he said now. "Not where my professional behavior would be a feature, not where our colleagues would be within sight and hearing."

Walter Forrest looked around him at the chattering, squealing, laughing, and observant people on the terrace. "You chose a fine place," he drawled.

"I would have met you anywhere."

"I've nothing to say to you, boy."

"I don't want you to say anything to me. I know anything you could say. But I do want you, and right away—like tonight—to go to Fox Creighton and tell him what happened Tuesday night of last week. Where you were, and with whom. Why Dorothy was out on the road with a loaded gun. Why I was not within reach when she was hurt."

The wide mouth smiled, but the pale eyes hardened. "There goes my lawsuit," he drawled.

"Damn your lawsuit!" cried Dr. Belze, his face white. "I want Dr. Creighton to know what went on that night. You can perjure yourself later in court—I don't know what you plan—but I want you to tell Fox the truth!"

Dr. Forrest picked up his glass. "I haven't the slightest idea of what you are talking about," he said.

Vil gaped at him. "You *know* what I am talking about!" he cried, his hands clenched on his knees. He could, literally, kill this man!

"Let's see," said Dr. Forrest. "Tuesday night, of last week. As I remember, the night my wife died on the operating table because the surgeon could not be located . . ." He lifted an eyebrow at Dr. Belze.

Vil drew a deep breath, he unclenched his hands and looked at them. He stood up. "You do need killing," he said quietly. "I suppose you know that Dorothy was on her way to do just that the night she wrecked her car."

Dr. Forrest laughed. "Will you so testify in court?" he asked.

"You, and Jane, would be amazed at what I could testify in court!" He turned on his heel and walked away.

Behind him, Walter Forrest no longer smiled.

* * *

To get away from the telephone, Fox told himself, he went for a walk after dinner that evening. He walked the boundaries of his home place, through the deep shadows of the pines and cedars. He went into the paddock, and looked at the new foal, he went to the barn, even through the greenhouse, liking the hot, loamy smell of the place. As he came back to the house, he critically studied it, the roof line, the chimneys—the deep terrace and porch at the back, the rosebushes, losing their color in the rising darkness. He'd have a drink and go to bed. He might or might not ask Story where Courtney had gone.

"Hello there."

He jumped. "Courtney?" he asked.

The swing creaked, and she sat up on the cushions. "Where have you been?" she demanded.

"Where have *I* . . ." He came up and across the flagstones, sat down in one of the deep chairs. "I've been right here!" he said loudly. "I came home at quitting time. I washed my hands and ate a proper dinner of—let's see—meat loaf and asparagus and new potatoes, and—"

"Vanilla ice cream with grape juice sauce," she concluded.

He stirred. "How do you know? You weren't here."

"Oh, I read Mrs. Story's menus. Frozen grape juice concentrate is delicious on ice cream. I tried it."

He sighed, and stood up. "I'm going to get a drink," he said. "Can I bring you something?"

"Maybe some coffee, if there is any."

"You won't sleep."

"I'll sleep. After the day I've put in."

He waited until he returned with his glass and her mug of coffee before he brought up the *"day"* business.

"You had one of your own, didn't you?" she asked.

"It seems that I have nothing but 'days,' " he confessed, sitting down heavily in the chair; the ice tinkled in his glass. "I can't remember when disaster failed to pay its daily call on me."

"Uncle Stephen," she murmured.

"It began before that, Courtney," he said. "I mark the beginning with a call Dr. Hawthorne paid us suggesting that we merge the two hospitals. Then it seemed a simple thing to declare that we would not consider such a ridiculous alliance. I didn't guess that, a week or so later, I would be admitting his daughter to our hospital which still smelled of the fire that had literally almost destroyed us. I didn't dream that he would ever ask us . . ."

"That death was a sad thing, wasn't it?"

"Very sad. She was a tiny girl, with soft, fine hair—a little darker than yours—and she didn't have a *chance*, Courtney! She didn't have one chance."

"I thought, maybe, when that happened—you know, her father taking her to you, and seeming to admit that your hospital was the only real one here—I thought that would break off all the bond issue election business and the closing of the two hospitals. But, instead, you closed your hospital . . ."

"Not me. The Board, the staff."

"It seems like you. I believe a lot of people feel that way. When I first heard the news on the radio—and later when you were on TV—it *was* you. So I wondered—What are you going to do now?"

Again the ice tinkled as he lifted the glass to his lips. "Do I have to do anything?" he asked.

"Oh, yes, I'd say that you would have to. Men have to do *something*. You're a doctor. I heard one of the lawyers at Uncle Stephen's funeral say you had done some fine work in research. A doctor had told him. Will you go back to that?"

Fox did not answer.

"Have you liked running the hospital better than you liked doing research?"

"I've thought I was hating the work I did here," he said musingly.

"But now you don't hate it."

"Now I feel only an emptiness. And you're right. A man should have, I suppose he actually does have, a life to live, a life of his own. Even if I just go on sitting here in a low chair, drinking Scotch, I'd still be having a life of my own . . ."

She moved, rustling against the swing's cushions. By then it was completely dark. One of the setters came up on the terrace and his cold nose rubbed Fox's hand.

"How old are you, Fox?" Courtney asked him.

Surprised, he sat up straight, his foot scraped on the stones. "What difference . . .?" he began. Then he settled back again. "I'm thirty-eight," he said gruffly.

"Mhmmmn. Well, you know, don't you, that a man not yet forty can certainly change his life if he wants to. Or he could even decide that the life he has is a pretty good one and put a lot of direction into that. He . . ."

"What about a girl of nineteen?" asked Fox.

"You're laughing at me."

"No, I'm not. You're nineteen and your life has changed radically for you during this busy two weeks' time."

"When you were having all those *days*," she agreed. "Yes, my life has changed, and I'm twenty, not nineteen. I had a birthday last Sunday."

"For heaven's sake . . ."

"We didn't need to mention it. But I'll answer your question. I certainly hope I could—that I can—change my life. Why, I'm fresh out of the terrible teens, and . . ."

"Were they terrible?" Fox asked, laughing a little.

"Of course. When you're a teen, you're nothing. You aren't a child anymore, with all those privileges of having temper tantrums and mud puddles and learning or not learning. And you're certainly not considered grown-up, with the privileges of *that* state. You know, able to decide what you want to do, and have your decision respected. If you tell a man you love him, he sheds the declaration like so many beads of water. If you do have a plan for your life, or if there are things you know you have to do, you have to be sneaky about it."

"Not sneaky, surely!"

"If you get tired of being ignored, or laughed at, you keep things to yourself. That's sneaky."

They were talking to each other, Fox realized, like two human beings on a level of experience and understanding. He asked her about Uncle Stephen—what sort of parent he had made.

"Oh, he was wonderful, in many ways," she said. "Of course, he felt a very heavy responsibility."

"Don't actual parents?"

"Sure they do. Some feel too much. And they love it; they don't want their children to grow up . . ."

"They know what being grown up means."

"Sometimes that's a part of it. Sometimes, even with teeners, they want to keep their daughters virgin. I don't mean in the sex sense. But untouched by hurt or grief. To keep their baby hair, as it were. And their sons too. Little boys' eyes, you know. They are wide, curious, trusting. It would be wonderful, parents think, if that innocence could be kept."

"But inconsistent with beards."

Courtney laughed. "Now you're bringing up a high hurdle. Maturity. What it is, why it is—"

"And wouldn't life be gruesome if it didn't come aound on time?"

It was very good to talk so. For too long, Fox had held himself aloof from this sort of companionship. Tonight he was not the doctor-Chief of Medical Services. Courtney was not the young, and perhaps foolish, girl he rather regretted taking on as a responsibility. They were just two people, a man and a woman, sitting there in the soft, warm darkness, talking about life, about young people, and people grown, ready to be grown.

"Teeners know, better than anyone else," said Courtney, "that there has to be guidance in life. They know they will have to take on that guidance, and some of them believe they don't want any help."

"Some of them don't want it."

"Not really, Fox. They are in a panic, and a lot of people in a panic get resentful . . ."

"And violent."

"Yes, that's the childhood temper-tantrum thing, left over."

"And made damn dangerous when the 'child' is six feet tall and weighs two hundred pounds."

"Could we go back to Dr. Hawthorne?" Courtney asked after a little time. "That situation has needed a lot of thinking about."

"What do you expect me to say about him? He's a doctor, he seems to run Union Hospital—he's rich, and popular in some circles."

"He's a charming man."

"Yes. How well do you know him?" Fox felt the green mold of jealousy tinge his words.

"I don't know him well at all," said Courtney. "One evening he introduced himself to me. I was with Hank Blair. Dr. Hawthorne said he thought I should know the town's leading characters, something of the sort. He was, as I say, charming. Which isn't a line I especially care for. Just as I don't like too much butter on a hot roll."

Fox rubbed his nose, which had suddenly developed an itch. "He was deeply hurt by his daughter's death," he said. "I know that to be true. And he won't get over that hurt very soon. But—perhaps I may have to expose him as a doctor, Courtney."

"Why haven't you done that before, if you can?"

"Because I live by certain ethical rules."

"And he doesn't."

"Well . . . on this particular point, perhaps he does. You know, Courtney, all doctors hesitate to squeal on other doctors. Their logic is: I may be in a tough spot some day. They don't bring charges readily, and you can scarcely ever get one to testify in court."

"But under some circumstances . . ."

"Yes. Under some circumstances, I suppose I would stand up and speak out."

"I'm glad this seems like a circumstance to you. Was that your reason for closing the hospital?"

He looked up, in surprise. "You're a smart girl, Courtney."

"I am smart enough. I've watched you, studied you. What do you have to expose?"

"Oh, a lot of things. For one, I could publicize his not being allowed to work under Medicare, and I would explain why."

"*I* don't know why, specifically."

"He turned in too many patients, too many calls upon them, too many treatments. He never dreamed that the Government would check . . . No, that is not what he never dreamed. He counted on his old people to be too senile to remember accurately. What he forgot, in at least one instance, was that senile patients have families, and occasionally one of these relatives will speak up."

"I see. And not be charmed, either."

Fox chuckled.

"What else?" Courtney prodded.

"What . . .? Oh. Well, he does some funny trading in self-dispensed drugs. This we can substantiate. He does various sorts of illegal medicine."

"Abortions?"

"And unreported gunshot wounds—some people pay enormously for that kind of medical care."

"Oh, dear. Would you get into that sort of thing, Fox? An exposé?"

"To save my hospital, yes."

"But—"

"It can be saved, Courtney. And I thnk it would be worth saving. I'd want to do it. It carries my name, you see. It means a great deal to me."

"I can see that it does. I've known that it does." She got off the swing. "I think you should expose this man," she said.

He seemed surprised. "I thought, maybe—"

Her fingers brushed through his hair as she passed behind him. "I've told you that I love you," she said. "I've understood you from the start."

Before he could move, or speak, her footsteps lightly skimmed the flagstones, the door into the wing opened, and closed. He sat on, smiling.

* * *

Alice Tunstall, preparing for bed that same night, was wondering as well about Fox Creighton. Her questions echoed Courtney's. Why had he closed the hospital? What would he do now? What would he do in the future?

Perhaps Courtney too asked what part she could play now, and in the future. Tunnie certainly gave it consideration.

She moved about her apartment, straightening things—magazines, newspapers. She turned out lamps in the living room, opened the draperies and looked out at the sky, at the moonlight.

She had, these past few days, spent hours like this one, debating whether there was anything she could do for Fox. She would, literally, do anything. He was a fine doctor, he had done an excellent job of running the hospital's medical services, but his personal life did leave a lot to be desired. A man his age, substituting a hospital for a wife and family, a home—Fox deserved more than that. He should have more.

So far as she knew, and she knew a lot, he was giving no thought to building up his personal life. Taking Courtney into his home had been the first contact he had made personally with any girl or woman. And that seemed not to promise much. Courtney was living at his home, she had come to the hospital a time or two, Fox had not known she was there. The hospital said she dated Hank Blair . . .

Well, Dr. Blair had his good points. But, if Courtney was interested in dates, in men, why should Fox be passed by?

Tunnie laughed, and went on to her bedroom. Fox was why. She knew that. He had brought Courtney to his home as he would have brought a valuable painting, to care for and protect.

Beyond that—

But there must be ways, steps a person could take, to make Fox look at Courtney, and see her—

There were things to be done. And Alice Tunstall could do them. Of course she would surprise everyone. Carolyn Cotsworth would go into a real tizzy. But that would be good. Yes, indeed.

* * *

The next morning—was it Thursday? Friday? Who noticed the days?

That morning, a man came to the hospital. He parked his car and walked up to the front entrance. Before that door there was a large cardboard sign, affixed to an easel. The man stood and read it, his head thrust forward, though the lettering was large enough, and plain.

Creighton Memorial Hospital, the sign read, was closed to the service of patients.

The man went around the sign, glancing back at it resentfully, and tried to open the front door. It was locked. He could see that there had been a fire, but there were people moving around inside—he even heard a telephone ring. He shook the door. Nothing happened.

He looked about him, back to his car parked in the street. There was a sidewalk along the front of the hospital, he went down to it, and followed it to the far end of the building, where there was another door.

This one was unlocked; he opened it and went inside. There was no one in the hall, no one sat behind the curved desk where one could expect nurses to be. The call board was dark. He walked along the corridor; there didn't seem to be any patients in the rooms. A wheel chair stood against the wall, a cart was further along . . .

He walked on, and coming out of what looked to be an office, he found a real, live man. He breathed a sigh of relief. A ghost hospital was nothing to joke about.

"Hey!" he said aloud to the big man.

Peach turned, his face surprised. "Who you?" he asked.

The strange man sighed again. "My name's Durkin," he said. "I came here with a problem—and I find the hospital closed."

"That's right," said Peach.

"What's your position here?"

"I'm Peach, an orderly. Just now Dr. Fox say I'm a custodian."

"I see. But isn't there someone . . .? Look, I'm a stranger here. I came to town just last week to take a job at the Chemical Company. It's out of town a ways." He jerked his head to the west.

"Yes, sir. I know about it. Lots o' Carson people work there."

"Mhmmmn! Well, you know—or maybe you don't—when you change jobs and go into a new company, you have to have a physical examination."

"Yes, sir. They come in here all the time. When we is open for business, that is."

"But what happened here?" cried John Durkin. "No, don't let's go into that. You were open two weeks ago when I came here for tests, and I had those tests, especially a urine test. Oh, boy, did I ever have a urine test!"

"Yes, sir."

"And then the hospital here was to send a report to the plant. I was given the job—I made arrangements for my family to move here from Illinois, I leased a house. And then, this morning, *boom!* I get fired!"

"Oh, man! What you do?"

"I didn't *do* anything, Peach. But my medical report went into the main office in New Jersey, and the doctor there, or somebody, decided that the quinine found in my blood showed me to be a dope user. A speed eater, a—well, the boss asked me if I shot heroin. I told him no! So he mentioned the quinine. Seems it's used to cut heroin. But when I told him that the quinine was medicine I took for a heart arithma—that's a jumping heartbeat—"

"Yes, sir."

"The heart's normal! It just gets this froglike jump; the quinidine slows that down and makes it regular."

"Yes, sir!"

"And the plant manager said that if I could get the doctor here to certify where I was using quinine, and why, to certify that there was no other evidence of heroin use . . ."

"And you can't find no doctor here."

"No, I can't. And I'll tell you one thing, Peach. I'm damn mad!" He stormed off, talking about lawyers, and the police. He'd find the doctor who'd done his physical, or somebody would pay. He was going to get his record set straight! Nobody was going to pin a user label on him. It wasn't only this job . . . Where would he find or get another job?

Yes! He was damned mad. He drove downtown, and stopped at the hotel for coffee. Fortunately the man he sat next to, and to whom he voiced his indignation, was Pat Kern, who agreed that labeling the man an addict on such evidence was terrible. There surely were ways to clear things up.

"Oh," agreed John Durkin, "there probably are. My doctor back in Illinois knows I take quinidine. But I still think that hospital had no business to close down."

Pat agreed with him. Then he identified himself as the mayor of Carson, ready to welcome a new family to town. "People say I do nothing but hang around this counter," he said, "but you are proof that the habit's not all bad. Now, let me see what we can do for you."

The first thing he did was to pay for Durkin's coffee. Then he took him to the mayor's office. He called the plant and asked them not to fill the position for which they had hired Durkin. Yes, he knew exactly what had happened, but he believed things could be straightened out there.

He smiled at John Durkin. "That's why I like being mayor," he confided. "It gives me clout. They will wait on further word from me. Now, let's see."

It took a little time, but the operator located Fox, and the mayor talked to him. He detailed Mr. Durkin's problem, and agreed that the doctor back in New Jersey must be an idiot . . . He hung up the telephone and turned to smile at his visitor.

Durkin was to go back to the hospital, he said. Dr. Creighton would look at his records. "You'll be all right. Fox won't call you a drug user if you're not one. And people listen to *him!*"

Durkin could guess why. With a friend like the mayor of Carson . . .

He found this Dr. Creighton just as dynamic. The doctor greeted John Durkin warmly, he spread the man's records out on the desk before him, he called Durkin's doctor in Illinois, identified himself, exchanged pleasantries, told of the difficulty, laughed at the other doctor's comment, arranged for a letter and a transcript to be sent to the Carson plant, and to New Jersey. Yes, he agreed, administrative processes could verge on the ridiculous. He then talked to the personnel office of the local plant, and with a smile put the phone down.

"You're all set, Mr. Durkin," he said. "You can go back to your job any time you care to. This silly charge will be removed from your record there."

John Durkin shook his head. He stood up and looked around him. "I never saw so much fur fly in an hour's times," he marveled.

Fox walked with him to the office door. Durkin looked out into the empty hall. "Shouldn't this place be working?" he asked. "Doesn't the town need its operation?"

"Yes, of course the town needs it," said Fox. "Just about as badly as you needed it this morning."

"I'd like to think my family could count on care here. I can see you've had a fire, but aren't you going to repair the damage?"

"Not just now. You see, there's a vote coming up to get money for a Government hospital here in Carson."

Durkin whistled. "Have you any idea or knowledge of what straightening out my record would take in such a hospital?" he asked. "Red tape wrapped around red tape! You wouldn't be a part of *that*, would you, sir?"

"I don't think so," said Fox. "My fur-flying talents would not be appreciated."

Mr. Durkin laughed. "But what are you going to do about that vote?"

"If you think of something to do, would you do it?"

"Yes, sir,!" said John Durkin. "I most certainly would!"

Fox held out his hand. "So would I, sir. So would I!"

* * *

When John Durkin went to his car, he was hailed by a man who had just driven up behind him. This man was driving a rented car, and he obviously wanted directions. Durkin went to him. Lord knew, he was in a mood to help anybody who might need help.

And he said so. "Could I help you?"

Yes, he could. The other man opened a wallet to display his driver's license. He was a Robert Ragsdale, attorney, from Los Hermanos; he had flown to Carson that morning, he said, and had driven to the hospital, seeking a client of his, a Miss Cotsworth who, he thought, was dietician—but —He gazed helplessly at John Durkin.

Mr. Durkin nodded. "The sign up there does say the place is closed," he agreed. "As it should not be." Quickly he detailed his experiences and their handling.

Then the two men tackled the problem of finding Miss Cotsworth. Durkin didn't think the dietician would be working, though perhaps someone inside could supply her home address.

"Oh, I have her address," said the attorney. "Why did they close the hospital?"

"Now, that's a very good question," said John Durkin, feeling like an established citizen dealing with the affairs of his home town.

In a half hour, Robert Ragsdale, attorney-at-law, was ringing the bell of the Cotsworth apartment. He identified himself from the lobby, and asked if he could see Miss Cotsworth for a short time.

A half dozen previous conversations with Carolyn had made him expect her to flutter before she settled down to what was a truly chisel-sharp business capability. So he waited until she said, but of course he could come up!

Once upstairs, in the prettily cluttered living room, speaking pleasantly to Mrs. Shelton, and waiting for Miss Cotsworth to sit down . . .

Thank you, yes, he would like a cup of coffee, please.

Oh, no, he was not ready for an early lunch. He hoped to get back to his office by one o'clock. Yes, he had flown. Now, if he could explain to her his reasons for coming . . .

Finally, he had his coffee. Finally, Carolyn sat down, primly, quietly, on the front edge of a chair. And Mr. Ragsdale was drawing two sheafs of paper from his brief-case.

"Is that the will?" asked Virginia breathlessly.

"Please, Virginia," said Carolyn.

"I suppose I should leave," said her sister.

Mr. Ragsdale shook his head. "Not unless you really want to," he said. "This matter could be of interest to you. You see—Yes, Miss Cotsworth, this is the will. In fact, the two wills, the two Mrs. Whiteside made and signed."

"Copies," said Carolyn Cotsworth, her mouth thin.

"That's right. But the Probate Judge has agreed that I might offer you the privilege of using the latest will of Mrs. Whiteside even though the original cannot be located. We thought, in our office, that you might want to probate and execute the estate of your sister as we know she wanted it executed. You could do that, by petition, since the changes are minor . . ."

"And it's what Clytie wanted," said Virginia breathlessly.

"No," said Carolyn. Her voice was clear, definite, and cold. "I think we should stay strictly with the law, and execute the will which you have."

"Putting the estate in trust would not be a bad idea, Miss Cotsworth," said Robert Ragsdale.

"I am quite capable of administering any business I have, Mr. Ragsdale."

"No one questions that. But you would be relieved of various responsibilities."

"Which I will gladly assume."

Mr. Ragsdale began to put his papers back into his brief-case.

Virginia cleared her throat. He glanced up. So did Carolyn, her eyes displeased.

"What . . . ?" Virginia asked. "What would happen, Mr. Ragsdale, if we found out what had happened to the real will, or ever found it?"

He smiled at her. "The will is in probate for a year. At any time we could open the case, and substitute the later will if it should be found. As to discovering what happened to it—then at least our puzzled curiosity would be satisfied."

"Thank you," said Virginia.

"I don't know why you ask such foolish questions," Carolyn reproved her. "Thank you for coming clear over here, Mr. Ragsdale. It was a lot of trouble for one question to be answered."

"Well, if you would have wanted to follow your sister's last wishes, we could have been busy all afternoon."

* * *

Alice Tunstall, from where she had been sitting on her third floor balcony, had seen the young lawyer arrive. The rented car, briefcase, black-rimmed glasses—she guessed at once who he was. She went inside, and opened her front door; she heard Carolyn greet and admit the young man.

"I'll go down there," she told herself. "I'll barge in and bolster Virginia's courage. She should tell that lawyer what she knows. Fox thinks she should . . . I'll do it!"

She did go down the steps, she did stand outside of Carolyn's door. But there years of self-discipline, of knowing what her own business was, and attending to it, took over.

"I'll go talk to Marion," she said. "I didn't promise Virginia not to tell . . ."

She found Marion making good use of what she called her short and unexpected vacation by cleaning house. She had begun with the living room.

"I hope that vacation of yours is not too short," Alice laughed, surveying the havoc already wrought. Draperies down, books off the shelves, "trash" heaped in the middle of the floor.

"Don't you expect the hospital to be back in business?" Marion challenged.

"I hope it will be. But I long ago stopped *expecting* Fox to do any fixed thing."

Marion shrugged and went on dusting books. She wore a blue denim jump suit, with a red bandanna tied around her hair. "If you don't want to help . . ." she said.

"I'll clear off a chair and watch," Alice offered. "I let Mr. Clean do my housecleaning."

"I should . . ."

"Certainly you should. I suspect you are working off frustrations."

"All I need is to be psychoanalyzed," said Marion plaintively. "Look, if you're not going to work, why don't you make us some iced tea and some sandwiches? There's cheese in the frige, hard-boiled eggs—lettuce—oh, all kinds of stuff."

Alice found the "stuff," and before she had finished Marion came to the kitchen. "I'll wash first," she said.

Though Alice had prepared their lunch on a large tray, the two friends decided to eat in the kitchen, and they were enjoying the meal when the front door opened and Maggie came in the apartment, calling, "Mum!" as she came.

"What on earth are you doing here?" her mother asked. "Why aren't you at work?"

"I am at work," said Maggie. "This is my lunch hour." She took a sandwich. "I had this terrific idea," said Maggie, sitting down. "You see, Laura Ann met me for coffee break this morning, and she told me what she was going to do with the money our grandfather left us. Do you know?" she demanded, pushing her long yellow hair behind her ears.

"Yes," said Marion.

"But that's crazy, Mum!"

Marion laughed. "Laura Ann doesn't think so."

"Well, I do. After I went back to work, I thought, and thought, about Laura Ann—you know? Her disloyalty and all. She could have kept the money and nobody would have thought much of anything—but to give it to Dad! Jeepers! So this is what I'm going to do. Now, listen. I am going to give my money to you, Mum." She sat back, her eyes happy. She ate her sandwich in large bites.

"Maggie," Marion protested weakly. "You can't. You shouldn't. That would be just as bad as what Laura Ann plans."

"In no way," said Maggie, with her mouth full. "Look." She drank some tea. "I know, and Laura Ann does too, what you have done for us, Mum."

"But, darling, you need the money. You and Patrick . . ."

"That's right," Maggie agreed readily. "We do need it. But I need to do this, too."

She stood up, she kissed her mother, she waved her hand at Tunnie, she picked up another sandwich, and ran through the apartment, slamming the front door behind her.

Marion and Alice sat silent, their faces awed and still. "Will you take it?" Alice asked at last.

Marion wiped her eyes with her napkin. "Don't you think I'd have to take it?" she asked. She was smiling, but another tear ran down her cheek. "Oh, Alice—"

"You could use it to buy her and Patrick a house," said Alice sensibly.

"Yes, I could, couldn't I?"

"Well, you think about it. I'll clean these things away."

She was back in her own apartment when she remembered why she had gone down to Marion's. She had not mentioned Clytie Cotsworth's will.

* * *

One could not believe that the days had passed, that even a week, and then three, had gone by. But they did go by, and election day arrived. The day when the qualified citizens of Carson, and its county, were to vote on the revenue bond issue which would, in time, bring a new hospital to their district. This was the day.

Fox Creighton did not vote until after five o'clock that evening. The newspaper had had a photographer at the polls early to get a picture of him. The evening paper did have pictures of other people voting. Dr. Hawthorne, the mayor—a little old lady who thought a "free hospital would be just the thing!"

Fox voted, and he went home, realizing as he drove into the grounds that he was looking forward to Courtney's being there. He was, he admitted, a bit excited at this prospect. They could have a drink, and eat dinner—take a walk perhaps. It was a good feeling to have that sort of companionship to look forward to. He had been a lonely man too long, a bachelor too long.

Courtney arrived one minute after he did, bringing the dusty station wagon up behind his car. What, Fox wondered, did the Story's do for wheels? That girl seemed to do a lot of traveling in the wagon.

She waved her hand at Fox. ". . . going to get a bath before dinner," she called. "I'm beat."

Well . . . She did look tired. Heaven only knew what she had been doing.

Fox went up to his own room, showered and changed into a loose shirt and slacks, came down again. The TV news program said that the polls were about to close, and began a résumé of what the election was about. Fox switched the thing off. He knew what it had been about. And, knowing, he had just sat on his duff and let things happen. He could have talked, he could have seen people and told what he felt and knew about a Government-supervised hospital, he could have brought out his proofs and attacked Hawthorne. He had done none of those things. He had closed Memorial Hospital, and sent patients out of town . . . Or to Hawthorne.

What had possessed him? Didn't he want to reopen Memorial, rebuild it? Of course the town had decided that he did not want to, that he was ready to abandon any obligation he might once have had . . .

They had their drink. Courtney came out to the terrace wearing a pink skirt, a pink and white striped blouse, her hair caught back with a silver barrette.

"You do look tired," Fox told her.

"I'll be all right when I've had dinner. I missed lunch."

"Why?"

She smiled at him. "Just forgot. When do we begin to get election returns?"

"Are you anxious?"

"Of course I'm anxious. Aren't you?"

"Guiltily so. Belatedly so. I realize that I haven't done the things I should have done."

"You've been here. Let's eat. My lemonade is making me giddy."

After dinner, he and Courtney elected to sit in the living room and watch the local TV station; the returns would come through that channel as soon as they were available.

"If we don't win, I'll die," Courtney assured him. She sat on her heels, and gazed steadily at the set, her hands clenched tensely, her chin thrust forward.

Fox watched her in concern. "Hey," he cautioned, "ease it off. Why are you so keyed up?"

She turned her dark eyes to his face. "Aren't you excited?" she asked.

"I've learned not to stake my whole roll on a thing like this election."

"But you have done that, haven't you?" she demanded. She got to her knees, and faced him. "Haven't you?"

"Well, Courtney . . ."

"Oh, go on and admit you are excited. I am. I really am. I've worked on this for weeks."

"Yes," drawled Fox. "I saw you with Hawthorne." His tone was as dry as sand.

She smiled at him, then threw a pillow to the floor beside his chair, and sat on it. "I was working," she assured him.

"And when you were with Hank Blair, too?" he asked.

"Oh, yes. He and I planned the whole campaign."

Fox straightened. "What campaign?" he asked roughly.

She put her hand on his, her touch was cool. "We had one," she said. "Hank and I—and the other interns as they got time off. We all five worked hard all day today. Bechars said the very last patient had left Memorial and they had no duty assignments."

They had not. "What did you do?" asked Fox, his voice strange. He felt strange.

"Well—" She waited while the announcer explained the process by which the returns would be given. And the first precinct total was recorded. Twenty-six for the bond issue, thirty-seven against.

"Out in the mountains," Fox told her. "Ranchers think any bond issue raises their taxes."

"Maybe thirty-seven of your hospital's patients live out there," said Courtney, and he laughed, shaking his head. "The issues have not been that clear," he told her.

"Oh, yes, they have," Courtney assured him. "We made them that clear. They knew—practically everybody knew—that it was a vote for or against Memorial and you."

"Courtney!"

She nodded, her face serene. "Oh, yes we did," she said. She kicked off her white shoes, and rubbed her stockinged feet with her hand. "We were at the polling places all day today. For all the days before— You see, Fox, we got copies of those petitions that were used to get this election."

"How did you do that?"

"We asked the mayor to see them."

"Pat?"

"He pointed out that anybody could see them. Not just your friends. And we made lists of the names, here in town, and out in the valley."

"Including Carolyn Cotsworth's?"

Courtney giggled. "We went to see her," she said. "Not me. Dr. Bechars. It took a little persuading to get him and Smith to work, but they did. All day today. And Hank and I—and that precious ambulance driver—"

"Almandarez?" Fox's face was incredulous.

"He talked to the Spanish," said Courtney, writing a new return on the legal tablet on the floor beside her. "We're a hundred and one ahead," she told. "We talked to every individual who had signed the petition. Well, to all whose addresses we could find—"

"But, Courtney," Fox said sharply, "not to patients!"

"Only if they were petitioners."

"And you talked to Miss Cotsworth. What results did you have there?"

"Oh, she said she knew you opposed the bond issue, but *she* thought that the single hospital would be a good thing."

Fox sat shaking his head.

"It was work," Courtney assured him. "Where do you think I've been every evening? And most days. I've put a thousand miles and more on the station wagon."

"I paid for the gas, I suppose."

"Oh, sure," she told him.

Fox leaned back in his chair. "What did you say to these people?"

"We told them what the election would mean, both ways."

"But weren't they all for Union? If they signed the petition?"

"Some were. Yes. Quite a lot said that Dr. Hawthorne and Union were a good hospital. I mean . . ."

"I know what you mean. So what did you say to them?"

"We asked them how good it was, specifically. That's where Hank shone. He knew right where to put his finger . . ."

Fox nodded; his green eyes were sparkling. "There's ninety-six plus," he told Courtney.

She wrote it down. "Then," she said, "we'd point out that Memorial was bigger, that it had room to expand, that it could get doctors and trained nurses. We spoke of the services it was equipped to give. Doing its own laundry got to a lot of people. And when they mentioned the fire, we'd say you could rebuild—that the hospital could. We didn't make much use of your name, though we did speak of Dr. Hawthorne, a lot. And a lot of people agreed that there didn't seem any sense in having a big bond issue if Memorial could reopen. They might as well keep the good hospital they already had; they sure missed it. And Almandarez did a magnificent job. He's a doll."

"Humph!" said Fox, reaching for the legal pad and marking down the latest numbers.

"He *is* wonderful," Courtney insisted. "He was. There were lots of Spanish names on those petitions."

"I'll bet he threatened those chicanos."

Courtney giggled. "I'll bet he did too. But Fox . . ."

"O.K. O.K. You did what I couldn't." He was totting up the score. "What I wouldn't."

"I could tell, that night you talked about ethics, you weren't going to make any speeches about another doctor."

He nodded, and showed her his score. The returns were coming fast. "I hope this works," he said.

"It is working."

"I can't imagine those interns—were they at the polling places?"

"Close by. They'd tell they were interns . . ."

"What did they wear? Whites and a stethoscope?"

"Oh, no, Fox! But nearly always the person they spoke to would ask if they were from Memorial. And they'd say yes, that Union didn't have interns."

He covered his face with his hand. "You really were interested," he marveled, after they had watched three commercials, and the election report resumed.

"Yes, I was," said Courtney.

"But why?" he asked. "You haven't been here long. To do all that grueling work . . ."

"I did it because *you* were interested. That's the reason."

To his own surprise, he could feel her excitement, know her enthusiasm, and in turn, he was stirred. The feeling was pleasant. "Are you going to celebrate if the bond issue loses?" he asked.

"Are you?"

"Well, I'll be relieved."

Courtney hugged her knees. "The trouble with you, Fox Creighton," she said, "is that you've got into the way of thinking old."

"What?" He looked at her alertly.

"Yes, you have," she said. "You've been doing your father's job here at the hospital. You took it on—you told me about that—and you thought you had to approach it like a man of at least fifty."

"Methuselah Creighton," he said dryly.

"Well, not really." She spoke very earnestly. "But your point of view does need adjusting. Your friend Pat Kern knows this, and he's good for you. My friend Hank Blair knows it, and he's been good for me."

"Possibly he'd be good for me too. I can see the point you're making, Courtney."

"Well, I'm glad you can. I worry when I realize that your best professional friend is Miss Tunstall, the nurse."

"She's a loyal, wonderful person, Courtney."

"I know she is. But as a friend, she needs some youthful relief."

"Which certainly you can give."

She looked quickly up into his face. No, he was not being sarcastic. She nodded. "And there's Dr. Blair," she said again.

"I like Blair. I was planning to keep him on at Memorial."

"That's good. You should get to know him better. Then, there's Dr. Belze."

"Belze?" He was genuinely surprised.

"Yes. You two could be friends . . ."

For several minutes, Fox said nothing. The returns were nearly all in; the bond issue had been defeated. Courtney turned off the TV.

"Do you think," he asked when she sat down again, "that I should let my hair grow?"

She drew a moon face on her legal pad. "You're laughing at me."

"Not me," he said quickly. "I wouldn't dare. What you kids have accomplished tonight shows me that you have your Ph.D. in this."

"Don't call us *kids*. Hank is thirty. But we do have a lot of nerve. We've ventured too far, maybe . . ."

"Oh, no. Because I realize—I've realized it, but the light has dawned. Except for Tunnie, Courtney, I've had no one here to criticize me and advise me. And any man needs that."

"I'm close to concluding that you didn't need me. Maybe the election would have gone this way without my barging in. You can run a big hospital, surely you can run your own life."

His hand fell to her shoulder. "I've done a fair job," he said. "A pretty good one at the hospital, but less than good personally. So—*fair* is the rating. I could have done better than that—it would have been easier on me. I can see that."

She laid her cheek against his hand. "I'm glad we won,"

He stood up. "You're dead-tired. I suggest you go to bed and sleep the clock around. I'm going to the hospital."

Chapter Nine

THAT NIGHT, every home in Carson—in almost every home—the TV screen glowed brightly, and people talked, score boards were shown like beautiful scenery, or horror pictures of a battlefield, depending on how one's interests ran. Vil Belze sat before the television set in the family room of his home. Jane was bathing the twins, and putting them to bed, always a lengthy process. He could hear the chatter and the clatter of the ritual. He himself had performed it often enough to know exactly what went on, what still must be done. He would sit here alone for another twenty minutes, at least.

Jane was staying pretty close these days, and nights. She and her husband had not yet spoken of the night when he had taken her out of that motel, and brought her home. Perhaps she had seen Forrest and talked to him. She could have, when Vil was busy at the clinic or the hospital. They could have made some plans.

Dr. Belze would not be busy tonight, and he was glad. Relieved was a better word. The way the vote was going perhaps work would shortly resume for him. But tonight the hospital would be dark; it would make no call upon the Chief Surgeon. He was relieved not to have to steel himself to work. These days, even his clinic work was a strain.

That damn lawsuit of Forrest's hung over him like a cloud of debilitating gas. He would fight the suit in court, but just now his every instinct was to fight the man with his fists. Though what good would that do?

There still would be Jane. She was fully as guilty as Forrest was. She knew it. Having failed in his appeal to Walter, she was the only one who could clear Vil of the charge

184

of negligence. If she would even go to Fox Creighton and tell him the truth; she could tell where Dr. Belze was that night, that he had been out of touch with the hospital because he was doing what any man would do under the circumstances . . . That the other man was the same one preferring charges made the whole lawsuit ridiculous. If the truth were known.

* * *

Fox did go to the hospital, more for reassurance that the place was still there, and waiting for the busy-ness that he would consider, plan, and very soon set in motion. He spoke to the watchman, he went into his office, and took a folder from his desk drawer. It was labeled Plan Number One. There was a Plan Number Two but he did not give it a glance. There was no need now to abandon the hospital, close his home, find some solution for Courtney . . .

Plan Number One was a thick folder. If implemented, tonight might well be his last free time.

He read it through, then put it back into the desk drawer, turned off the lights and drove home again. There was lamplight behind Courtney's curtained windows. The dogs came running to him, and he patted them, then walked down the road with them, letting them run across the fields, calling them back. He enjoyed the walk as much as they did. The stars blazed white hot, and seemed close at hand. A curved moon lay upon the mountaintops. Now and then a car would come long this road which led to homes like his own, set into acres of desert land, gardens and orchards.

Plan Number One would get thicker, if he were not careful. Another car was coming, and he ordered the dogs to heel as he stepped into the ditch, and cursed below his breath. This was just the night to meet up with Perry Hawthorne.

He hoped the big car would sweep by in its cloud of dust, but no such luck. Hawthorne saw him, recognized him, and backed up. "I was going to your house," Dr. Hawthorne told him.

Fox could think of nothing to say to that announcement.

"I realize that you have been taking the bond issue thing as a personal contest between you and me, Creighton."

"Shouldn't I have taken it that way?" Fox asked, hearing his father's voice in his, remembering Courtney's charge. He relaxed the stiffness in his spine, softened it in his tone. "I considered it a time for a good fight, Hawthorne."

"All right. You fought that good fight, and you won. I was on my way to congratulate you."

"No need for that . . ."

"I felt there was. After the way you tried to help Christie, I should have called the whole thing off."

"Could you have done that?"

"I could have tried. You—"

"Look. I am dreadfully sorry about your daughter's death. It was a tragic thing. But nothing was done, or could be done, for her."

"I accept that," said the father. "I blame myself for not knowing her condition earlier. I knew she was small, and tired easily—I wish I had been a better doctor, a good doctor where she was concerned."

"I'm sorry," Fox said again. "And so is Dr. Belze, I feel sure."

"He's a good surgeon, isn't he?"

"I think so."

"He had one advantage. The case was not a personal thing with him, as I made it for myself. And for you too."

"Oh, no! I never make a medical case a personal thing, Hawthorne. I approach them first, last, and always as a doctor. Only."

"I guess I have to believe you. Otherwise you wouldn't have taken my girl in."

Fox sighed, and wished the man would drive on.

"Are you going to reopen Memorial now?" Hawthorne asked him.

"I could. We'd need extensive repairs, and we'd like to expand."

"So would Union," said the other doctor. "I suspect it's the hospital which should close down."

"Oh, don't do that!" Fox cried. "This vote tonight—over nine hundred people backed you up. They probably want exactly what you give them."

"I guess so. And we make money. But you'll rebuild . . ."

"And add that other wing too?"

"Maybe. You have the money, don't you?"

"I don't know. Of course just the details of reopening, letting contracts for repair, working around the hole in our guts—I won't have time to get into mischief for a month or two."

"It would be a job," Hawthorne agreed. "Well—hold your dogs. I'll turn and go back—or could I give you a lift?"

"Thank you, no. I was getting some pre-bedtime exercise."

"Sure." the headlights went on. "By the way, how's Courtney?" he asked.

Fox felt his every muscle harden; his head went up and back. For this—this *creature*—to speak so familiarly . . . "She was well when I left the house two hours ago," he said stiffly.

The engine started silkily. The doctor's car was a fine one. "Don't tell me you're all doctor there too, Creighton."

Fox was furious. He was sure his face betrayed him. It was only by a great exertion that he said nothing. He held the dogs' collars and stepped off the road.

"How old are you, Doc?" Hawthorne called.

"If you'll excuse me, it's getting cold."

"It does that out here on the desert. Good night, Doc."

Fox waited until the dust had subsided, then, with the dogs set free, he began to run up the road, toward his home. What Hawthorne had said—implied—was what Courtney had said.

Though age had nothing to do with how Fox felt toward Hawthorne, or his hospital—or Courtney.

He went into the house, and upstairs. Knowing that the way he looked at his age had a great deal to do with—everything.

At noon the next day, the Carson Town Council met to canvas the bond election votes, and to decide what the district now would do about a hospital. Pat Kern, of course, was presiding and for ten minutes he listened to some rather heated talk about their city's need for a hospital, about Fox Creighton's not having any right to close Memorial. It was licensed by the State, wasn't it? Couldn't he lose that license?

Seeing that he was expected to answer, the mayor said that the councilmen seemed to forget that Memorial Hospital was a private institution.

So was Union.

Not in the same way. In applying for nonprofit status which gave them tax relief, Union had obligated itself in various ways to the community. The city attorney could brief them on such things. As, the mayor suspected, their own capable attorneys could tell them about Memorial's obligations.

"Damn it, Pat, we need the place open and running, if

only to handle emergencies. Now you call the police and tell them you need an ambulance, they say to call Union. We just plain got to have a hospital and right now!"

"Oh, I agree with you," said the mayor. "Could you tell us how we should go about it?"

"No, but the cream on your whiskers says *you* have an idea."

Pat laughed. "I asked Fox Creighton to come down here and discuss the matter," he confessed.

He got up, went out of the room, and returned with Fox whose face and manner were bland. The mayor explained the situation to him saying that since the bond issue had failed to get the majority of votes, and since Memorial Hospital had been closed, the Council was ready to examine means to secure adequate hospital care for the city, and its immediate neighbors.

"That could be a problem," Dr. Creighton agreed. He wore a blue denim jacket and trousers, tailored well, fitting his lean body precisely. The red and white handkerchief at his throat was silk, and his boots were handmade, of glovelike leather. His audience appreciated the costume.

"I will remind you," said the doctor, "that Carson does have Union Hospital."

"But we had yours, too."

Fox smiled.

"I know we played the damn fool and set up a vote to get another hospital it would take two years to build."

Fox waited.

"All right," said the councilman. "We were wrong. We knew we were wrong when we called that election."

"You had no choice, did you?"

"It didn't seem so at the time. But now—well, the simple truth is, Doc, we need Memorial Hospital. We need it right now!"

Fox stood up. "It's available," he said quietly.

"This minute, Doc?"

"Oh, there are details. Like a boiler, the steam has to be built up. Suppose you attend to such details as are in your jurisdiction, and I'll go back, talk to the Board, and maybe unlock the front door." He walked out of the room, the light shining on his red head.

"Did he promise us something?" asked one of the men, looking anxiously at the mayor.

"No more and no less than he's always promised you," said Pat. "A good hospital, if you want it."

Fox went back to the hospital, to his office. He took off his jacket and got out Plan Number One, opened the folder on the desk blotter. Plan Number Two he threw into the wastebasket.

He had his secretary and the switchboard operator busy when Marion Clark and Alice Tunstall came into the room. Fox looked up and frowned. "I said tomorrow morning," he protested.

The women gestured at their garments. Alice in a gray and white striped suit, Marion in a red shirt and black slacks. "Tomorrow morning," Marion agreed. "Ready to work. But today, Fox . . ."

"Today I am as busy as three flea-bitten dogs," Fox assured them.

"We won't take long," said Alice. "if you'll let us say what we came to say."

He frowned, then sighed, and finally laughed. He threw his pencil down, and rubbed his hand through his hair. "Let's have it," he agreed.

The women sat down. Both were smiling. "You tell him the goodie part," Alice told Marion.

"All right," she agreed, leaning toward Fox. "Do you know what Laura Ann and Maggie plan to do with the money their grandfather willed them, Fox?"

"Yes. You and George got cut in.

Marion looked shocked.

"He's teasing you," warned Alice. "Tell your story."

"All right, but I wouldn't want you to think, Fox . . ."

"I don't," he assured her. "Now tell me what Nancy has cooked up. At seventeen, she could produce a dandy idea."

"At seventeen, she just has," said Marion with vigor. "Fox, that girl—she went up to Alice's at the crack of dawn this morning . . ."

"Eight-thirty," said Alice.

"For Nancy, that's when dawn cracks. But that girl actually asked Tunnie here how much it would cost for her to train to be a doctor."

"A doctor like Marion," said Alice huskily.

Fox was smiling as widely as they were. "But that's great!" he agreed. "Really great."

"And we all feel just wonderful about it," said Marion, her eyes misty.

"She'll make it. Thanks for telling me. Let's see. I'll mark her down for an internship nine years from now."

"You'll just about get Memorial started up by then," said Marion.

"I should," he agreed.

"You're calling the personnel and staff back . . ."

"And I have a Board meeting lined up."

"When do you think we'll admit patients and get to work?" Fox shrugged. "That depends on the town," he said.

"I see. You're going to let them sweat."

Fox smiled at her. "When you girls came in, you indicated that you had more than one goodie to bring me."

"Only one goodie," said Marion.

"All right, let's have the not-so-good."

"Well, have you talked to the Cotsworths lately, Fox?"

"Why should I?"

"Did you tell Carolyn to report in tomorrow?"

"As a matter of fact, I didn't. I thought I should talk to her first."

"About hospital matters, that would be."

"You have something else on your mind?"

Marion and Tunnie looked at each other. Fox stood up and took his denim jacket from the clothes tree. "Let's go," he said. "I'll ride back to the apartment with you. I won't take my well-known car."

"The way you're dressed you could be riding your Appaloosa."

Fox buttoned the jacket. "You don't like this outfit?"

"I like it. And my girls would flip. All three of them."

"Fair enough." He herded the women before him out of the office. "Be back in an hour," he told his secretary.

"Do you think," he asked when they were in the car, "that you could get Virginia to one of your places?"

Marion looked at him. *"Virginia!"* she echoed.

"Watch the road. Yes, Virginia. I have something to say to her."

"She'll come up to my apartment," said Tunnie, "if I ask her, and we wouldn't have the interruptions there."

"And how!" agreed Marion. "Can we listen to what you have to say?"

"You might as well."

They managed to get up to Alice's apartment without meeting Carolyn, though what she might have seen from the windows was anyone's surmise. Alice unlocked her door, told them to go in; she'd go downstairs again and fetch Virginia.

This took a little time. Virginia was puzzled. She could not imagine what Dr. Creighton might have to say to her. But, oh, yes, of course she would go up. Carolyn was out, but she'd leave a note for her."

"All right. But don't mention Fox."

"No, I'll just say where I am."

This was accomplished; Virginia powdered her nose and brushed her hair. "Oh, come *on!*" cried Tunnie. "Fox is a busy man!"

"Of course he is. That's why . . ."

Alice almost dragged her up the steps. They found Marion and Fox in the kitchen, eating crackers and cheese. Invited to join them, Virginia smiled shyly. "I had a big lunch," she said.

Alice got out ginger ale, then she too sat at the table.

"Fox?" she prodded him. "Virginia left a note, telling Carolyn where she would be."

"I see. Well, I did have some things to say, Mrs. Shelton. If you remember a certain problem concerning your sister's will was brought to me."

"Yes, I know," said Virginia. "But—do you know what she is planning to do, Dr. Creighton? Carolyn, I mean."

"Heavens, no," he said. Marion and Alice were looking at her apprehensively.

"She says she's going to work at Union Hospital. She says there is good work to be done there."

"I am sure there is," Fox agreed, his face like a rock. Marion's and Tunnie's were torn by a half dozen emotions. Surprise, amusement—apprehension again. "And I think her decision is a good one. She would want to stay here in Carson probably, and we shan't be needing her services."

"Aren't you going to open Memorial ever again, Dr. Creighton?" Virginia asked.

"Oh, yes. But we shan't have Carolyn in employment *ever again.*"

"I see."

"I hope you do, dear. Tell me, do you have to live here with Carolyn?"

"Do you mean financially?"

"Partly that. Mainly, are there sentimental reasons, any feelings of loyalty, that make you . . ."

"No, there are not. I can live anywhere I like. Maybe in

the same town where my daughter lives . . . not with her, of course."

"Wouldn't she be glad to have you?"

"Yes, she says she would."

"I think you should make such plans, Virginia. Because, in considering your situation here, with Carolyn, I am ready to advise you to fight your sister on that will business. I would suggest a lawyer, I would give any testimony I could —your friends would. If Carolyn has committed a felony, she should be brought to account."

Virginia's face was white, then her cheeks burned poppy red. "Oh, nobody has ever fought Carolyn," she whispered.

Fox stood up. "Then it is high time someone did. You'd have a lot of support in this, my dear. And of course you are the only one to begin this suit. The executors of the will would help, I feel sure."

He pressed her shoulder; Marion stood up. "Stay with her," said Alice. "I'll drive Fox back to the hospital."

"She won't fight Carolyn," said Fox, as they drove along.

"I never knew you to involve yourself this way," Alice told him.

"But I do think she'll move," Fox continued.

"It just isn't like you, Fox."

"How," he asked brusquely, "does one avoid involvement? We live in each other's pockets. I never would have expected to get involved with Perry Hawthorne."

"Oh, but that worked out so well!"

"I hope so. And I hope the Cotsworth tangle straightens out too."

"To some extent, it will."

Fox began to chuckle, and Alice glanced at him. "I'm just speculating," he said, "on Carolyn's adventures in Hawthorne's hospital."

"You think maybe they deserve each other!"

"That too. But I think, for once, our wonderful Carolyn is going to be put down a notch."

"Or even two." And Alice also began to smile.

Chapter Ten

HE THANKED Tunnie for bringing him "home." She caught the word and smiled at him. "Finally," she murmured.

"Oh, go about your business!" he cried. "I have a Board meeting."

"I see the cars. And Pat Kern's too."

"He's just being nosy."

"You don't want me to stay?"

"No. I'll stop by afterward and tell you what happens."

The Board members were gathered, Pat Kern with them, in the front hall of the hospital. "Do you have business here?" Fox asked his friend rudely.

"I hope so."

Fox greeted the Board members. When all had assembled, the chairman suggested a tour of the hospital. "You've seen it," said Fox.

"Many times. Even after the fire. We think we should make this tour with a view to the possibilities for reopening, for repair, and possibly additional building."

Fox's eyebrow went up. "Then let's start."

They made the tour, nine men, and three women, of the Board. The mayor, Fox, and the hospital administrator. Then they went back to Fox's office where chairs had been brought in. He gave his desk to the chairman, and went to sit beside Pat Kern.

The chairman had a few comments to make. He mentioned the insurance appraisal, and the money available for repair. He said that he expected little disagreement with his opinion that the hospital should be working again. "Could we, Fox?"

He shrugged. "Under restricted conditions," he agreed. "How about personnel?"

"With a few exceptions, they are on stand-by orders. We had patients here until only a week ago, though we have not admitted any for some time."

"I see. Then you could be operative."

"Yes. I think so. For a time, anyway."

"For the time it would take to make repairs and replace equipment?"

"Yes, sir. That would be, I estimate, six months."

"What about expansion?"

Fox's head lifted. "I have dreams, and architect's plans, for expansion, sir. But the money . . ." He shook his head.

"Are your plans of the sort—say, could we begin with a unit, keeping future ideas and plans in mind, and work toward them?"

Fox frowned. "Well, we could build a third floor to extend over the two wings we already have, move all our surgical and maternity cases up there. We could build wings back into what is now the parking area, or forward across the front lawn. One wing, or two. Start with basement and first floor, later add one or two other floors. These would accommodate the services we need and will need. Clinics, outpatient services, physiotherapy, more pediatric beds. Orthopedic. I have the plans."

"Would your architect be available for specifics as to cost and time?" asked the chairman.

Fox frowned. "Everything would be available, sir, except the money to do those things, or even to begin. One two-story wing could cost five hundred thousand dollars. The third floor additions would cost that . . ."

"One million, five hundred thousand, would cover your whole idea," said Pat Kern musingly.

Fox looked at him, turning in his chair to do it.

"How many beds would you add, Fox?" Pat asked him coolly.

"Seventy-five, over all. But the main addition—"

"I know. Would be services. Could you accept this idea, Dr. Creighton? To go ahead with the repair of the hospital, get your architect to draw comprehensive plans . . ."

"I have those."

"With pictures?"

"Renderings they are called. Yes, I have them."

"Paid for out of your own pocket?"

"Well . . ." Fox got red. "It's none of your damned business!" he shouted.

Everyone in the room laughed, and he managed a grudging smile. "I'm sorry, Pat."

"It's O.K. You've yelled at me before. What I'm getting at: as you saw for yourself earlier today, the City Council wants hospital service for Carson. We have some funds available, and we could get more funds. Through revenue bonds, or a special tax—to give us the service we need now, and will need as the town grows. We have prospects that it will grow. Would you accept this sort of help from the city?"

"Are you asking me or the Board?"

"We're asking you because we want you to continue on as Chief of Medical Services."

"I see." Fox sat thoughtful. Then he cocked an eye at his friend. Everyone was watching him. "We just beat a bond issue election that would have meant Government red tape . . ."

"We are talking about local involvement, not Federal bureaucratic takeover. Perhaps the banks would invest in such a project, industry, and, along with the city, own stock, sit on the Board. It would be quite different from a Federal hospital. This would be locally owned and run, with the interests of our locality always in mind. If you could get us a model of the proposed hospital, if we would stage a proper campaign, Carson would get its own larger hospital, with you in charge."

"I'm one man, Pat . . ."

"You'd like to get us started, wouldn't you?"

"I'd sure try."

"All right. Any plan we'd work up would give the present Board, or its individual successors, a big voice, along with citizen members—though I think your present members can be called citizens, and civic-minded."

Fox nodeed. "Of course they are. Me too, if you'll believe that. It's just that medicine . . ."

"I know. And we'd give you authority as Medical Services Chief, we'd keep hands off. If that would be what you want."

"With a good medical staff, yes, it would be what I'd want, and have to have." He got up and walked about the room, every eye upon him. "We always did need to enlarge," he said at last, as if persuading himself. "Ever since I came here I've known that. We could give real service to the town, and to the outlying areas." He whirled and faced

Pat, almost accusingly. "You didn't mean the whole thing?" he demanded. "Two wings, *and* the third floor?"

Pat laughed. "The whole thing, you crazy goat. I am sure we could swing it. So—how soon can we tell people? I know a woman who is holding back having her baby until she knows Memorial is back in business."

"Can she wait until tomorrow?" Fox asked, and grinned at the sigh of relief that swept the room. "One thing I'd like to clear up," he said. "One thing for now, that is. If you can be so sure, Pat, that the city will do this, why did we ever get into Hawthorne's bond election?"

"Or have a fire?" asked Pat, keenly watching his friend.

Fox stood frowning, slim, tall, and strong in his blue denims. He fingered the handkerchief at his throat.

"The people needed to be scared," said the mayor, "and they were scared, but good, by the weeks you gave them of doing without Memorial."

"Well, the fire scared me!" said Fox. "I guess we needed that too, eh?"

"Oh, now, doctor . . ." protested the administrator.

Pat put up his hand. "I'll agree that you did need the fire," he said.

"I don't think you set it."

"I've not the guts. But I did see where we might use it. And Hawthorne's election, too. Now you and the city will be together on this."

"I shouldn't be listed as essential," said Fox thoughtfully.

"You won't be *listed*. But if the new Board can count on your continuing as medical officer, if no change there is announced . . ."

"Would you have abandoned this opportunity on my say-so?" Fox demanded.

"You know how the expansion should be carried out, Dr. Creighton," said the Board chairman. "We only know the results we'd like to have."

Fox nodded. "Fine. Then we'll get right on with it. We'll open tomorrow, and we'll start to repair. With the certain prospect of new building, we'll make our plans accordingly. I'll have a medical staff meeting tomorrow morning. Oh, we'll be having lots and lots of meetings!"

"You have a fine staff here."

"We do. Miss Cotsworth and Dr. Forrest have both resigned. Both were capable people, but they can be replaced.

We'll need more fine and capable people, of course, and we'll get them."

Pat Kern stood up. "I'll report to the Council. You'll have some of your meetings with them, and the people we expect to cooperate with us. The Council and I are excited about this thing, Fox. And unless you set the fire deliberately, we feel as if Providence had stepped in to solve the medical problems of Carson."

"It must have been Providence," said Fox, "though I am glad such help was available. And I'll say that I am glad to be getting back to work. Will you make an announcement, Pat?"

"Yes, tomorrow morning. When we can say the hospital is in operation. We'll want you and the chairman of the Board to join me for that announcement."

It took another hour. There was excited talk; Fox's rolls of plans were got out and examined. He then phoned the architect in Denver . . . But finally he could start home after what seemed to have been an endless and ultra-busy day. He stopped at the "sorority house" to tell Tunnie and Marion to report to the hospital for duty the next day.

"With patients?" asked Marion in surprise.

"They'll be coming. I'll have a notice in tonight's paper, and on the radio, that we'll be open. I've contacted everyone I could. We'll have a full staff meeting first thing tomorrow."

"Big news, Fox?" asked Tunnie.

"Big enough. You'll like it."

"I know I shall; you seem to. Marion, tell him our news!"

"Oh, yes," she said. "It may not equal yours, but, as you say, I think you'll like it. After you left, Virginia Shelton told me that she had decided she would move out of Carolyn's apartment, that Carolyn wouldn't need her share of the expenses, and that she was going to go to the lawyers in Los Hermanos—tomorrow, she said—and tell them about the will, what she knew and suspected."

"They'll have a record of that special delivery letter," said Fox. "And I am glad if she will make the fight. I'll help her if I can."

"You're going to be busy at other things, aren't you?" asked Tunnie slyly.

"I hope to be," he answered so smugly that the women laughed.

"If she does these things," said Marion, "Virginia is resigned to the fact that Carolyn will find a way to punish her."

"How in the world will she do that?" Fox asked.

"Oh, she can," Marion assured him. "Remember, she's a wonderful woman."

Fox sighed, and ran his fingers through his thatch of red hair. "How," he asked, "did we ever get into all the things we have been into this past month? Death, wills, fires . . ."

"And life," said Tunnie quietly.

Fox nodded. "I suppose you're right." He stood up to leave. "Did I tell you, Marion, that I was pleased at your news about Nancy?"

"You mean the money and her study of medicine. Oh, yes. I'm very happy about that myself. I think she'll stick to it, too."

"And you can begin to live some sort of life of your own."

"But I do live my own life!" she protested.

"No, you don't. Everything you have been doing has been for the girls."

"Because I wanted to."

"All right. But now I think you should divorce George . . ."

"I can't do that, Fox. George needs me. He has nothing in this world to lean on except the knowledge that I am here. Something firm and reliable."

Fox opened his lips to reply, then he shook his head. A month ago he would have answered her quickly, assuredly. "Nobody should *need* another person," he would have said. But now . . .

"O.K.," he said. "I'll see you girls tomorrow."

He left, and Marion and Alice looked at each other in surprise. "What's got into him?" asked Marion.

"I think I know," said Alice. "So I am going upstairs, Marion. I have things to do before tomorrow, plans to make."

That evening, which was a hot one, with a strong wind coming down from the mountains and bringing dust with it, Vil Belze brought the children indoors, and closed the house, relying on the air conditioning to keep them comfortable. Jane protested, but he mentioned the dust, and she shrugged.

"It's their bedtime anyway," said the doctor. "I'll attend to that if you like."

But the telephone rang, and, by habit, he answered. So Jane took the twins back to their room. When she returned, she found Vil sitting thoughtful over some papers. "Budget?" she asked.

He glanced at her. "Not ours. I just heard that the hospital will be open tomorrow for patient admission."

"But aren't their operating rooms still out of commission?"

"They are. We'll make do with Emergency, though repair is to start immediately, and some expansion as well."

"Oh?" She picked up a magazine.

"It seems a rather large industry is coming to Carson, with adequate hospital service a requirement. So we are building. Dr. Creighton asked me if I would be Chief of Surgical Services, which will involve supervising the new surgical facilities, the repair of our two old o.r.'s and the addition of another. I am to be consultant in those things."

"Well! You seem to be doing all right."

"I hope so. I'll need to get some new surgeons. Forrest has resigned." He did not look up from his papers.

Jane stiffened, and the magazine slipped from her lap. "Who told you that?" she asked sharply.

"Didn't he tell you?" asked her husband.

She made no reply, but sat, biting her lip, and tapping her slipper toe against the end of the heavy oak coffee table.

"I think it was by request," Vil said.

"You seem to be riding high at Memorial," Jane told him, her tone waspish.

"I would like to think so. I would like to think I could stay on there, and do the work Dr. Creighton is asking me to do."

"Can't you?"

"That depends on you, Jane."

"Why on me?" Jane Belze had a classically beautiful face, high cheekbones, perfect nose, eyes well set. She skinned her light brown hair severely back to display this beauty.

"I would like you to tell Creighton why I was not at the hospital, why I could not be located, the night Dorothy was hurt and died."

Jane shook her head. "You know I won't do that."

"I think you should."

"I can see why you think so, but for my part . . ."

"Has Forrest tried to see you since that night? Has he told you that he was asked to resign from Memorial?"

"What difference does that make? I haven't tried to see him. There's talk enough."

"I know there is talk. About his lawsuit, and about me. That is why . . ."

Jane got up from the deep couch. "I won't do it," she said.

"Then I am going out to Creighton's . . ."

"To tell him yourself?"

"No. Just that I am going to have to leave Carson."

This startled her. "But you can't, Vil!"

He shrugged. "I can't. But I'll have to. I'll be at Fox's for about an hour, I think. Any calls . . ." He was outside, and going to his car.

Nostalgia already had seized him. He did not want to leave Carson; he did not want to leave his pretty home, or the hospital, his clinic office. He would miss his occasional visit to the Creighton home, that gracious place of sweeping drive, wide lawns, clustered trees, and the lantern-light above the wide front door.

Story admitted him, and Fox came at once into the living room. "I have been chained to the telephone," he said.

"I know you are busy . . ."

"You can't believe how busy. I am making lists of lists. Do you realize what is going on, Belze?"

"You gave me a slight idea, and I wish I could be part of it."

"But—"

"Yes, I told you that I would be. But then I was counting on Jane's agreement to tell you about the night when Dorothy Forrest was killed."

Fox made a wry face, and shook his head. "Can't we forget that night?"

"You, maybe. Me, never. But I did hope—Though, since my wife won't help me, Fox, I just cannot stay on in Carson."

"Well, you just cannot leave me now. So suppose you tell me what happened that night."

"I'll sound like a whining, injured fool."

"All right. I wouldn't recognize you, but let's have it. No holds barred. Would you like a drink first?"

"No." Dr. Belze sat hunched forward in his chair; before he finished, he was pacing the carpet, Fox watching him. He told the whole thing. His ignorance that his wife and best friend were betraying him, his unwillingness to believe

Dorothy when she came to him with the story. He told of the second night, the woman on the road with a gun—his own search—not knowing that Dorothy had wrecked her car. He had found Jane's Jaguar, and Forrest's . . .

"I went to every room in that motel unit," he told. "I still can see those flat doors. Pink, yellow, green—and I found them. My wife wrapped in a blanket, my friend—"

Fox got up and mixed a drink, brought it to Dr. Belze. "If you tell that story in court . . ." he said.

"I don't plan to tell it in court. Forrest knows I could tell it and prove the facts. He knows I won't tell it. He expects me to settle the damned lawsuit and keep silent."

"I told you that he was no longer to be on our staff."

"I know. But the suit . . . If Jane would tell the story, clear my name . . . She could, and there would be no lawsuit."

"And you feel one would embarrass us at this time?"

"Wouldn't it?"

"Yes. It would. So you have to make her tell."

"How can I?" asked Vil, drinking deep from the highball glass.

"Fight her. Be rough with her. Play dirty if you must."

"It won't do any good."

"It will do good. A couple of kids showed me this week that fighting solves things, Belze, when the right is on your side. I'll even predict that Jane will love you for doing it.' "

"Agggh!"

"Try it, and see."

"She's probably with him right now."

"With Forrest? Not likely. He's left town."

Belze thought about that. Jane had not seen nor heard from him; she had not known that he'd been asked to resign; she wouldn't know that he'd left . . .

"Did you know all this story," he asked Fox, "before I told you?"

"No. But I knew that Forrest was not behaving as a doctor should, or as a friend should. A Chief of Services has all sorts of problems, Belze. Handling cases like Forrest need not be one of them."

"No, it shouldn't." Vil stood up.

Fox held out his hand. "I'll see you at staff meeting tomorrow morning."

"I hope so. A lot depends on how I come out with rough-talking my wife."

"I'll see you," said Fox.

* * *

The full staff meeting took place the next morning, and left the hospital personnel too stunned, too delighted, too excited, to spoil the TV announcement that was made by the mayor, Dr. Creighton and the chairman of the Board at eleven o'clock.

But, the night before, Miss Tunstall had decided on her course of action, and the excitement of that morning only gave her increased determination to take a hand in Fox Creighton's affairs. He probably would solve this particular thing for himself, but just now, especially, she wanted to make sure that he would.

She talked to Courtney on the telephone, and when Fox returned to the hospital in the early afternoon—there had been a lengthy meeting over lunch with bankers, politicians, the Denver architect, the Council members, Fox and Pat Kern—Miss Tunstall's name was first on the list of the appointments his secretary had made for him.

He was not suspicious. The supervisor of nursing services well could have items to take up with him. "Ask Miss Tunstall to come in," he said readily, busy with straightening his desk, and glancing at his mail.

He looked up, smiling, at the nurse in her sparkling white. "It's good to see you back in uniform," he said.

"Yes, doctor. I—"

"Did you think our news was exciting this morning?"

"Oh, of course. I just hope I can find nurses to keep pace with you."

"You will. We think now, Tunnie, that we can get local financing and won't need a city election for a bond issue. Of course the city will give us the two hundred thousand it has—from its new-industry funds, you see—and—"

"Fox."

He looked up at her. "I'm rattling?"

"A little, and I enjoy it. I think we'll do a lot of enjoyable talking before we're through."

"But just now you have other business."

"Well, yes, I do. So if I could have your attention . . ."

"You have it." He leaned back in his chair. Today he had worn a navy blue suit with a light blue shirt and a dark green tie. He now wore a white jacket over the shirt.

"I talked to Courtney this morning," said Alice.

"I told her at breakfast what was happening."

"She said you had. She was very happy about the hospital."

"I think she was. She's going to come down here and work."

"Yes, I know that, too. I think it's a fine idea. And I hope you will think my idea is a good one."

"Oh, I probably shall. What is it?"

"I am going to take Courtney into my apartment. To live with me."

The smile faded from Fox's eyes. Mentally he repeated what Tunnie had said. Then he leaned forward across his desk. "But why?" he asked.

"You're going to be most awfully busy for the next months. There's going to be a great deal of busy talk-talk in town about the hospital expansion. And if Courtney is living with me, things will be more proper where you are concerned. You should not be hampered, or even bothered, by gossip just now."

Fox laughed. He threw his pencil down on his desk, leaned back in his chair, and laughed aloud. "Well, good old Queen Victoria Tunstall!" he said.

Alice smiled ruefully. "With the things I see going on today, I find a great attraction in the Victorian, Fox."

"As a matter of fact, I often do too. But, Tunnie, have you forgotten the Storys?"

"No. I haven't."

"And Courtney is with me just for the summer vacation months."

Alice said nothing.

Fox flushed, and anger burned in his eyes, etched deep lines about his mouth. Then his face got redder, and redder than that. "O.K.!" he shouted. "Have it your way! It might be better, if you think so."

"It's not what *I* think that matters, Fox."

"But, good Lord, Tunnie, I'm twice that girl's age!"

"You're not, just for the record. Though age has nothing to do with it. Courtney—any woman—why, Fox, there isn't a female in this hospital, of any age, who wouldn't marry you, given the chance!"

"Agggh!"

Tunnie nodded. "I know. You don't want any of them. And I don't blame you."

Fox smiled at her. "You're not so bad," he told her.

She stood up. "Thank you very much. Well—come to see us, doctor."

He walked with her to the door. "You or Courtney?"

"Both of us. We'll both be there. Along with the Cotsworth sisters."

"But Virginia . . ."

"She won't leave. The two of them may quarrel; Virginia will tell us what she knows. But she won't leave Carolyn alone."

"Mhmmmn," said Fox musingly. "You know, that's a very strange thing . . ."

"Oh, our apartment house is strange."

"I'd say it was just about the most respectable in town."

"And you think, these days, that isn't strange?" She touched his forearm. "Get back to work, Fox. I'll go help Courtney move."

"Tell her to keep and use the station wagon. Have you told her, Tunnie—will you tell her why you want her to move?"

"She knows."

"I suppose she does. Well—tell her I'm coming to see her."

"She'll know that too."

By six o'clock, the move had been accomplished, and Courtney was sitting across from Miss Tunstall, eating strawberries as the dessert for their dinner. The evening sky was a tender blue, the little-sheep clouds over the mountains were beginning to glow. Then the front door opened, and Carolyn Cotsworth came bouncing in, a plate of her pretty cookies in her hand.

"To welcome Courtney!" she announced brightly.

"Thank you," said Courtney. "It was a lovely thing for you to do."

Carolyn stayed with them for perhaps five minutes. She did not mention Virginia, nor Memorial Hospital. She left, saying that she had a meeting at the church.

Courtney escorted her to the door, thanked her again for the cookies. When she returned to the dining room, Alice was taking the plate of them to the kitchen and was opening the white pail marked Trash. The cookies slipped off the plate in a little stream, and Alice closed the pail.

She looked calmly up at the startled young girl. "Hasn't Fox taught you to fight infection?" she asked.

Courtney looked very puzzled. "The cookies were pretty . . ." she murmured.

"I know. But molds, fungus—they can be beautiful, lovely—and poisonous."

Courtney finished eating her strawberries. She looked sad. "Fox hasn't made any attempt to teach me much of anything," she said, as if she reminded herself. "I don't know that he even likes me, Miss Tunstall."

"Oh, nonsense!" cried Alice. She began to clear the table, and Courtney said she wanted to wash the dishes.

"There's a dishwasher."

"All right. But I'll clean things up. I can. I really can."

"I'll believe you, child."

"You know," said Courtney, busy at the sink, "When I first saw Fox Creighton, I fell immediately in love with him."

"Every woman does that, Courtney. I told him just today that he could marry any one of all the females in his hospital."

"Including you?" asked Courtney, smiling mischievously.

"Oh, sure. Including me."

"But I can't marry him," said the girl in the red and white dress. "Though I told him that I loved him . . ."

"You didn't!" said Alice, laughing.

Courtney looked up. "Why not? Was it the wrong thing to say to him?"

"Well . . ." said Alice. "What did he say to you?"

"He laughed at me."

"Then what happened?"

"When he first brought me to his home, he ignored me."

"He's a very busy man, Courtney. And especially since you've been here. Not that you were to blame."

"I know. Then—after that, he scolded me."

"What for?"

"Well, for following him to the hospital. And for having a date with Hank Blair."

Alice shook her head.

"But, finally," said Courtney, snapping the switch on the dishwasher, "finally, he would talk to me. I've liked that."

"I don't blame you," said Alice. "I don't believe anyone ever got that far with him before." She followed Courtney to the girl's bedroom. Courtney had put hand lotion on her palms, and stood rubbing it in, gazing at the clothes still in dress bags on the bed.

"And now I'm quitting," said Courtney. She tossed her hair back from her face, and with one swoop she gathered the dress bags into her arms, and started across the hall.

"Where are you going?" asked Tunnie in dismay.

Courtney lifted her chin above the heap. "Back home," she said. "Back to Fox."

"What will he say if . . .?"

"I'll tell him that I love him," said Courtney. "This time he will listen to me." She opened the door and plunged down the stairs, around, and down again. Alice heard the outside door open; she heard the car door slam. And Courtney returned, running up the stairs.

"Oh, he'll be angry," she said as she passed Alice, and went on to the bedroom. "Then he'll get over it." She opened a suitcase on the bed.

"He didn't bring me to his home," she said, "because he thought I was a girl he could make love to."

"Well, of course *not!*" cried Alice. "To him you were a human being with a need."

"That's right," said Courtney, scooping shoes off the closet floor. "And I know that. And I fell in love with him because I knew what he was doing. Then of course, the way he looked, and talked, focused my love, and made it a physical thing."

Tunnie opened a drawer and began to put clothing into the open bag, tucking lingerie around the shoes, adding some folded blouses. "I thought I was helping you and him," she said.

"You have helped," Courtney told her. "You helped me decide what I wanted to do."

"Or to do what you wanted to do?" asked Alice.

Courtney turned impulsively and hugged the tall woman.

"Hold on a minute," Alice told her. "I brought you here to help Fox as much as you."

"But Fox will like my coming back. You'll see." She started for the door with the suitcase, and some coats over her arm.

"Wait, Courtney . . ." said Tunnie. "You can't go back there just because you want him to believe you love him?"

"Oh, yes, I can!" said Courtney happily. "And this time

he'll believe me. Everything will be lovely, and proper, too, Miss Tunstall. Even Dr. Hawthorne will have to think so. Because, as you know, Fox is a man to do the right thing by a girl."

Have You Read these Bestsellers from SIGNET?